CW01210023

# The Melting Dead

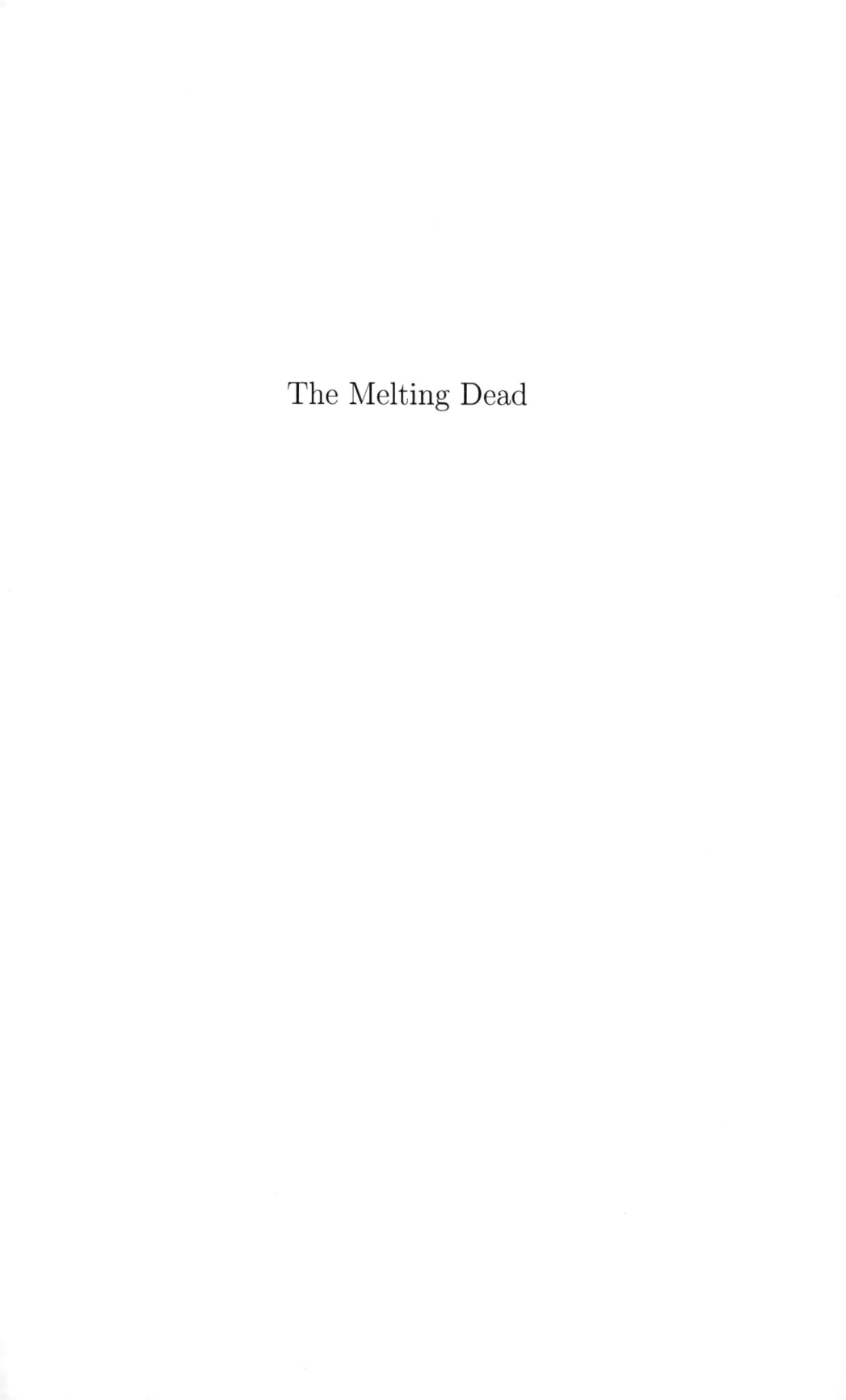

# THE MELTING DEAD

*Doug Lamoreux*

Copyright (C) 2013 Doug Lamoreux
Layout design and Copyright (C) 2017 Creativia
Published 2017 by Creativia (www.creativia.org)
Cover art by Cover Mint
This book is a work of fiction. Names, characters, places, and incidents are the product of the author's imagination or are used fictitiously. Any resemblance to actual events, locales, or persons, living or dead, is purely coincidental.
All rights reserved. No part of this book may be reproduced or transmitted in any form or by any means, electronic or mechanical, including photocopying, recording, or by any information storage and retrieval system, without the author's permission.

# ACKNOWLEDGMENTS

Jenny McDonnell – Nothing works without Jenny;
my island in the storm.

Mitch Lamoreux – For his expert knowledge of the Mississippi River and his valued opinion.

All the horror fans that "get" it.

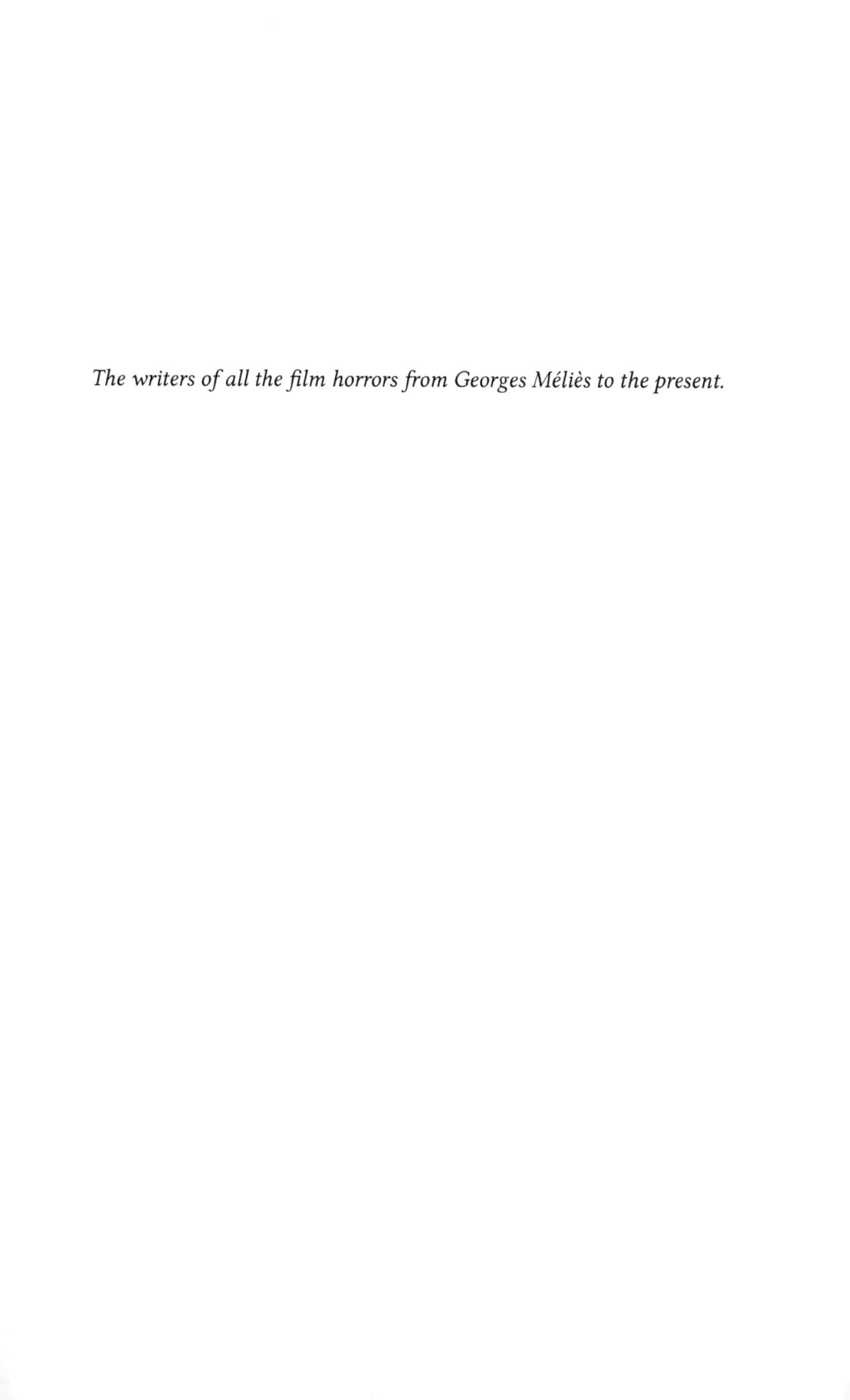

*The writers of all the film horrors from Georges Méliès to the present.*

# ONE

At the risk of being crude, Angela looked as if she'd been yanked through a knothole. Her eyes swam in pink puffs of flesh, tears streaked her cheeks, a smudge marred her jaw. Her hair was disheveled, her clothes filthy, torn, blood spattered, and burned in spots. Yes, burned. She was running like she'd never run before. Uphill through the woods, out of breath, aching in every muscle, running on her last ounce of strength. She hadn't a step left in her, still she ran on, gasping, shooting terrified glances into the darkness behind.

As she ran, she failed to hear any of the *normal* sounds of night. No nocturnal animals scampering in the brush, no creatures slithering in the grass, nothing flitting past on night wings. Not even crickets. Nothing but her gasps, her footfalls – and the unearthly sounds of the thing chasing her. The leaves crunched and branches snapped to its uneven step as it, whatever it was, pounded the path behind. Its occluded breath, growing louder, drawing nearer, threatened Angela like an opening theme from a horror flick, *Suite for String Orchestra, Tubular Bells, Malcolm is Dead;* music to scream by, music to die by. Its throaty panting gave way to a guttural howl. The thing was hot on her heels and closing.

All seemed lost... when the dawn arrived.

Angela experienced a rush of hope as brilliant rays of orange, white, and gold burst through the trees. But that hope was fleeting. The cavalry had not arrived in time. It wasn't the light of salvation. Rather, it was the dawn of the dead. It cast long shadows through the woods while, at the same time, ominously lighting a clearing ahead like a spotlight on a stage. Lights up, she was afraid, on the final act in the theater of blood. Angela had no choice. She left the path, crossed the clearing in eight panicked strides then, gasping in terror and exhaustion, pulled up with no more room to run.

"No!"

She caught her balance at the brink of a sheer rock cliff. She swallowed hard and gaped over the edge taking in the hundred foot drop to a surging river below. Her mind reeled. Her stomach rolled. She took an involuntary step back. Her cognitive senses took an instant to catch up. She was trapped.

She turned to stare back across the clearing to the woods on the downhill side. She dropped her arms to her sides, flexed her fists, and fought to master her breathing. Was she afraid? *YES!* Still… If it was the end, she decided then and there, let it come. She was Angela Roskowic, wasn't she? Her old man's kid? She'd meet this like she met every challenge in life – head on.

The morning breeze chilled, blew through her hair and torn clothes, brushed her beads of sweat, turning her skin to goose-flesh, and sending a shudder through her small athletic frame. Behind her, Angela heard the water surging below. At the timber line, before her, she heard the snap of twigs and crunch of leaves heralding the arrival of her pursuer.

The thing broke through the trees.

Angela screamed – and bolted upright in bed. Just like the heroines did in the old horror movies she loved so much. She eyed her surroundings in the gloom and, finally, recognized them; her own bed, in her own room, in her own apartment. Angela caught her breath. It had only been a nightmare. *The nightmare…* again. For the fourth night in a row. Four times the growling thing had chased her through the woods and to the brink. Four times she'd found herself trapped and facing death. Four times she'd screamed herself awake.

She'd been a mess in the dream and, no doubt, looked worse now it had passed. Angela sat drenched, her too-big flannel night shirt clinging with sweat, her hair matted, her breath coming in pants, and a rivulet of saliva escaping the side of her mouth. *Ugh*, pretty. She wiped her chin with her shirt-sleeve and collapsed back on the damp pillow.

Like most actresses, most directors, most people of the theater, Angela was a night person, not much good in the day. Facing the normal world was challenge enough. Now, with her nights being ruined by crazy dreams… *Ugh!* Who needed it? She lay there, slowing her breathing, blanking her mind, willing her muscles to relax. She looked at the bedside clock and groaned with relish.

"Whatever you do," she told herself aloud, "don't fall asleep again. It's time to make the doughnuts."

To heck with nightmares. She had places to be, people to see. If she didn't get going, Angela knew, the day would wind up one big trip through hell.

Four hours later, following a shower, toaster pastry with sprinkles, and a few last minute chores at the theater (she'd procrastinated the day before), with a cup of espresso driving away the remnants of her nightmare and her comfy-as-an-old-shoe Maverick driving away the last of the two hundred miles from The Windy City, Angela motored through Savanna, a sleepy northwest Illinois town on the east bank of the Mississippi. If she'd read the map right, she had nearly reached her destination.

One of the great thought-thinkers at the last meeting of their Chicagoland Directors' Guild, to the question of where their next convention ought be held, had boldly suggested a retreat into the wilds beyond the city. A "get away and play" as he called it. Of course, with the exception of a film shoot in South Bend, he'd never been more than five miles from the heart of the Loop. Someone else would have to arrange the affair. Angela as, one, the committee's recording secretary and, two, the only member not at the meeting, was nominated and immediately elected. She had no more experience with nature than the others, but that would teach her to miss meetings.

That was five days ago. Four fruitless days of rehearsal followed, with a *guest* director that made Scrooge look open-minded and amiable, with a cast of young performers straight out of *Village of the Damned*. Each one followed by a night of rotten sleep and the recurring nightmare. Four nights of being chased in a senseless dream. And it was senseless. What dream, after all, could be more hair-raising than the frightening world of the theater? Moreover, Angela was a horror film nut. Monsters didn't scare her, she found them a blast. She was gaga for all things Gothic. So why was she having a nightmare? Why a nightmare set in the woods? She wasn't afraid of the woods, she just wanted nothing to do with them. She was a Chicago girl, born and bred, and didn't go anywhere without plumbing. And why the dark faceless thing on her heels? Chi-town was full of things willing and eager to chase you. You didn't need a walk in the woods for that. But what needled Angela most about the dream was her own ravaged condition. The torn clothes were nonsense; she pitied the guy ever laid a hand on her without the okey-dokey. Likewise her dreamed exhaustion was patently ridiculous. When she wasn't in a show, staging a show, or catching a fright flick, Angela kept fit by running marathons. (The personal challenges of the sport gave her a rush.) She may have needed tip-toes to peek over a five foot wall, but she could jump one with no trouble. It would take a heck of a run to wear her out so completely. The dream made no sense.

Anyway, the nightmare was behind her and the trip from the city. The reason for the trip could now occupy her mind; the mission foisted upon her to scout the sticks for a retreat venue. But she may as well have been on a journey to the far side of the sun. Outside of her comfort zone, she cruised through Savanna feeling as if she'd entered the creepy small town territory of *Salem's Lot* or maybe *Let's Scare Jessica to Death*. The sidewalks at that early hour were virtually empty. The few gaunt figures out and about silently followed her progress down the street with the deliberate stares of Stepford wives. She'd freely admit she wasn't being fair to the locals but couldn't help feeling what she felt. In Chicago, a million people might pass by but none paid you any mind. But in that tiny river town… It wasn't that Angela minded attention, she just preferred to be on stage playing somebody else when it came.

At the hard curve in the middle of town, between the Lutheran Church and the Fire Station, Angela passed a sign reading '*Marina*'. In a phone call three days earlier, she'd been told specifically to pass the sign, and the marina, by an insistent and gabby Park District big shot and to keep heading north. She drove through two traffic lights, in total, and found herself already heading out of town. Gorgeous rock bluffs with sheer cliffs, not unlike the one in her dream, the *Palisades* according to her map, imposed to the right of the highway. Then, thankfully, on the left appeared the sign she had been directed to look for. Despite the fact it made no sense at all, she turned left onto Marina Road (which she now knew didn't lead to the marina), crossed a series of railroad tracks, and eased into the gravel lot of something called *Miller's Landing*.

Ahead, for as far as she could see to the left and to the right, surged a gray-green superhighway of water, the great Mississippi River. Angela had arrived.

In one way, Angela soon discovered, the boonies, like the city, were governed by the maxim '*Hurry up and wait*'. She'd forced herself from bed, escaped the city madness, nursed the old Maverick across the state, and arrived safely, only to find the door locked and the landing office vacant. She looked out over bobbing boats, wooden piers, and beyond the concrete incline to the water (for the launching of boats, she imagined), considering her options. Someone named Arthur should have been waiting to give her a boat ride. There wasn't a soul about. How, she wondered, would she get to the island?

An island retreat; that's what she was getting the Chicagoland directors into.

Prior to that moment, the nearest Angela had been to the Mississippi was a four-week run of *Show Boat* in summer stock. Now, finally, she saw the river for real and saw it come to life. The birds were everywhere, big black and white birds that looked like pelicans and majestic birds that were certainly eagles (though she didn't know Gold from Bald), soaring passed each other overhead. On the rocks beside and beneath the dock, frogs croaked, snakes hissed, and all around the hidden *things* in nature leaped and slithered and made their presence known. She couldn't see the fat daddy cats and walleye hanging low along the shoreline, but they were there. She could hear the big mouth bass break the surface with a splash and, though Angela knew only that they were fish, she wondered if they weren't giving the fin to the few anglers visible up and down the way. The rapid river current slapped the rip-rap on both the Illinois and Iowa shores. (That was Iowa over there, wasn't it?) Barges, flat, rusting metal monsters asleep at anchor, waited for the day's work to begin. It was all quite amazing. But one look told her that, while Old Man River might *jes' keep rollin' along*, he was too wide-awake, wide, long, fast, and cold for her to swim. As in her nightmare, Angela was trapped and had no choice. She would have to wait and hope Arthur and his boat put in an appearance.

Resigned, committed, and with her mind now free, Angela heard music. From radios and receivers in boats and barges up and down the water, as the station identification of a local radio show danced on the Mississippi valley air. "*W-O-M-R. Old man river ra-di-o!*" She heard the sprightly jingle from at least one of the cars, or trucks, or campers in the parking lot; had probably been hearing the broadcast all along but had blocked it out. Who listens to commercials after all? Now she heard it plainly, the first sign of civilized life the city girl recognized that morning.

As the song died, there boomed the gravelly voice of a female radio host. "Yes, it is, moms and dads, boys and girls..." Three packs a day, Angela guessed. "This is your charming and delightful, ol' Aunt Sal. And right over there, shoving another cinnamon bun in his pie hole, is my sidekick, little runny-nosed Eddie. Hi, Eddie!"

"Hey, Aunt Sal," came the laughing reply, over the air, from the depths of their studio.

Sal Cartwright, Savanna's most famous radio dee jay, didn't just sound like a frog, she looked like one and had, sitting in her WOMR radio seat, since the training wheels came off Caesar's chariot. Eddie Lanfair, her co-host, his headphone cord stretched to its limit, his mouth jammed with pastry beside the snack wagon across the studio, had been with her for half that time.

"On this beautiful morning," Aunt Sal croaked, moving the flexed microphone arm above her desk closer to her mouth, "we need to start off with a warning."

Choking down a sticky bite, licking his fingers, Eddie raced back to his seat and told his mic, "Say, sounds serious, Sal."

"Whoa. Easy on the alliteration, Eddie, you'll hurt yourself. But, yes, a warning. We want to inform our faithful listeners that the south end of Mississippi pool thirteen will be closed today."

"What?!" Eddie asked in mock surprise.

"That's right, Little Eddie," Aunt Sal said, scanning the news release in her hand. She rattled the paper in front of her microphone for effect. "Says right here… No lock and dam traffic due to dredging below the Rock Island."

"The river never closes, Aunt Sal!"

"It does today, you lying little rat. Pool thirteen is open for recreation, the Bellevue lock and dam is operating as usual, and the river is open for commerce to the north, but don't travel south today because there's nowhere to go past the island. And the Clinton lock and dam is closed to traffic."

Eddie grabbed his kazoo and blew a wheezy sigh.

"Yes," Sal agreed, picking up another sheet. "…it's sad. But here's a story from the NP news wire to cheer you up."

"Oh, boy, what is it?"

"Well, Eddie, it appears we get a meteor shower this morning."

"Hey, a fire in the sky, that's cool!"

"Oh, wait, wait. No, it isn't. Says here… we probably won't see it."

Eddie blew his kazoo again.

"Yes, sad," Sal agreed. "Meteors strike the earth all the time, the experts say, but their spectacular night time displays are apparently a dud in the daylight– What's that?" Interrupted, Sal looked up and through the four-by-eight soundproofed glass separating her and Eddie, in the booth, from the control room engineer on the other side. "I'm being corrected over my head phones. Erwin, the super genius MIT grad who's running the sound board in this broken down

Savanna radio station, is correcting me. He says, they're not meteors if they strike the earth. Just a second." She laid a hand to the headset cupping her ear. Erwin's lips moved behind the glass. "Okay, great. You can go back to sleep, Erwin. All right, folks, here's the facts."

"The 411?" Eddie chimed in.

"Don't be hip, Little Eddie. I'm giving our good listeners the scoop on meteors and you're making an asteroid of yourself."

"Sorry."

"Yes, you are. But back to the subject. If these flying space objects hit us, meaning planet earth..."

"The big blue marble?"

Sal glared daggers. Eddie wilted and she continued. "If they hit, the objects are meteorites. But that's rare. Meteoroids, that's what they're called in space; meteoroids usually burn up in our atmosphere."

"My rhoids are always on fire."

"Can it, squirrel!"

Eddie cut into his own laughter, suddenly confused. "Well, wait. Then, what's a meteor?"

"A meteor is– Shut up, Erwin, I got this. The fiery tail trailing the meteoroid is the meteor."

"Really?" Eddie asked. "That's so confusing."

"Only to you. These burning space rocks are something to see at night, so they say. But on a bright morning like today, not so much."

"Wow," Eddie said without excitement. "So, if we aren't going to see it, why the hell are we talking about it?"

"Oops," Sal said, feigning concern. "Put a quarter in the potty mouth jar, Little Eddie!"

"What? Just for saying 'hell'?"

"Yes, siree, Bob. Go ahead and hit her twice for repeating it, you blockhead!"

Sal and Eddie had listeners from Dubuque, Iowa to Moline, Illinois, both sides of the river, and boats in-between. But four individuals in particular were ignorant of that morning's broadcast. Those four, occupants of a battered Econoline van pulling into the *Bait and Switch* Gas Station and Convenience Store on the north end of the one-blink-and-you-miss-it town of Sabula, Iowa, were assaulting their senses with the Ramones' frenetic *Beat on the Brat*. The van jerked to a stop by the outside pumps. In the vehicle, a hand slipped between the seats to poke the CD player into silence. The radio took over and Aunt Sal continued whooping on Little Eddie in dulcet tones of dumped gravel. "...while you pay up, you little freak." Two coins *tinked* atop a pile of change (presumably in a glass jar) and Sal spoke again. "There you go, Toilet Tongue. Now that's done... On behalf of our sponsors, Pool 13 Pools and Crappy's Tattoo Parlor and Bar, I get to tell the listeners we're looking at rain this afternoon and more rain tonight. But, for now, it's a fine Saturday morning on the quiet Mississippi."

The red head behind the steering wheel, startling not only for her gorgeous hair but for her ghost-white skin and the ring in her nose, poked the power button and put the radio out of their misery. Her name was Norene and, of the four, she looked the most like a human being. But she was desperately nervous and couldn't stand anymore noise. The others, Dex, her boyfriend, cracking his knuckles and breathing deep in the passenger seat, Gar, their leader, and Falcon, Gar's girl, locking and loading handguns in the back, were replete in their ghastliness in frightfully dyed hair, black leather, severe makeup, tattoos, and piercings; Goth nightmares all. And all four as nervous as cats.

"Leave it run and be ready," Gar told Norene. The lizard's eye contact in his left eye, and his rooster foot necklace, unsettled her. She nodded and looked away. Gar turned to the others. "Everyone stay cool. Don't go shopping. Keep to the plan and this will be child's play." Falcon and Dex both nodded. "Let's do it." Gar shoved the van's side door open and he and Falcon hit the ground running. Dex slipped from the front, between the seats, and followed hot on their heels.

"Y'all be careful," Norene called in the sweetest little southern fried accent. Like children released to play, they raced across the lot in a mad parade.

Dex overtook them, reached the store first, jerked the door open to a welcoming chime, and held it. Gar and Falcon, brandishing their weapons, hurried in. From the van, Norene heard Gar shout, "Get 'em up." Then Dex disappeared inside too.

# TWO

Believe it or not, when the bandits first hit the store Billy Pratt, the cashier, was more frightened of their makeup and clothes than he was of their guns. He'd been robbed before with weapons ranging, swear to God, from a ball bat to a chainsaw. He'd seen plenty of guns but he'd never seen anything like these people. Freaks, that's what they were. Society discards pouring through the door, waving pistols. Billy didn't mess with freaks.

"Fill it," Falcon shouted, throwing an empty linen bag at him. "And don't fuck around."

Leather, tats, piercings, and paint, the woman meant business. At least Billy thought it was a female; some kind of jungle woman or cycle slut. Billy didn't know much, but he knew when to do as he was told. He tapped a key on the cash register, *ding*, and the drawer slid open.

Dex circled round the counter and pushed past him. 'Course, Billy didn't know the fella's name. All he knew was the guy was a big African-American (the others looked white) in leather, with spikes at his collar and wrists, and he was no stranger to a gymnasium weight room. The fella didn't say *'Boo'*, just started cherry-picking off the shelves; cartons of cigarettes, boxes of cigars, bottles of whiskey, and one of vodka. (Billy didn't know, but vodka made Norene horny.) The loot disappeared into Dex's bag as fast as he could snatch it.

Falcon jumped the counter sending Shrine Circus coupons, the contents of a *'Need a penny, Take a penny'* tray, and impulse buys from condoms to caramels flying into the air. She landed on her feet on the other side, crunching the rain of peanuts, key chains, and miniature Horoscope booklets beneath her heavy jump boots. She snapped open her own bag and grabbed one of the lottery displays. With no time for unraveling the tickets, she took the whole plastic carousel.

"You little punks!"

The shout, from the back of the store, startled them all. They looked up to see a tubby 50-something man charging from the store room, down the gum and breath mint aisle, with a Louisville slugger over his shoulder. This was Ferenc Blasko, the store's owner, and Lord was he mad. Gar, standing lookout in case of such an emergency (as Falcon saw it), loitering uselessly by the *Zingers* (in Dex's opinion) saw Blasko coming, without being seen. Gar used the butt of his gun to smash the old boy and send him reeling into an endcap display. Blasko hit the floor in a hail of antacid tablets and beef jerky.

Dex sped up his activities. Falcon paused in her thieving to enjoy the heady violence. She threw Gar a smile of twisted glee then, riding her adrenaline wave, turned back on Billy and jammed her gun in his nose. "Let's go!" Falcon relished the fear in the cashier's eyes and celebrated by wagging her split tongue in his terrorized face.

"Let's go."

It was the same phrase, muttered at the same time, by a different person in another setting. The mutterer, Professor Paul Regas, stood alone recalling a recent conversation and growing annoyed.

"Come on, man. Let's go." That's what Malcolm, eh, Dr. Richard Malcolm had said. His colleague, a lit prof at the same college Paul taught Geology (the small l and capital G were how Paul thought of each), had been insistent. "Come on. You said you'd teach me to rappel. Let me steal a few days of your vacation. Let's go." So the getaway was set. They would make a weekend of it, bosom pals, rock climbing in the wilds; first the Mississippi Palisades and then on to the Rock Island.

Paul shook his head, knowing he should have known. Vacations never worked out and this one was holding true to form. Like a nincompoop, he'd waited all Friday, yesterday, on the bluff overlooking the Palisades and river valley (and later, below the sheer cliffs) for his fellow professor to put in an appearance. But Malcolm, probably helping a leggy undergrad with her homework, had failed to show. As you do not rappel alone, the day was wasted. In the evening, Paul caught a boat for the Rock, their next scheduled destination, telling himself they'd merely had a miscommunication.

Rock Island Park, officially, had yet to open for the season but the caretakers, an old couple named Aaron, and the park superintendent, a talkative Mr. Towers, received him cordially and let him stay. Made him comfortable, in fact. He'd had a restful night's sleep and rose with the sun to find Malcolm still a no-show. Now Paul greeted the morning, outside of the facility's big community house, a stone's throw from the central fire ring, wondering why he'd agreed to the excursion? Wondering what to do about it now? But the cloud hanging over the outing had a silver lining, the rock cliff (from which the island got its name) was there, he was there, and the river valley was lovely, even for college professors soured on adventure. Paul looked to his gear, two rope bags and a duffel piled on a picnic table, and sighed. With nothing to do but wait, he might as well double-check the gear and hope for Malcolm. Paul grabbed the duffel but, before he could unzip it, was interrupted.

Harry Towers, the park super, led a man in clerical garb from the main building and off the porch. Paul had caught a glimpse of them earlier, from a distance, when they'd arrived with the caretakers. (Where the Aarons had gotten too, the professor hadn't a clue.) The man of God was tall, thin, with wispy gray hair, a white dog collar, a suit in Johnny Cash's color scheme, and a wide smile; Barry Fitzgerald without the crust, Paul guessed. It was a guess. The professor patronized neither the cinema nor the hallowed halls of organized religion. Towers looked exactly as he had the previous night, short of height, pink of face, red of nose, with a middle mound keeping his feet a secret from him. He had a tendency to talk incessantly and was even then. The religious leader followed, smiling patiently, trying unsuccessfully to work a word in edge-wise.

"I'm certain, Father Snow, your young people will have a terrific time here on the island."

"I'm sure they will–"

"Kids always do when they put their minds to it, eh, Father?"

"Please, Superintendent, it's Reverend, not Father. I'm–"

"Then, come to think, you probably wouldn't know about kids, I suppose, being a priest and all?"

Paul grimaced, embarrassed for Towers. The fat fool was talking so much and so fast he couldn't hear himself being offensive. Reverend Snow was not a priest, he was a minister; a horse of a different color. Paul wasn't a church-goer but he wasn't an idiot either.

Towers, chattering like a crazed magpie, having missed the one sentence the poor guy had gotten out, was off to the races again. "I've got a young woman coming, she should–" Towers interrupted himself to look at his watch. "She should be here. Organizing a reunion, or a team get together, or something. I don't remember if it was a high school or college, she may have said. Well, it makes no difference. I think our island park will fit her group admirably. I mean as well, I expect, as it will fit yours."

The reverend attempted a reply but Towers cut him off. "We'll tour the trails now and she'll soon be here. Oh, she is late. But she'll be here soon, I'm sure. We can tour the buildings together? Our trails are gorgeous this time of year. But, just between us, you wouldn't want to be lost here near dark."

Towers spotted Paul, exclaimed excitedly, then steered the reverend towards him. "Good morning, Paul. Uh, Father Snow, let me introduce you. Dr. Paul Regas."

"Reverend," Snow corrected, reaching for Paul's hand.

"Professor," Paul corrected in return, giving it a shake.

Towers hadn't heard either. "Not a medical doctor, I think," Towers corrected himself, incorrectly. "A scientist of some sort… looking over our facilities before we're actually open for the season. We do try to accommodate when we're able. Paul, Father Snow is touring the park in anticipation of some church function or other."

Paul and the reverend shared muted smiles, brothers in suffering. The minister turned to the park official and tried to speak, but Towers cut him off.

"It just occurred to me I may have given you the wrong impression," the superintendent said. "Paul doesn't work here, he's one of our visitors. The park wouldn't have any use for an archeologist, would we? Well, I've another group organizer coming, I don't know if I mentioned her or not, some sort of teacher or other. We'd better get a move on. I'll give you a quick peek at our trails." Towers started away with the minister, tossing an, "Enjoy yourself, Paul," over his shoulder. Yakking, he disappeared with the reverend past the old barn theater and down one of the marked trails.

Bemused, if not amused, Paul watched them go. When they had vanished into the trees, he shook his head and returned to his gear. "Nice talking to you, reverend," Paul muttered aloud. "No, I'm not a doctor. No, not an archeologist either, I'm a geologist. Mr. Towers? Yes, he is a babbling idiot."

Dex, Falcon, and Gar raced from the store, their arms loaded with bags of loot and bottles of booze. They piled through the side door of the waiting van. Falcon head-butted Dex. Gar landed atop Falcon and pulled the door closed, shouting, "Go! Go! Go!"

At the wheel, Norene panicked. She tromped the gas pedal and slammed the transmission into drive. The engine revved, the tires shrieked, and the van lurched. What happened next seems impossible. It happened all the same. The van hit a collection of pallets leaning against a display of bagged fertilizer. It rode the lead pallet like a ramp and, to Norene's horror and shocked exclamations from those in the rear, flipped the van with a *crunch* like a movie stunt car onto its passenger side.

Billy ran from the store, his mouth a wide O, adjusting his glasses to gape. "Ho-ly Moses!"

Torn bags of horse manure littered the pavement, A pungent aroma filled the air. The van shook on its side while disgusted shouts, screams, and unintelligible grumbles escaped through the driver's side – now the top – window. Norene's feet (she'd fallen into the passenger seat), were visible through the sideways cracked windshield. No one else could be seen at all. The rear door fell open. Gar climbed from the wreck, slipped on the brown skating rink they'd created, and nearly fell. He caught the door, grimaced with repulsion at the smell, waved his gun at the cashier and shouted. "Get back!"

No hero, Billy retreated into the store as fast as his legs would carry him.

The driver's side window shattered and Falcon, using Norene, the seats, and the steering wheel as steps, pushed herself up and out. The van rocked. She swore, lost her balance, and half-jumped, half-fell off the door onto the wrecked display. Ankle deep in broken fertilizer bags, shaking with rage, she let fly with an aria of profanity.

As it was hardly the first time she'd been stepped on in life, Norene quickly recovered from her trampling. She found her knees and crawled into the back of the van while, outside, Gar was yelling to her and Dex. "Grab the stuff and get the hell out."

Blasko, the store's owner, sporting a knot on his forehead, appeared at the door. Gar saw him and pointed his gun. The storefront window beside the old man exploded. Glass flew. Signs highlighting the deals of the day shredded and fell. Windshield fluid deluged the floor and sidewalk on both sides of the frame.

The 'OPEN' sign was closed for good. Blasko hollered, threw up his hands, and disappeared back inside.

But Gar hadn't fired. Stunned, the gang leader turned to see his old lady, now on the ground beside the van, waving her smoking gun. "Falcon!" he yelled. "I told you, no shooting."

"Did you tell the southern belle not to smash up the van?"

"Baby–"

"Piss on that, Gar," she growled, waving at the muck on her boots and leathers. "I may or may not be full of shit, but I'm not getting caught covered in it!"

"I know, dearheart, but try to maintain. No shooting, if we can help it." He goggled at the shot out window and demolished storefront then turned, putting it behind him. He yelled to the van. "Come on, you two. We haven't got all day."

Dex staggered out, limping, a bag of loot in his left hand, the palm of his right pressed against his forehead. A red stream of blood ran from beneath his hand, around his eye, and dripped on his jacket. Norene followed him out, crying, "Dex, ya' aw-right?" He ignored her, letting Gar help him through the pool of horse manure.

Falcon brushed past them back into the van. She cursed, to the sound of breaking glass, then stuck her head out. "Get your asses back here and help me." She disappeared again.

Inside, Falcon collected the surviving loot, scattered to all corners of the compartment, shoved it back into bags, and the bags to the open rear escape. When Norene showed her face at the window, Falcon all but exploded. She grabbed the neck of a shattered whiskey bottle and wagged it at the red head, screaming, "I ought to use this on you." Norene cried in desperate apology.

"Falcon," Gar shouted in. "We don't have time for this. Let's go!"

Silently promising to smack the worthless bitch later, Falcon threw sacks of lottery tickets and cigarettes at Norene. "Take these. Do something right for once."

Loaded down, the Goth thieves left the wrecked van and the lot on foot.

Sabula, the *'Island City'*, was a sliver on the world separated from Iowa by Sabula Lake and from Illinois by the Mississippi River. The town was nine blocks long and four wide, discounting both the two mile elevated road leading in from the north bridge and the south marina. The Bait and Switch sat on the north end of town, on Highway 52, the east-west causeway north of the lake, connecting the town with the landlubbers of Iowa proper.

Trailing broken glass, dripping fertilizer, and (here and there) spots of blood, Gar shouldered the limping Dex down the middle of Broad Street and away from the wildly rearranged convenience store. The girls, their arms loaded with loot, followed after.

# Three

For all the excitement elsewhere around the river valley, there was none at Miller's Landing and nothing on the horizon. The landing supervisor had finally arrived and opened his office. Angela had expected, unfairly she admitted, a sinister banjo player with bad dental work, but couldn't have been more wrong. He was a perfectly normal, if quiet man, willing to help but not really able. He had no clue where her river taxi was. His call to the island, on her behalf, had gone unanswered. He offered to rent her a boat if she wanted but Angela, aware she was no Tippi Hedren, decided against it.

Alone on the pier, there was little to do but pace and look around. She'd given up worrying about missing her island tour. What would that accomplish? It was the fault of her hosts, if she remembered her instructions, and Angela was certain she had. They said they'd send a boat. Instead, to pass the time, she gave in to her inner nerd and started mental pushups, taking in her surroundings and, with imagination, deciding which horror films they placed her in. The novice would have ogled the docks and simply named the biggie, *Jaws*, and its sequels. (*Jaws III*, set in a Sea World knock-off, didn't count.) And the rip-offs, *Barracuda, Tintorera, Tenticles*. Each the same movie, in an ocean setting. By adding a boat landing on a river, it got tougher. *Piranha, Humanoids From the Deep*.

Speaking of rivers… Angela paused for a look, saw nothing resembling a boat heading her way, and exclaimed out loud, "Poop."

She returned to her game, adding an island destination. *Piranhaconda*. "Meh, try harder." *The Island of the Doomed*. "There you go." Was Cameron Mitchell waiting downriver, she wondered, with his blood-thirsty tree? *The Island of the Alive? The Island of Lost Souls?*

"Are we not men?" Angela asked the sky, mimicking the last film's *Keeper of the Law*. Then she looked about in sudden embarrassment, hoping she hadn't been heard. "Are we not foolish?" she asked under her breath. "Are we not completely bored?"

The river current rocked the moored boats, the boats thumped the pier, and Angela sighed. She wandered the dock, waiting, alone.

From a bird's eye view, perhaps one of the many pelicans or soaring eagles, the Rock Island looked like a bowling pin designed by Picasso or Dali. It sat on angle in the river channel three-quarters of the way south in pool thirteen. On its north end, near the top of the pin's head, was the park campground where Paul Regas readied his gear. It featured a community building with meeting hall and second floor dormitory, an attached nature museum highlighting the flora, fauna, and fun of the great outdoors, an old refurbished barn with activity center and theater, and the usual outside accoutrement one found at a camp. Southwest of the campus, downriver on the island above the pin's neck, was a mountainous rise through the timber that halted suddenly at its famous rock cliff. The cliff faced south-southwest, with a sheer drop to a small cove, and offered visitors a magnificent view of Iowa to the west, the lock and dam leading to pool fourteen to the south and, in the distance on a clear day, the Quad cities of Illinois and Iowa. The wide southern bottom of the island, the pin's base, dropped to low-land and was taken up almost entirely with dense woods dotted by tiny clearings and threaded with nature trails. At the southeast tip of the island was another, smaller cove, well-hidden by nature. None entered it and few spoke of it except, of course, Harry Towers.

Towers had led the Reverend Snow down one of the many paths and well into the thick of the south timber. He'd filled the poor man in on the park facilities history, flora, fauna, available menu, rules, including the in-season operating hours of the museum, and had now moved on to gossip. At no time during the walking tour did the park authority let the minister get a word in. "You know, Father," Towers was just then saying, "I don't mean to be a babbling idiot."

"Excuse me?" Snow asked, taken aback. "Oh, and please, I'm not–"

"Well, I should tell you… Have I mentioned the Harpers?" Towers asked. "Good God. Pardon my French, Father, but good God! Let me tell you about the Harpers." He paused for a moment, to consider his words, a rarity for the superintendent. The silence was deafening and Snow might have slipped in a sentence had the poor man not been caught off guard. But the moment passed quickly and Towers was off again. "The Harpers, you'll find, are known of by everyone in these parts but talked about by few. Technically, legally, they're squatters. But, of course, they don't see it that way. Ellis Harper, the leader and patriarch of their clan, considers himself a settler in the tradition of his forefathers. A year ago, in late fall, when the park – and all of the Rock Island – was closed for the season, Ellis rowed up with the whole family and just moved in, lock, stock and barrel. There's a small inlet, sort of a notch cut out of the southeast corner of the island; they had the nerve to name it *Harper's Cove*. You can't see it coming downstream, but heading north, it's an odd dark spot in the overgrown trees. Anyway, he built a cabin of tin and plywood in a clearing near the inlet, on public land, and installed his clan. And he refuses to leave. He nailed a 'NO TRESPASSING' sign to a tree and another reading 'HOME SWEET HOME' to a wall in their cobbled up shack, eh, so I've been led to understand. He dug an outhouse; yes, an honest to God outhouse! Put a rocking chair on the porch and called it good."

The reverend stared, speechless.

"Exactly," Towers said, nodding. "What can be said? Ellis Harper is a widower, a father of three, some sort of military veteran, and a mean river rat. He's homesteading on our park island and he defies anyone to do anything about it." Towers pointed, his plump hand trembling, down one of the gloomy paths. "Their shack," he said, "is at the end of that trail."

The reverend couldn't help but look and wonder.

The big city, big money weekenders, living four months a year in expensive homes on either side of the river, might have called Ellis Harper an eclectic lone spirit, a Renaissance man or, to the greenies among them, a civic-minded recycler. That's if they'd bothered to look his way. Of course they didn't. The born and bred locals, who not only looked but stared from a distance, considered him a bum. The truth lay somewhere between. Ellis was a good old fashioned junk dealer from Cairo, the most southern town in Illinois. (So southern, squeezed in between Missouri and Kentucky at the confluence of the Mississippi and Ohio Rivers, his whole family sounded like kin to Scarlett O'Hara.) Piles of wood, rusting farm implements, car parts, old appliances, barrels of scrap wire, tarp covered what's-its, and weed covered who's-its filled the clearing around his cabin as evidence of dedication to his work.

That morning found his family to home. Jay, the eldest son, coming from the outhouse he and his daddy had proudly dug and built, tugged up his coveralls and got back to work. Knowing they'd be rowing down to Clinton beginning of the week to turn in scrap, he flipped back a tarp and resumed his search for copper amid the stacks.

"I'm never leavin' home." The statement and the voice belonged to Crystal, the middle child and only daughter, and had come from her favorite tree. She was a sassy teen, on the verge of womanhood, and spent a lot of time in the branches of what had always been her thinking place, just thinking. "I'm never leavin' home at all."

Caleb, the youngest, beneath Crystal's tree, two hops from the porch, wrestled in the high grass with two fat German Shepherd puppies. The pups, their coats equal parts gray and black, still had a momma. She was named Spot and was asleep on the porch. The pups were luckier than him, Caleb thought. His momma left 'em not long after he was born. They'd been alone with their daddy ever since. That was life, as far as he could see; things just up and left. "You got no choice about leavin'," Caleb shouted up to his sister. "Ev-ybody leaves. You'll have to too."

Crystal ignored her don't-know-nothing baby brother. "Daddy, I'm never leavin' home."

"Didn't say ya had to, baby," Ellis replied from his porch rocking chair.

His daughter, in shorts and a tied top, dropped, hanging upside down, from her perch in the tree. "No," she said. "I mean never."

"Never's a long time, Crystal."

"The law goin' to make us leave?"

Ellis spit. "Ain't talkin' bout the law. This is our home. But some day you'll trade a boy your heart fer his wallet. Then you'll leave. It's how things is."

"Nope. This is my tree. I ain't goin'." Crystal sat herself back on her favorite branch and searched what she could see of the sky. From somewhere above, distantly, she heard something. A rumble maybe? But what in the sky on a beautiful clear morning could rumble? "Daddy," Crystal called out. "You hear that?"

Ellis stopped his rocking, squinted, and listened. He growled with his brows. "Another gall-derned motor boat. Jay, get on down to the cove an' take a peek. If it's a group o' them picnickin' pricks chase 'em to their side o' the island. If it's the law just hurry back here."

"Don't sound like a motor boat to me," his oldest said. Jay listened hard. "Don't hear it no more."

"Don't argue, boy. Get down there."

"Yes, sir," Jay said, starting away on the run.

Caleb let loose a pup and jumped up, shouting, "Can I go too, Daddy?"

"No, Caleb," his father said. "You stay here." The child put the brakes on. Pouting but knowing on which side, and by who, his bread was buttered, Caleb returned to his dogs. Ellis, rocking again, smiled and nodded. "That's my boy."

Rufus Nelson's nickname was *'Rough'*, had been since he broke Susan Baker's arm jerking her off the playground slide in the third grade. That was a long time ago, decades before he'd been elected Jackson County Sheriff. In the time since nothing much had changed. Nelson was still Rough.

He rolled his toothpick with his tongue, from one side of his mouth to the other, studying the wrecked van in the parking lot of the Bait and Switch. He hadn't believed it when he'd got the call but there it was, bigger than shit, an old Ford on its side like the carcass of a felled dinosaur. He took in the shot-up storefront. He took in the full-bodied fragrance of spilled gas, leaking oil, and horse manure. He took in the fresh painted front door of the City Hall not thirty yards away, catercorner across the street, and he shook his head. Yup, it looked to be a head-shaking day.

One of his squad cars blocked the front entrance to the lot, its lights doing a blue-red dance. On the far side, stringing yellow 'crime scene' tape from street lamp, to stop sign, to phone pole was his best deputy, Melissa Renee. Rough was never much on the idea of police women, but Melissa sure shut him up there. She was a good girl and, as soon as she had the rubber-neckers (weren't many yet, but there would be) blocked out so's they couldn't tramp any evidence, she'd start on the government nonsense; calling the hazmat wizards, Environmental Protection sharpies, and the photo and fingerprint scientists up from Clinton. All the BS they could have skipped if the perps hadn't fired a gun in the commission of the crime. Bastards. All the crap Rough hated to deal with. Yup, Melissa was a good girl.

Something, an unusual sound, like a distant rumble, caught his attention and Rough looked to the sky. (Melissa looked too; she didn't miss a trick.) He panned the blue west and saw nothing, slipped his sunglasses into place, panned the east and saw the same; not a plane, not a storm cloud in sight. Though the radio was calling for rain. He and his deputy shared a shrug and she went back to work. Rough tugged his gun belt back into place; tended toward the gut as he was, it had a habit of slipping. He headed around the parking lot mess, past the shot-up window, and into the store.

Jay Harper heard it plain as day, louder than before; the rumble. His daddy said it was the boat motor of some snoop but, search the river as he might, he couldn't see a boat anywhere. He stood beneath their homemade sign reading 'Harper's Cove', hung from a tree above their overgrown and sagging pier, and looked. Their small empty row boat tapped the dock with the slight movement of the water, but that was all. The river was clear to the south. Jay left the cove, circled around through the weeds and trees, through the heavy brush, into the cattails and prairie grass on the island's open southeastern shore. He looked up and down to the east and saw there was nothing to see. The river was empty. But the rumbles continued.

Jay wouldn't argue with his daddy for all the tea in China, that was for sure. Still he didn't believe the noise had anything to do with snoops, the law, or the Mississippi. He thought, was almost certain, the strange sounds were coming from the sky. He looked to the wild blue yonder, but saw nothing but a few wispy clouds. Funny, it sure sounded like it came from the sky.

Inside the Bait and Switch, Billy had the store's First Aid kit out of the back room and was doing laps around Blasko's head with a roll of gauze. The store owner held one of those 'popped' ice bags to his noggin and was trading hands around Billy's doings to hold it in place.

Rough Nelson helped himself to a large coffee in a paper cup. "They get anything else, Ferenc?" he asked, sniffing the brew.

Blasko grunted, probably from the pain, maybe for attention. "I haven't had time to check, sheriff."

Rough watched three sugar cubes sink from sight. "Let go of his head, Billy, so he can check."

Billy did. Blasko got up to have a look around the store, while the clerk asked, "Why aren't you chasing them, Rough?"

Rough took a long first sip before looking up. "Do I chase people?" He pursed his lips and blew to cool the coffee. "I got the causeway blocked to the west. I got the bridge blocked to the north."

"Why?" Billy asked, sticking his nose in further. "We told you they went south."

"Yeah, I got south," Rough said dryly. "Then where'd they go, genius?"

Billy shrugged. Rough shook his head, so much for south.

The chime, surprisingly still intact above the door, rang as Melissa stuck her head in. "Rough, you got a few seconds?" The sheriff assured her he'd be right there and his deputy ducked back out.

"That's it," Blasko called from behind the counter. He came around front, crunching across the spilled do-dads littering the floor. "All my cash, everything in the till, all my lottery tickets, half my smokes, a bottle of Smirnoff, two Captain Morgan's, and a couple bottles of VO."

The sheriff shook his head. "With Jack Daniels right there on the same shelf. I am depressed." He took another sip and gave his cup the stink eye. "You switch coffee brands, Ferenc?"

"You want to criticize it," the store owner growled, "pay for it."

Rough studied the disaster of tossed shelves and scattered merchandise. "Don't look to me like you could make change." He turned, in no hurry, and started for the door.

"What if they grab a boat?" Billy, hurting his brain trying to detect, asked the sheriff's back. "There are plenty around. They'll get away."

"Not to the south they won't. They can't get off the island unless they do steal a boat. If they go to the trouble, they can't get out of the pool to the south. They're dredging and the Clinton lock is closed." Rough paused at the door for a long slow sip. "This isn't Los Angeles, Billy, it's Sabula, Iowa." He stared past the busted window to the wrecked van in the lot. "You were robbed by the Addams Family. They're on foot. Judging by the blood at least one is limping, hopping, or being carried. They aren't exactly invisible, boy." He took another thoughtful sip. "Just hold your water. As long as a bass is a fish with gills, it's just a matter of time."

Rough pushed out of the store.

# FOUR

When Sheriff Nelson, who didn't chase people, and his favorite deputy arrived at the Bait and Switch, saw the wrecked van, instituted the first road blocks, and began to discuss the manpower necessary for a search, the armed robbers were less than two blocks away.

With Gar slowed by the injured Dex on his shoulder and Norene too idiotic to put up with any longer, Falcon had taken the point. She led them, running, for a block and a half in plain sight down the town's main drag. Dressed in black leather and studs, with explosive hair and fright makeup, trailing manure and blood, she hollered over her shoulder – in Falcon's own special diction – to remind her man they were going to draw more attention than seemed advisable. "We need a fucking plan!"

The notion of swiping a car was considered and quickly abandoned. Vehicles with keys left in the ignition were bound to be scarce and no one in their ragtag group knew how to hot wire an engine. Besides, Gar told them, the cops would soon have the roads blocked. It made more sense, he said, to keep their eyes peeled for a boat with a reliable looking outboard or, better yet, with keys in view. People were less careful about boats.

"What we gonna to do?" Norene asked.

"We're surrounded by water," Gar growled. "What do you think we're going to do?"

Falcon got it, of course; was way ahead of her old man. Still she had a problem. As thin as the town of Sabula was water showed between the houses on either side of them. Falcon was perplexed as to which direction offered the best chance of escape. She finally decided with the foolproof *eeny, meeny, miny, moe* method and led them through a yard to the right. One town block, two Fbombs, and a "Son of a bitch" later she stopped dead in her tracks, staring at the enclosed and inescapable Sabula Lake. She'd chosen wrong. Falcon grit her teeth. Norene cried. Gar took a deep breath, spun Dex, and started back to the east, growling, "Come on."

Sirens sounded, again, in the distance.

Falcon once more took the lead. (Really, she had had it with Norene.) They cut across Madison Street, through a yard headed south again, back across Broad to Pearl, then to the wide Mississippi River. Damn! Not a boat dock in sight. There were a number of private piers back to the north, where they'd come from, but nothing nearby. No one in the group made a peep but silently, each in their own way, were cursing their rotten luck. Dex, limping and using Gar for a crutch, was supporting more of his own weight now as they headed back up to a tree-line even with the River Street row of houses. Norene followed, still crying. Falcon passed her, slapping her red head as she went.

Only three blocks remained, the last without trees for cover, to the end of town and the mouth of what a fancy sign insisted was the *'Island City Harbor'*. The mini-marina featured five short piers berthing several dozen boats. One local, an old-timer near the pilot house with a bent back and a short clay pipe, sat watching them. He saw the approach of the oddly dressed quartet, with the leather-clad Falcon in the lead, and took them for trouble. He stared as Falcon darted from one boat to another checking for keys. He silently puffed his pipe, considered the situation, then hid his face behind his newspaper. From then on, he actively ignored them. He didn't get to be an old codger by being stupid.

None of the boats had keys. Falcon swore, at the situation, then at Norene. Gar told her to shut it. He told them all to cross their fingers and head further south.

"There are only two houses left," Falcon complained. "Then we're out of island."

"I can count, babe, and I can see."

"Then what?"

"Then we swim," Gar shouted in exasperation.

"Swim, my ass." Falcon jerked her head in Norene's direction. "I'm making a raft out of the Georgia peach." She shuffled the bags of loot in her hands and took off running.

Gar shuffled the limping Dex under his shoulder and started after her. Norene, sniffling and unable to wipe her nose for the three bags she carried, brought up the rear.

They'd run (and hobbled) six blocks, a mile and a quarter, from the Bait and Switch and, as mentioned, were about out of island. The penultimate house showed neither car nor boat and Falcon passed it without slowing. She picked up speed as she entered the yard of the last house on the left. There, moored at a tiny dock in the back, bobbed a brand new boat. The stern of the craft was painted with a blue ribbon and the name *Sabula Pride*. Doubting how high that bar could be set, Falcon nevertheless felt her own pride at the discovery. She whistled and pointed. "Gar!"

Coming on, he and Dex saw what she did, a beautiful boat with a monstrous built-in motor and a fancy mini-roof over the driver's seat and console. Best of all, the sunlight glinted off of a set of keys dangling from the ignition.

"Are we really goin' to steal a boat, y'all?" Norene asked. "Ain't we in enough trouble aw-ready?"

Ignoring her, Falcon set her loot over the gunwale and jumped in. Dex handed her his bag then, with Gar's help, got himself aboard. Gar took a seat at the wheel. Norene climbed in last, whining, "Y'all, this is a bad idea."

"So was wrecking the van, Norene!" It was the first sentence Dex had uttered since the accident.

Norene couldn't believe her ears. "Oh, nice, Dex." She crossed her arms, sat heavily, and looked away. "Go ahead and bring that back up."

"What do you expect?" he demanded. "Look at my head."

"I cain't. 'Cause I don't want to see ya ugly face."

"All this foreplay is boring as hell," Falcon hollered.

Gar turned from the wheel. "Why doesn't everybody have a great big cup of shut the fuck up!"

"Hey." Everyone froze in place. "Hey!" They traded looks and realized as one the new shouts were coming from outside of the boat. Then came the sound of a slamming screen door.

"What do you think you're doing?"

They turned to see a pair of hippos wrestling in a denim sack. Then, one by one, realized what they were looking at was one colossal man in coveralls running their way. The bandits didn't know John Henry Pucket from Adam.

But they knew an enraged boat owner when they saw one and this fat bastard was spitting fire.

Gar turned the ignition key expecting, the way their day had so far gone, nothing but the metallic grinding of a bad starter or the hiccups of a faltering engine. But, to his surprise and delight, the boat motor turned over, started on the first try, and immediately settled into the purr of a well-stroked cat. Something had finally, *finally*, gone right for them.

Thank God, Gar thought. Because, despite the man's outlandish size, John Henry was picking 'em up and laying 'em down. He'd almost reached the little dock. And Falcon, being the incorrigible minx she was, was drawing her handgun. Dex flipped the mooring rope free and shoved them off. Gar gave the throttle hell.

John Henry hit the dock as if it were a diving board and launched his behemoth body into the air.

The boat's stern sank as the motor bit into the river and the *Sabula Pride* roared away. The resulting arc of water soaked John Henry as he cannon-balled through it, hit the river, and disappeared beneath the surface like a harpooned orca. Nothing remained but the gleaming wake of the stolen boat.

John Henry wasn't the only *John* on the river that morning. Not with John P around.

John P's favorite song was Jimmy Dean's *Big Bad John*. No, he wasn't six-foot-six, nor did he weigh two forty-five, nothing like it. John P was a thin, pale, mild-mannered fisherman. In fact, the biggest, baddest thing about him was his wife. She ruled the roost, which is why John's greatest moments in life were spent alone on the river. He'd had one of those mornings, so far, knocking the crafty monsters dead on the Running Slough, a backwater that was virtually a river of its own on the Iowa side of the Mississippi north of *Santa Fe Beach*. And he was having one of those moments now. John P grinned over his morning catch swimming laps in his boat's live tank, lowered the bench seat cover, and took the wheel in hand. He fired up his faithful outboard and puttered back toward Miller's Landing. It had been a good morning for little 'big bad' John.

He didn't know who she was, the tiny brunette, pacing the pier as he motored that way. She looked kinda bored, and sorta depressed, and maybe she needed a little help. Not that John thought he could be much help, but she was a looker. He wasn't a dirty old man, not by a long shot, but had he been twenty years younger, or she ten years older… He saw her brighten visibly as he drew near.

It was nice to see a smile on a young woman's face at his approach. Yes, sir. And it wasn't his imagination. She was smiling bright as the morning sun.

On her side of it, Angela pulled up in her pacing as a small motorboat came her way. There was one man aboard, a skinny old man, sitting at the steering wheel. It appeared her wait had finally ended. The old guy was an Arthur if she'd ever seen one. "Good morning!" Angela called out, waving.

"Morning," the boatman replied, touching the bill of his worn cap.

"You're Arthur, I hope?"

"Excuse me?"

She raised her voice over the idling motor. "Are you Arthur?" She twisted her lips, unable to remember the last name. It didn't seem to matter. From his frown, it appeared they were both about to be disappointed.

"No, I'm not, Arthur. Sorry." The young woman sagged visibly, looking as defeated as John suddenly felt. It had been a long while since a young woman had smiled at his approach; a long while and counting. "They call me John P." The name meant nothing to her, of course. Why should it? "Just getting in a little fishing," he added, excusing his presence. "Eh, headed down to the island, are you?"

"Rock Island," she said.

"Yes," John smiled. "But which? Are you going to the town of Rock Island or headed out to the island named for the Rock?"

"Oh, I didn't know there were two. It's supposed to be an island with a summer camp."

"Thought as much when you said Arthur." John nodded knowingly. "Arthur Aaron, he's the groundskeeper."

"That's it, Arthur Aaron. He was supposed to pick me up, but... so far," she pointed to the empty river. "No Arthur. And no ride to Rock Island."

"*The* Rock Island," he corrected.

"*The* Rock Island. I had a tour scheduled but I'm already late."

"I'm not surprised. I know Arthur," John said. "Tell you what, I'm going to catch holy hell, er, heck, 'cuse me, from my wife for being late but, I'll give you a quick lift down there, if you want."

"I'd hate to get you into trouble."

"Aw," John waved it away. "It's just a couple of miles."

"That would be wonderful. I'd really appreciate it." His boat bumped the pier lightly and Angela took hold. Then she took his offered hand, stepped aboard, and sat on the bench behind him. He flipped a lever and the idling motor dragged them back from the pier. Clear with room to spare, he flipped the lever again, turned the wheel, and they started downriver.

"I really do appreciate it," Angela repeated, shouting over the growl of the motor. John waved it away. "It's beautiful."

"What's that?"

"The river. I've never seen the Mississippi before. It's beautiful. And big."

"Bigger than you know," John said with a laugh. Then Angela discovered how she would be paying for the ride. The only thing John P loved more than fishing was the river itself and he shared that love whenever he could. Angela got more than a ride; she got a lectured tour.

In no time at all, she learned they were on the fourth longest, tenth largest river on the planet. That, not counting the drainage basin that reached into Canada, the river flowed entirely in the United States. That the headwaters of the Mississippi rose in northern Minnesota and twisted downriver, through twenty-seven lock and dam combinations, to the Gulf of Mexico. That the Army Corp of Engineers, and their locks, deserved all the derision that could be heaped upon them for their attempts to control the river. "As if anyone could," John P laughed. "Man's hubris."

Angela nodded her agreement. "Men are like that."

John did a double-take but left it go. If there was one thing he'd learned from marriage it was when to let something go. Best get back to his tour, it was safer.

"The section of the river between each of the locks," he told her, "is a numbered *pool*." He released the wheel and spread his arms. "We're on pool thirteen. If you were to see it from a plane or one of them fancy satellites, pool thirteen looks like the front half of a snake." He pointed over the stern to the north. "She comes south out of the number twelve lock and dam at Bellevue, Iowa, then she slithers southeast, then south again in a meandering S." He pointed over the bow to the south. "The pool grows wide and oval, like a snake's head, north of the Quad Cities. Then the whole river skinnies up to barely nothing going into the number thirteen lock and dam at Clinton. Looks just like the snake's flicking her tongue out."

They motored quickly past Savanna on their left. On the river, headed the opposite direction, none of the emotionless early morning roamers could be seen. And the little town, in Angela's opinion, looked entirely different, less foreboding, almost quaint.

"You just left Miller's Landing," John P declared. He pinked with embarrassment. "Eh, sorry. You probably know that. What I meant was… The river fishermen and the out-of-towners, the weekend warriors, put in at the landing." He chucked his thumb to the left as they passed another group of piers featuring, mostly, tied up houseboats. "This here is the Savanna Marina. These are the permanent residents, the old-timers and the long-timers. The landing launches sport; the marina docks leisure." John P laughed.

Angela chuckled herself. She'd had to brace herself to make the trip. And, all the while, couldn't help but wonder if she had what it took to succeed in her mission. To her surprise, she'd just discovered one of the locals already considered her a sport.

No sooner had they left Savanna behind than John pointed to another smaller town coming up on the right side of the river. "That there's Sabula, Iowa." One block inland, red and blue flickering lights competed with the morning sun to be seen. John P both saw and recognized them; obviously the police. Without thinking, he muttered, "Looks like someone stepped on their dick."

Then John turned bright red. "I am so sorry," he told Angela, suddenly sweating bullets. "I'm used to being alone out here."

"Meh," she replied. "Don't worry about it. I've heard worse. I work in the theater." She pointed back to Sabula. "I thought I heard sirens earlier, but I wasn't sure."

The old guy, yet to recover from his gaffe, had pulled out a red farmer's hanky and was furiously wiping his neck. Angela felt for him and tried to offer relief by changing the subject. "So where exactly is this island?"

"Eh, a couple of miles downriver," he told her, waving over the bow. "Right in the middle of the stream, not far from a speck of a town on the Illinois map called Thomson."

Angela nodded. "Whereabouts on the snake?"

John stared, confused for an instant, then laughed aloud. "In her neck, right at the base of the head."

John Henry Pucket's stolen boat had blown by the Rock Island and, using John P's metaphor, was racing across the wide oval head of the great Mississippi snake with Gar at the wheel. They passed a buoy wearing a bright sign lettered in red reading '*LOCK AND DAM CLOSED*'. Gar throttled the motor back nearly unseating his passengers. Their wake ebbed and the boat settled to rocking with the river current.

Distantly stood the angled concrete walls and iron red workings of the lock and the great drop of the dam, gateway to the Quad Cities and environs south, shut down for the day. While, in the river pool this side of the dam, rising from the water like a metal serpent from beneath Loch Ness, was the Corps of Engineers' massive dredger already hard at work. The machine howled like the creature it looked to be, gobbling silt from the river bottom by way of a huge vacuum, lifting it to the surface, and pitching it from the maw of an upper exhaust shoot onto a growing pile of muck on the western bank. Outside of the distant beauty, regardless of the awe-inspiring mechanics of the dredger nearby, all was frustration for the boatload of Goth bandits. Their escape to the south, they now saw, was entirely cut off.

"Damn it!" Gar shouted, slamming his hand on the wheel. "We should be on the road and half way to Dubuque by now."

"Oh, y'all," Norene whined. "I'm so sorry I wrecked the van."

"Shut up, bitch," Falcon screamed, "or I'll kill you."

"Yo. Don't yell at her," Dex said, coming to his girlfriend's defense.

"You shut up too, pansy," Falcon growled, refusing to back down.

"Falcon, Dex, knock it off!"

"All I did was say I was sorry," Norene said. "Ain't no reason for her to be ugly."

"We're tired of hearing it," Falcon barked. "You fucked us all. We're all going to jail for armed robbery. It's your damned fault and we don't forgive you."

"I'm not going to jail." Gar gunned the engine. He turned Pucket's boat on a dime, shifting his passengers – and their loot – again and nearly tossing Norene out. They started back upriver.

Arguing as they were, with John Henry's boat motor revving to beat hell, none aboard heard the rumbles in the sky; the same rumbles heard throughout the valley that morning. Neither did they hear one particularly high-pitched whistle. They were oblivious to the fist-sized object that raced over their heads like a missile; the first blazing space rock of the predicted meteorite shower. The cosmic stone splashed into the river in their wake, hissed gray steam, and disappeared beneath the surface.

# FIVE

Crystal dangled from her tree, her biscuits hanging lower than her shorts. Ellis, out of his rocking chair and sorting loose wire in the yard, saw her accidental display, frowned, and grumbled, "Cover yourself, girl."

"Daddy!"

"Daddy nothin'," Ellis insisted, headed into the shack. "You're a spectacle. Cover yourself!" Crystal dropped to the ground and yanked her shorts back in place.

Caleb was still laying with the pups in the grass. Spot had joined them and the boy, using the mother Shepherd as a pillow, called to his sister. "How come Daddy don't let no one come here?"

"Cause people try to make us leave our home," Crystal answered without interest.

"How come?"

"Daddy says the world's gone mad." She picked a wild flower, the first she'd seen that spring, and spun it in her fingers. "They say we're squatters."

Her little brother persisted. "What's a squatter?"

"Daddy says it's people do for themselves without givin' the gub-ment a cut."

Caleb lifted one of the puppies towards her. "Here's your cut."

"Get that flea bag away," Crystal said, pushing his arm with her foot. "Yer ignorant." Spot, moving only her eyes, issued a low growl. "You shut up too, Spot, y' ol' mad dog."

"Daddy!"

That shout was Jay's, coming at them through the trees. Caleb looked up. Crystal looked around. Ellis stole a peek out of the shack's sole window. Their eldest brother, Ellis' eldest boy, appeared on the run from the trail to the cove, calling, "Daddy, there isn't no boat."

"I can hear it," Ellis insisted. "And I'm pret near deaf."

Sure enough there it was again. The air was alive with rumbling, louder now, insistent and coming on. Jay turned to what sky he could see through the trees. "I hear it," he said. "I didn't say I didn't. I hear it too. But I can't see it. A boat went by like blue blazes headed south a bit ago but that wasn't the same noise at all. And there's nothing else on the river by the cove."

Yet it continued, the rumbles, louder now, soon joined by the oddest high-pitched whistle any of the Harpers had heard before. Jay, in the yard, and his daddy, in the shack window, shared questioning stares. Those stares quickly grew to looks of alarm. The rumbles increased. Crystal, wearing fear like a mask, took hold of Caleb's arm. Having none of it, Caleb pulled away. He dropped the puppy he was holding and turned to the sky, searching the clouds. Spot whined and turned a circle. She snatched up one of her pups by the scruff and hauled it under the porch. The other chased after her momma.

Suddenly, and with no warning, a fiery baseball dropped from the sky and slammed into the tin door of the Harper's shack with a thunderous *BANG*. "Jumping Jezuz," Ellis shouted from inside. Jay stared mutely. Caleb yelled "Creepers!" Crystal just screamed.

The door was horribly dented and all but destroyed – with a hole in the center Caleb could have stuck his head through. The rock (it hadn't been a baseball at all, but a rock), charred black and still on fire, bounced to the porch and into the grass. Spot, hiding with her pups, howled. Ellis swore.

What happened next can't even be accurately described; it can only be told.

More rumbles and more whistles followed, one on top of the next, each louder and scarier than the last. Then it hit, a literal shower of rock rain, fast, hard, and sharply angled as if driven by a gale-force wind. Those in-the-know would later call them meteorites, but to the terrified Harpers they were just rocks, one after another, pea gravel to soft balls in size, black, burning, and hot. They strafed the yard hitting trees, junk, and shack with *whistles, pings, and bangs.*

As Jay ran toward the shack, a meteorite hit him square in the back. He felt his spine snap and went down with a shout. Crystal screamed again. Caleb dove to the ground. While Ellis, caught behind the broke door and unable to get out of the shack, hollered "Find cover!" Small fires sprung up amid the wood piles, tarps, and foliage wherever the hot rocks struck anything that would burn. There followed screams, shouts, and howls beneath a quickly building blanket of smoke.

A fatal hour had come to the island. A few of those just introduced were about to die. But that was the good news. For, in the midst of the falling flaming terror, no one could know or understand that there are far worse things awaiting man than death. And sometimes, *sometimes*, dead is better.

There came a rumble that dwarfed those before. Then came a shrill nerve-rending whistle. A huge meteorite, big as a medicine ball, smashed the porch roof and crushed the Harper's shack.

"That was something!"

John P's boat was adrift with the river current. John had abandoned the motor and Angela her seat. They stood beside each other staring in awe at the sky. "The radio said you wouldn't see it," John said breathlessly. "But we did. Right over our heads. Meteors. A meteor storm. That's what it was too, a storm. Those things came over like they were on the attack."

Angela stared into the vast open sky, if anything, even more jazzed than her pilot and guide. How many times, in how many movies, had she seen that scene played out; *War of the Worlds, It Came From Outer Space, The Crater Lake Monster, Alien Dead, The Blob*. An honest to goodness attack from space and she'd witnessed it for real. Still looking to the clouds, she followed the path of the falling meteors downriver. "Do you think they hit anything?"

John saw her concern. "*Nah.*" He stared after her, considered the question again, and decided he agreed with himself. "*Nah.* Landed in the river, I imagine. Nothing to worry about." He retook his seat. "Well, I better get you to the island – for both our sakes." She sat too. He started the motor and gave it some gas.

Moving again, John had to speak up to be heard over the motor, breeze, and rushing water. "So where was I before we were rudely interrupted?" He laughed. Angela smiled. "Oh yeah, I was filling you in on Arthur Aaron. Listen, don't take it personal if Arthur did forget you. He's apt to do that. His wife, Hilda, she's a good gal, but she's a tad pushy. Well, Arthur's way of pushing back is to slink off and get himself a snoot full."

"You mean he drinks?"

"Let's just say he's saving Hilda the expense, and the undertaker some work, for when the time comes; he's embalming himself now." Angela laughed, a real

*The Melting Dead*

laugh this time. John liked the sound of it and kept on. "Rumor has it Arthur's got flasks hid around that island like Easter eggs."

"No, really?" Angela asked. They laughed together, not at Arthur, merely at the thought.

When the laughter faded, John shook his head and sadly added, "Some say Arthur isn't what he used to be. Fact is, he's pretty much what he always was."

As it happened, Arthur *had* forgotten Angela. He'd forgotten half the items on Hilda's latest 'To Do' list. And, regrettably, he'd forgotten the time.

He'd also forgotten that morning's predicted meteor storm and had missed the falling rocks entirely. His attention had been on the ground as he roamed the island's north timber collecting kindling. Now, burdened with an armload of sticks, he peered from the bushes at the edge of the timber to the clearing at the backside of the community house. He looked, specifically, to the kitchen door for any sign of his wife, the park's camp cook, his help-meet and nag, Hilda, puttering about. He saw none – and decided to take a chance. Awkwardly, balancing the firewood, Arthur worked a flask from his back pocket. The bottle, he could tell by feel, was on fumes. But things were what they were and a tiny bracer was better than none at all. He pulled the stopper with his ill-fitting teeth, swallowed all she had, licked his lips, and tucked the empty away. Fortified, Arthur left the trees on a bee line for his workplace.

He should have paused a moment more. As it turned out, he was out of the trees but not out of the woods. No sooner had he reached the small garage (or large tool shed), and dropped his firewood atop an existing pile, than there came Hilda's mean and motive-filled shout, approaching on a tear from the kitchen, to the accompaniment of the slamming screen door. "Arthur!" The old groundskeeper stepped from the shed, pushing the door closed behind him, preferring to take whatever it was his wife intended to deliver in fresh air on neutral ground.

"Arthur," she repeated, closing in, "haven't you gone for that drama teacher yet?"

"Yes," he said, clicking his teeth. "Left hours ago. Have no idea when I'll be back."

"Don't you be smart, Arthur Aaron. Don't you even. That poor woman's going to be waiting."

"Why, it's too early, isn't it?"

"For heaven's sake," Hilda said. "Early came and went a long time ago."

Arthur looked at his watch, frowned, and tapped the crystal. "My watch stopped. I don't understand that. That's a new battery too, damn it."

"Language! Go and get that teacher."

"All right. All right. I'll finish here and clean up first."

"Lot of good it'd do a dirty old man like you to clean up. There's no time to finish anything. Not that you were doing anything. As it is, you'll be lucky if she's still there."

"You think it's time?" He looked at his stopped watch again.

"For heaven's sake, Arthur. Which part of 'You are already late' do you not understand? You're a good man, but you are brain dead. Brain dead and walking around."

Arthur sighed, nodded, and disappeared back into the shed.

Hilda turned in exasperation, took in the yard on the side of the house and a good chunk of the campus, and gasped aloud. There he was, that college rock scientist, coming from the rest room out-building, with a front row seat to her spat with Arthur. She'd had no idea he was there. He stopped beside one of the picnic tables piled with equipment. Red with embarrassment, but determined to mend the situation, Hilda headed his direction. "I'm so sorry, Dr. Regas," she sang, twenty feet off. "I didn't know you were out here. I'm so embarrassed, yelling at poor Arthur right in front of you."

Paul, doing his best *not* to see and overhear, no longer had a choice. "Don't worry about it, Mrs. Aaron," he replied with a smile. "That's what husbands are for, huh? Oh, and, not that it matters but, I'm not really a doctor. I'm just a college professor. Or just Paul. Paul will do fine."

He was so modest, Hilda thought. And handsome. Arthur had been handsome once. "Oh, all right… Paul." Though it wouldn't have seemed possible, she reddened even more. Avoiding eye contact with the professor, Hilda ogled the picnic table spread from one end to the other with ropes and do-dads – without any idea what any of it was.

For the record, it was two tall cylindrical bags at the end of the table holding ropes coiled like rattlers; the first, a 60 meter climbing rope for a simple rappel, the other a fast rope, hopefully unnecessary, in case of an emergency. A third bag, a large duffel, lay open and empty. The gear it usually carried made up the organized mess on the table, now inventoried and examined in the ever less likely event Paul's colleague showed and they went climbing. Hilda understood none of it, the rolled webbing, cordage, slings and anchoring runners, the personal retention lanyards, the assorted hardware, carabiners with gate clips, quick links, ascenders, and descending rings, a fast rope descender he had no intention of using, a 6 mil rope for tying safety knots, several rappel devices (an ATC and a figure-8 descender), a full harness, of course, leather gloves to stave off rope burns, and a helmet to protect his noggin from rock fall. Everything needed for a man to fly – straight down.

"Are you doing..." She waved a hand over his accumulated gear. "...something scientific?"

Both laughed. "Purely recreational," Paul said. "A little rappelling to get the blood flowing."

It was all Greek to Hilda. Or maybe Spanish. Spread out, it looked like the tools of the Inquisition. All for an endeavor as frightening as anything those old torturers might have dreamed up. "Oh," she said, a tremor in her voice. "You step off a perfectly good cliff... with just a rope to hold you?"

"If my partner ever shows up, I am, absolutely!" he said, beaming. "That's what I call freedom."

"One man's freedom is another's fear," Hilda said. Then, moaning, added, "I don't like heights. I can't think of anything more frightening."

The park was perfect for the youth group getaways Reverend Snow had in mind. Nearly perfect, that is, save for two bothersome points. The first was an oddity he'd noticed there on the southern portion of the island. The nature trail upon which they walked seemed wholly devoid of nature. There were plenty of trees and plants and, if one looked, budding spring flowers and, if one smelled, all the fetid and rotting post-winter underbrush a nose could stand. That was all right. But, inexplicably, there wasn't a bird, bug, or squirrel to be seen. Not one. The second item had passed quickly and was merely an annoyance, but he'd noted it all the same. Construction of some sort was underway nearby, for the air had only just been filled with low rumbles and nerve-wracking whistles. Not the sort of thing to go with peaceful contemplation and perhaps, the reverend thought, not a good omen. He would like to have asked the park superintendent about both. But successfully asking Towers anything, Snow had discovered, was beyond his ability.

Just walking the trails with the man took decided effort, a healthy dose of humor, and such a large helping of patience that, Snow was certain, he'd never receive value for the cost. At the risk of his immortal soul, the reverend found himself building a grudge toward the superintendent and, worse, developing hurtful – perhaps evil – thoughts aimed directly at the swine, eh, the man.

To add insult to injury, Towers, in Snow's opinion, ought not even have held his position. On top of being loud, tiresome, and uncouth, the superintendent was desperately out of shape. They were clearly on one of the longest walks he'd taken in the recent past, as Towers had for some time been sweating like a pig, breathing like a winded ape and, now, could barely negotiate the path. Despite his dislike of the fellow, the reverend couldn't help but fear for his well-being. What, Snow wondered, would he do if Towers suddenly suffered some cardiac event and burst his obese heart?

Despite his struggle for breath, the superintendent talked on. "Now, don't get me wrong," Towers said. "You being a man of the cloth and all. I'm not saying they're scary exactly. They're just different, with a capital D. They're squatters, right there on the corner of the island."

Reverend Snow shook himself, and his uncharitable (and perhaps sinful) drifting thoughts, back to the moment at hand. The superintendent had evidently returned to attacking his favorite nemesis, the unseen but infamous Harper family, again. The reverend smiled attentively.

"Just arrived one day on the river, far as I know, the whole clan. From Cairo, they say, eh, not Egypt. Illinois. That's right next to the Tennessee border and, my God, do they sound like it. Eh. Pardon me, Father."

"I'm not–"

"Just stepped ashore," Towers interrupted, still uninterested in whatever it was the minister was not. "Planted a flag, figuratively of course. Hauled in materials from some junkyard, looks like, and built a cabin. They put up a plywood shack in a little clearing there, with a porch of all things, and called it home. They built a dock at the inlet where they came ashore like it was Plymouth Rock or some such foolishness. They even named it after themselves, did I tell you, called it Harper's Cove. Now before you ask, everybody asks, why haven't we evicted them? The fact is, we have. They've been evicted by the court, they just won't go. The local law, the Savanna police chief, is too nice a fellow to initiate a shooting war over a portion of the island the size of our campfire ring, his words. The local Iowa sheriff would love to kick them out, or shoot them, but that part of the island isn't in Iowa, it's in Illinois. He can't take action on an Illinois court order."

The superintendent's monologue was interrupted, finally, by a woman's scream. A shrill scream that tore through the trees. It startled the reverend and froze him in his tracks. Unbelievably, Towers took no notice and kept on talking. "I have no interest in the matter, you understand," the superintendent said. "Not personally. But I have my clients to think about; visitors to the park." It came again, a terrified woman's scream. "You can certainly see my point–"

"Mr. Towers, please!" the reverend shouted, embarrassed at having to scream himself to shut the man up. The park official halted, gobsmacked by the reverend's rudeness.

Distantly, a pained male voice joined that of the woman. Both were screaming.

"My heavens, don't you hear that?" the reverend asked. "Those screams? Is that your Harpers?"

Towers had no choice but to hear them now. "I-I d-don't know," he stuttered. "It would have to be. Yes. The girl, Crystal, and one of the brothers, Jay or… Who's the young one? Caleb."

"Their names aren't important now!" The minister took off running, in the direction from which the screams had come, shouting over his shoulder, "Come on!"

"Wait," Towers hollered. "Don't do that. If we just show up out of nowhere, Ellis Harper will shoot us!" The reverend ignored him, running on. Towers threw up his hands, sighed in desperation and, putting his bulbous self in motion, reluctantly followed.

# SIX

Harry Towers, or anyone for that matter thinking the Harpers lived in a junkyard before, had a surprise coming. The small clearing claimed by the squatters as a homestead had now been claimed by smoke. The shack, what could be seen of it through the acrid gray swirls, had collapsed and was wildly burning. The roof was gone but, in a cruel joke, the fragile porch railing remained untouched, giving it the appearance of a church pulpit over the wreckage.

Crystal, the only family member still on her feet following the cosmic barrage, coughed and waved her hands before her searing eyes, crying out, "Daddy! Caleb! Jay!"

She turned in place, searching but seeing little, wondering what in heaven to do. Somewhere in the yard, beneath the smoke, she heard a groan. "Daddy? Caleb?" She heard it again and a voice calling her name. She followed it and, finally, found her older brother face down on the ground with his coveralls on fire. Crystal dropped and slapped at the flames, tamping them out.

"Where's Caleb?" Jay screamed.

Crystal, crying, couldn't catch her breath to answer.

"Crystal, where's Caleb?"

"I don't know," she supped. "I cain't see Caleb or Daddy."

"Find Caleb. Never mind me and Daddy. Daddy was in the shack. He's dead. My back's broke, I can't move my legs. I can't help you. Find Caleb. Find him!"

Crying, fighting for breath in the smoke, Crystal rose to search the rubble. "Caleb! Caleb!"

The Reverend Snow arrived on the run at what the trees suggested was a clearing. "Dear God," he exclaimed, his mouth hanging open, as he fought to see through the heavy smoke. Towers arrived a moment later, huffing and puffing.

"Land sakes alive," the superintendent cried between gasps. "The Harper place was never anything to look at but... Now!"

Snow scowled, resenting the new monologue. It wasn't necessary. Even through the smoke it was plain to see the place was destroyed; a burning shambles.

"Ellis Harper!" Towers shouted, coughing and fruitlessly waving at the smoke. "Ellis? Are you folks all right?"

The reverend, unwilling to wait for an answer, disappeared into the cloud. Endless talk was cheap. He intended to help, if he could. Whether led by providence or merely luck, Snow quickly found the eldest Harper boy, Jay, and was flabbergasted by his condition. He lay face down, his clothes burned and his body broken. But he was still alive.

Towers moved more cautiously, around the thickest of the smoke, to the other side of the clearing. He found Crystal on her feet and, physically, uninjured, crying for her baby brother. Towers dived in helping her dig through the debris. In short order, they found Caleb unconscious beneath the porch. Towers pulled him free and handed him to his sister. "Get him away from here, Crystal. Get him out of this smoke." She did as she was told and carried her brother away and into the cool woods.

Towers remained behind determined to search the wreckage for their father. "Ellis!" he shouted. He took a breath, climbed the porch through a spiral of smoke, and dug into the wreckage of the shack.

The reverend found a rain barrel in the yard and, better still, a cup hung on a nail beside. He ladled a drink for the boy, wet his handkerchief in hope of offering some comfort, and headed back. Jay had been right, his back was broken. He was badly burned, in searing pain, and had a desperate thirst. He drank with Snow's assistance, crying the whole while, and fighting to catch a breath. The reverend tamped his sweating forehead, praying for the child, crying himself.

Picking through the rubble, Towers continued to shout for their missing father. Then he lifted a sheet of scrap tin that had once been part of the roof. Under it, glowing red-orange beneath a crust of black char, was the cause of the destruction; a big roughly round meteorite. The heat radiating off the rock was beyond belief. It hit Towers. He screamed and dropped the weathered tin, covering the superheated space rock again. But the damage was done and, horribly burned, Towers screamed on.

John P idled the motor and slowly maneuvered his boat toward the island park's east dock. He waved his hand inland, introducing, "The Rock Island."

As if he'd given a cue, a flock of birds, all kinds and colors, exploded from the trees. Angela squealed, John yelled, both ducked covering their heads as the squawking and flapping eruption moved at, around, and then past them. As quickly as they appeared, they peppered the sky, scattered, and were gone. "What in blazes scared them?" John cried out. Then, recovering, said, "Never seen nothing like that. Birds of different feathers flocking together. Never seen nothing like that."

Angela, trying to catch her breath, couldn't help but be reminded of Hitchcock. Nothing new there. As she'd already experienced that morning at the landing, any unexpected emotion in her life, extreme boredom to extreme anxiety, triggered her nerd defense mechanism. It filled Angela's head with the titles, greatest quotes, and best moments from the comfy horror films upon which her dear old dad had raised her. And the startling avian explosion had instantly given her *The Birds*.

"It's a morning for sights," John P said. "I'll give it that. Speaking of which…" He pointed to a faded green rowboat with a rear outboard moored at the dock. "That's Arthur's boat there. Hard telling where Arthur is." He shifted to neutral and let his own vessel drift in. Angela was out of her seat, thanking him, and moving to abandon ship before they bumped the pier. Once they did, he gave her a hand over.

She cleared the gunwale and looked hopefully back. "You're coming, aren't you?"

"No. Sorry, but you're on your own." John pushed off and waved as he drifted away. "I'm glad to have been of help but I need to get home." He pointed to the mouth of the path. "The campus is straight down that trail."

"Thanks."

"Don't mention it," John replied and meant it. She had a nice smile and that last one had been meant for him. That was worth the hell his wife was going to loose on him. He waved again, turned the boat, and started back up river.

With the island behind him, and plenty of river ahead of him back to the north, John P took a good long look at his dash. He frowned and gave one of the gauges a couple of solid raps.

Meanwhile, Angela left the east dock and started down the island trail.

The reverend stared, astonished and horrified.

In the wreckage that had been the Harper's shack, the scorched park superintendent was on his knees, hands raised to the heavens, fingers clenched in agony. "My God," Harry Towers screamed. "It burns! Like fire!" He continued to scream and rant.

Reverend Snow felt for him, the Lord knew he did, the poor man; the burns, the pain. But he also sincerely wished Towers would shut up. The screaming, the agonized rambling, was heartrending, sickening, and terribly frightening. The minister wanted to approach, to help, but knew he dared not. Whatever had burned Towers would burn him as easily. What good would that do? Perhaps he was rationalizing, but what good would it do? Towers screamed on and on and, dear God, why wouldn't he shut up? If only something would happen to make him shut up!

As if in answer to his unspoken, perhaps unholy, prayer the cabin wreckage convulsed. The splintered wood and torn tin pulsed as if something beneath was trying to rise up and free itself. With a crash and a groan, the debris lifted and fell aside. An irradiated and hideously burned Ellis Harper burst from beneath. He shrieked. He stumbled out and off the porch rise, teetered, pitched forward, and fell to the ground. He lay there as still as a stone. Ellis was dead.

The reverend stared, eyes like fried eggs, mouth hanging, unable to move. The fires crackled, the smoke billowed, and Towers like the flee in the elephant's ear continued to cry, ramble, and scream; background music to the horror.

Then with seemingly no instigation Ellis' corpse shook. There arose a sound described a century before by Poe as *"a watch... enveloped in cotton."* Snow heard it and feared he'd lost his mind or, at the very least, that his imagination had taken flight. Surely Ellis Harper had been dead as a mackerel. Now the reverend heard the beat of the squatter's tell-tale heart. The horror continued. The corpse's arms shot out, his burned hands gripped the ground. Ellis pushed himself to his knees. With his eyes glowing like red coals, his burned face pulsing with irradiated menace, the Harper patriarch slid his feet beneath him and stood.

"My God, Ellis," the agonized Towers shouted. "What's happened to you?" He raised his burned hands, pleading, "What's happening to me?!"

Ellis stepped over the smoking debris to the park super still on his knees. He grabbed Towers by the hair and yanked his head back. He bit the exposed throat, clamped his teeth, and pulled. Flesh tore and Towers' scream abruptly ended. Ellis spit the wad, skin, fat, muscle, and vocal chords, onto the ground. The silence that followed was alarming and Ellis, despite his own intense pain, basked in it, growling, "I've… wanted to do that… for a loooong time." He licked his lips, relishing the sticky sweetness of the park man's blood; hell and heaven, brimstone and treacle. Then the undead Harper stood again and inhaled the rotten sulfuric smell of the burning meteorite as if it represented the first day of Spring.

Snow screamed, staring but no longer seeing or, perhaps, seeing but no longer understanding. He stumbled backwards, spun awkwardly, and ran into the woods. The reverend ran, down the trail, then off the trail into the thickness of trees, stumbling and mumbling, unhinged. "I tell you the truth," the reverend screamed to the tree tops, "unless you eat the flesh of the Son of Man and drink his blood, you have no life in you." He laughed, roaring, and he ran. "Whoever eats my flesh and drinks my blood has eternal life, and I will raise him up at the last day." He howled and he ran. "For my flesh is real food and my blood is real drink. Whoever eats my flesh and drinks my blood remains in me, and I in him."

Dodging this way then that, circling back upon himself, laughing hysterically, the raving Reverend Snow disappeared into the woods.

Ellis, looking considerably healthier than when he died, stood licking the blood from his fingers. Behind him, the dead, burned, and just now returned Towers stood up with glowing eyes. He tried to speak, producing nothing but a gurgle as juices ran from the hole in his throat. Hearing another cry of pain, Ellis climbed over the smoking debris. Towers followed him into the yard.

The eldest Harper boy, immobile on the ground and unable to defend himself, saw red eyes first, then a face in the fog coming his way. "No, Daddy! No!"

Ellis dropped down over his son, his bloody mouth open, his tongue hanging. Then his glowing eyes shot wide with terror. He howled and pulled away. A covered stack of wood lay on fire beside the boy. Buried in the burning tarp was the source of its ignition, another of the hot space rocks. It was this glowing shard of meteorite that terrified Ellis. The undead Harper, violently repelled, scrambled back to his feet and away, leaving Jay to himself. Towers backed off as well.

Ellis knew Jay was not the only fish in the river. There were others. "Crystal," he shouted, sounding himself as if he were under water. "Caleb." He searched the smoke-clouded clearing around the ruined cabin but came up empty. He turned and started into the woods. "Crystal. Caleb."

The Towers-thing, gurgling through the hole in his throat, followed after Ellis.

# SEVEN

Angela had yet to conquer her nerves following the strange flight of the birds upon her arrival. Her senses remained on heightened alert and, unfortunately, her nerd defense mechanism was running on overdrive. Without meaning to, she made her way carefully through the tree-shrouded gloom of the island imagining the gloomy forests of one fantasy film after another, *The Lord of the Rings, The NeverEnding Story, Labyrinth*. But as the eerie timber thickened around the winding trail, as the foliage crunched and snapped beneath her feet, the fantasies faded and the horrors crowded in, *Long Weekend, Dead Weight, The Evil Dead*.

Something howled in the distance off to her left and she halted frozen in her tracks.

Angela didn't like that. She loved horror from a theater seat, or the safety of her couch, but didn't need a howling in the woods. She stared into the timber off the trail, uselessly. For there was nothing to see and, as quickly as it had arisen, the sound had gone. She heard only silence; an unnatural silence, in her opinion. True, she knew nothing about the outdoors, but weren't timbers noisy with wildlife? With the chirping and skittering of everyday critters? Since the birds had flown, there'd been nothing. Now a howl? What kind of creature, she couldn't help but wonder, living on a river island in the middle of nowhere howled? Maybe she was mistaken? The howl, after all, couldn't have been real. Could it?

Angela returned to the trail and, hesitantly, started down the path through the trees again. She tried to force her racing thoughts away from whatever creature might be roaming the woods. But it was no use. All on their own, they'd switched categories on her. The fantasies were gone entirely, replaced now by a cascade of fright flicks featuring, of course, howls in the gloom. *A Company of Wolves. Wolfen. The Brotherhood of the Wolves.*

Crystal had carried her brother on her shoulder, from the scene of their burning cabin, into and through the woods on the south end of the river island, for as long as she absolutely could. She'd carried him all the time, as big sister and surrogate mother, when he was little. But he wasn't little anymore. She was running out of steam. Besides, he was awake now, and coughing miserably, and crying about the smoke in his eyes. "I'm sorry, baby." She put him down, grabbed his hand, and took off running again pulling him along.

Crystal and Caleb popped out of the woods and crumpled in the high grass on the bank beside the river. She tore a piece of fabric off her top, wet it in the cold Mississippi, and bathed his eyes and face. "Does that feel better, Caleb?" she asked in a whisper.

In the woods behind, she heard her father calling. "Crystal," Ellis howled. "Crystal!" But there was something wrong with his voice. The horrid noise frightened her. Worse, she could hear her daddy, and what must have been Mr. Towers, crashing through the trees. Their carrying-on, branches snapping beneath their stomping feet, their shouts and tortured breathing, should have spooked the wildlife, the small critters and the birds. It should have sent them racing and flying in fear. But it hadn't. Crystal noticed it the minute she'd entered the wood with Caleb; the animals were all gone.

She turned quickly to look over her shoulder. There again, a pained cry, then the growl of her own name. Behind it came Mr. Towers gurgle in the trees. They were getting closer.

"Crystal?" Caleb lay awake now in her arms, his eyes wide with fright. "What's happening?"

"*Shush.* I don't know, baby," she told her brother. "You got to do something for me. You got to go get Mr. Aaron."

"I don't want to leave you."

More breaking limbs and another shriek, louder now. They were closing in. "I'm afraid."

"I know. But there's no time to argue," Crystal said. "You gotta get help. Get to the campgrounds and get help!" She lifted him to his feet and gave him a shove. "Go."

Their daddy and the park man burst through the trees on the other side of the clearing. Crystal gasped in horror at their burned and bloody conditions, their frightful red eyes. They weren't human no more. Bloodsucking freaks, that's what they were. Caleb saw it at the same time she did and took off like a shot. He vanished in the thicket. "Caleb!" Ellis cried, and dove into the trees after his son.

"No, Daddy!" Crystal screamed. Then she remembered the other man, the other thing. She turned back quickly to see Towers raising his fat charred hands in her direction. He mouthed speech but, owing to the missing voice box, produced nothing. A gurgle escaped the jagged hole in his throat. Crystal screamed, jumped out of his grasp, and darted into the woods. Dripping gore, Towers trudged into the trees after her.

*Moon of the Wolf. Scream of the Wolf. Werewolf of London. The Howling.*
"My God," Angela muttered. "You're just now getting to The Howling? How could you have forgotten The Howling?"

She was still alone, and talking to herself, playing her silly movie game, and badly enough she'd embarrassed herself. She needed a life. But why bother, she wondered, when she was making such a mess of the one she already had? The involuntary game in her head had, apparently, come to an end. The horror movies had gone for the moment, leaving only the gloomy trail in the woods, and her sometimes gloomy thoughts – and whatever lay beyond.

But then she rounded one last slow curve and, to her relief, the wooded path ended. A large white community house came into view through the trees. And Angela stepped into what had to have been the park's campus clearing.

Before she had the chance to wonder 'What next?' she spotted an athletic, good-looking man packing equipment into a duffel at one of the picnic tables. She was late for her meeting, and feeling as if she'd somehow failed the Chicagoland Directors' Guild, but suddenly things were looking up. Maybe the tour wouldn't be so bad after all. Angela cleared her throat to draw the guy's attention, raised her arms theatrically, smiled, and called out, "Well, here I am."

Paul Regas looked, saw the compact brunette, and returned her smile. "Morning." She obviously wasn't Dick Malcolm, so he still wasn't going rappelling. But, whoever she was, she wasn't doing the scenery any damage. Maybe, Paul thought, things were looking up.

Paul and Angela, strangers, each had their own perspectives on their chance meeting. There was another, a third view of the situation, of which neither was aware. On a trail, in the woods on the other side of the clearing, Caleb Harper – running for his life – saw the community house coming into view through the trees. He didn't know Angela or Paul. But he saw a lady across the way in the mouth of another trail. He made out flashes of a man in a light colored shirt not far from her. He saw the end of his own trail and ran for it breathing hard – too hard to get a word out. And Caleb heard the rhythmic thud of his daddy's footfalls immediately behind him.

But he was almost there. Almost to the big house where Mr. Aaron might help. Or maybe those folks in the clearing. Almost there. *Olly olly oxen free.* Three more steps–

Ellis grabbed Caleb by the collar from behind. He jerked his son backwards and clamped his hand over the boy's mouth. He pulled up panting, shaking, unintentionally burning the child with the radiating heat born of the meteorite as he wrestled to hold him and keep him quiet.

Angela heard something. Paul too. Both looked, Angela straight on, the professor over his shoulder, across the campus to one of the many trail heads leading into the woods. Neither saw anything. The path was empty and all appeared quiet. Paul shrugged. Angela smiled and whispered, "Something wicked this way comes."

Ellis had carried Caleb back, away from the mouth of the path, then off the trail and into the trees. There, he dropped heavily to the ground. Ellis held Caleb down and bit him deeply in the side of the throat. Caleb flailed violently for a moment then ceased to struggle altogether. Ellis sat back on the leaves with a rustling crunch, pulled his unconscious and wounded son onto his lap, and drank deeply, relishing the warm tang of iron and sating his bloodlust.

Almost immediately, Ellis' burned and decomposing flesh began to mend itself, to rejuvenate. The longer he indulged in the blood feast, the better he looked. He lifted his head, gasping for air, blood running down his twisted chin. Red eyes gleaming, he stared down at his lifeless Caleb and whispered, "That's my boy!"

"Angela Roskowic." She offered a hand and Paul gave it a shake. "Sorry I'm late. There must have been some mix-up. I thought you were sending a boat?"

Paul stared with absolutely no clue what she was talking about. But, considering how very cute she was, and the growing likelihood he would not be rappelling again today, decided to play along. That, of course, would require his winging it. "I apologize," Paul said with a smile. "It's been one of those days. I am glad you made it."

"Thanks." They shared a stare. Angela cleared her throat. "Did you want to show me around?"

"Yeah. Yes. Absolutely." With his gear stored away, Paul zipped the full duffel and slid it to the edge of the table near the rope bags. He placed his helmet atop the pile, then gave Angela his undivided attention. He clapped his hands, looked around for a place to begin and, finally, pointed. "Eh, the community house. As good a place to start as any. Dormitory… upstairs."

She followed his gaze to the windows of the second floor. *Werewolf in a Girl's Dormitory,* she thought. Then she mentally kicked herself for thinking it. She turned, eyed the path by which she'd arrived, and told herself, 'Forget the howling in the woods. Let it go.'

"Uh, and showers of course," Paul said, going on, still pretending he knew something about the place. "Dining room, kitchen, and meeting room on the ground floor."

Angela turned back, smiling brightly. "All right. You lead and I'll follow."

"And what did I just say?!" Sergeant Lester Vance shouted into the phone.

His boss wouldn't have liked it. The police chief demanded professionalism, particularly from his highest ranking man, and didn't like voices raised to the public. Heck, Vance didn't like it either. He liked to be nice when he could. But the grumbler, eh, citizen, on the line was outdoing himself and, in all honesty, was really pissing Vance off. The sergeant was near his wit's end and, out there, had a tendency to raise his voice. Besides, the chief wasn't in the office.

"What did I just say?" Vance repeated, no longer shouting. He had control again and spoke, low and slow, with menace. "I said I would let the chief know, Ben. Didn't I?" He paused to listen, didn't like what he heard, and replied, "There is no point in getting nasty. Listen, there's a robbery happened across the river this morning. Their Sheriff's Department may very well need our assistance. That means I've got to clear the phone and keep it clear for– No, I'm here by myself at the moment– You know, Ben, there's an old saying, goes like this, 'You can catch more flies with honey than you can sitting in jail for shooting your mouth off.' Yes, I thought you'd see it that way." Vance cradled the receiver and stepped to their radio. He pressed the 'Send' key. "Savanna HQ; Savanna One."

Atop the bluff, two miles from the Police Station, on the high side of the sleepy river town, at the wheel of his patrol car and just heading out, Police

Chief Carter Cross yawned and took his first sip of coffee. His radio squawked. "*Savanna HQ; Savanna One.*" The tinny voice of his frustrated sergeant demanded attention Cross wasn't quite ready to provide. He sipped again but the radio was insistent. "*Savanna HQ; Savanna One.*" Cross balanced his cup on the dash and grabbed his hand mic. "This is Savanna One. Go ahead, Lester."

"*Sorry to start your morning this way, chief, but Ben Nath is kicking up a fuss again. Just called.*"

Cross sighed. Why, he wondered, couldn't they start the day with an exciting convenience store holdup like the county across the river? Or a nice friendly murder for that matter? Was that too much to ask? Why did it have to be the chronically unhappy, impossible to satisfy swamp rat, Ben Nath? "Let me guess," the chief asked his radio. "Poachers? Or is it loud campers on the island?"

There followed radio haze and laughter. "*Got it in two. It's the island.*"

Cross sighed again and told the mic. "Ten-four. I'll talk to him."

So much for a nice drive and a quiet cup of coffee. With Ben working up a head of steam, regardless of the excuse, no one would find peace until someone pulled the thorn from the old boy's paw. Cross turned the squad, following the nose-bleed angle of the street down off the bluff, then turned again for the main drag, headed for the far southern reaches of the small town on the big river.

"The kitchen's great," Angela said, still following Paul's lead, out through the swinging doors into the community house main hall, the commons; a wide open area, with folded tables and stacked chairs at the ready, suitable for meeting, dining, or dancing.

"I'll take your word for it. What I know about cooking could dance on the head of a pin," Paul said. "But Mrs. Aaron, Hilda, she's the wiz, a great cook."

"The lady cleaning upstairs?" Angela asked. She'd gotten a glimpse as they'd passed the dorm bathroom; a reflection in the mirror of an older woman shaking her booty to the too-loud sound of Big Band music as she cleaned around a commode. She and the mop seemed to be having the time of their lives and Angela and her guide, opting not to interrupt, got away without being seen.

"Right," Paul said. "You'll love her when you meet and talk to her. She's a hoot. Her husband's the groundskeeper." Then he added with a laugh, "Good ol' Arthur."

"I heard about him on the boat trip over. My pilot, John, must have been one of the local gossips." Seeing no light dawn in Paul's eyes, she added, "John P."

Paul shook his head. "I haven't had the pleasure."

"You don't know him?"

"Can't know everyone, I guess."

"No. I guess not," Angela said suspiciously. "I just assumed. Seems like such a small place."

Paul nodded noncommittally. "But it is a big river." He pointed to the door. "Did you want to see the campus?"

"Yeah, sure," she said. Then, smiling, she added, "Absolutely."

Paul led her out, past the two weather-worn picnic tables (and his gear) where they'd first made their acquaintance, to a ring of eight, seven or eight foot long, log benches in a catawampus octagon around a circle of assorted round river stones and white jagged rip rap dotted by an ash pit at its center. Paul flourished a hand. "The fire ring," he said.

"That one I knew," Angela replied in monotone.

"Yeah, thought you might." He pivoted. "What's next?" He pointed to an old round barn on the far side of the clearing. "The theater's great. Well, it's really a big barn with a stage, but–"

"Theater! I'm in theater. That's what I do. Actor and director; a theatrical director. That's the group I'm scouting a meeting place for… the Chicagoland Directors' Guild, remember?" He didn't appear to. Nice-looking guy, she thought, but thick as a tree. He gave no sign he knew what she was talking about. She'd given him the lowdown over the phone when she arranged the tour. Apparently, you didn't need to be smart to run a park camp. Whatever… they had a theater!

Poor thing, Paul was thinking, still thinks I'm Harry Towers. Well, nobody said you had to be smart to direct a play. There seemed little sense in informing her at this late date. Paul left his thoughts and rejoined reality in time to notice Angela had abandoned him. She was headed for the barn, on the run, shouting back over her shoulder, "Come on!"

Paul hurried to catch her. But that wasn't happening. Angela could run. She beat him to the building with plenty to spare but, politely, waited for him to get there and let her in. "The thee-a-tah," he said, throwing his arms wide as they stepped in. "Room for a prom, or a scout jamboree, or a meeting of gilded Chicagoland directors. Or push the chairs to the side and do *The Sound of Music.*"

"You mean *Sweeney Todd,*" Angela said. "I love it!"

There were no seats, just a wide-open floor (as round inside as out) with scads of folded tables and stacked chairs against a section of the wall as in the commons hall. Across the way was a large modern fireplace with a neat pile of chopped wood nearby at the ready. Not far from that was a small mobile wet bar, with no obvious evidence of wet in sight, and a dark and empty popcorn machine; both waiting for an audience. A stage occupied the far third of the building. Fronted by a proscenium arch, with a work area to the rear right (backstage left) full of furniture and props and a deep hidden wing to the left (backstage right), filled with God only knew what. There were lights, curtains, the whole shebang. Stairs on either side accessed the stage from the floor.

Angela ran for those on the right and took to the stage, singing, "Let's put on a show!"

Caught up in her infectious good humor, Paul joined her. "My uncle can build the sets."

Angela laughed. "My aunt can sew the costumes."

"Aha!" Paul shouted. "There's no need. Come on. I've been snooping."

Backstage right overflowed with set pieces, flats, plywood, a work table, tools and what-not; plenty of what-not. Above the ceiling, running the depth of the wing, with a wooden ladder leading up, was a crow's nest for storage. Paul hurried into the wing, climbed the ladder, and disappeared.

"Snooping?" Angela asked. She turned, searching the wing. "Hey!"

Paul had vanished.

She stared up at the crow's nest, so deep and dark only a brave crow would enter, and called out, "What do you mean snooping? You run the place. Why do you have to snoop? Hello?"

# EiGhT

"Harry? Harry?" Seeing nothing in the dark, hearing no answer from the crow's nest, Angela hesitantly took the ladder rungs in hand and started to climb. "Mr. Towers?" At the top, she peered into the gloom. "Mr. Towers?" She strained to see deep into the loft.

An amber light snapped on. Angela yipped.

The light threw harsh shadows on the scattered props and set pieces, on an open steamer trunk, and on a figure standing before it; a vision straight out of hell's own opera. Draped in a crimson robe and a matching red flowing cape, clutching a brown staff his own height, wearing a wide-brimmed black musketeer hat (with a gargantuan green feather depending to the side) atop his head, and a face – that was no face at all, but a grinning skull with eye orbits that sank into black nothingness.

Angela yelped. She lost her grip on the ladder and nearly fell. She clutched at the rung, caught her breath, and stole a second look. As shocking as the cloaked figure was, he stood unmoving in a richly theatrical pose, with one hand on the staff and one on his breast. All indications were he, it, appeared content to remain posed. Angela raised a suspicious brow.

Then the skeletal figure spoke, in Paul's muffled voice, crying out, "Costumes!"

"Don't do that! You don't do that to someone on a ladder. You scared the life out of me. I could have fallen and broken my neck." Angela climbed the rest of the way up and into the crow's nest. She hurried to Paul's side, yanked off his skull mask, and shouted, "I want a cape!" She turned to the trunk. "What's in the box? What's in the box?"

To tell where Ben Nath lived might give you the notion he was a transplanted Cajun, an old swamp cat with a cabin full of dried lizards and stuffed toads, using the river marshes as a stand in for his beloved bayou. That would be romantic. It would also be nonsense. The truth was Ben, a born and bread native, lived by himself on a Mississippi back channel beyond the southernmost edge of town, south of South Street, west of the *Great River* (walking, biking, and hiking) *Trail* winding its way through the lowlands from Savanna to the Quad Cities. Ben was a loner, because he liked being alone and, there's no denying, because he was a mean old bastard with whom nobody else could get along. You couldn't see his place from the town line but, if you knew where to turn and beyond that where to pull off, it was just a short hike – when the river was low and the land dry – through the thick trees to the shifting bank of the channel beside which his house sat on stilts. In other words, the middle of nowhere. Chief Carter Cross, having answered Ben's chronic complaints for years, knew where to turn off. He parked his squad with no enthusiasm, took another sip of coffee as a bracer, then took to shoe leather through the trees and the deep grasses.

He was spotted the instant he reached the other side of the small backwater timber. Spotted and targeted as Ben stormed from his shack and down his rickety steps like a Tasmanian devil.

Ben Nath was a nasty piece of work. He was as disagreeable as any three men, but short the body parts for one. He was missing the lobe of his left ear, every other tooth in his head, and the three middle fingers of his right hand (leaving him what looked like the pink claw of a Mississippi blue crab). One eye was hidden by a squint but that, Cross thought, was more attitude than ailment as it wasn't always the same eye. Ben was small, wiry, and so bull-legged he looked like a rider in search of a horse. No doubt his mount had taken all the bitching it could stand and run off leaving the ornery cuss on foot. If that wasn't enough, Ben's sweat stank of beer and garlic, he screeched like an owl, and blasphemed every time he opened his mouth. A real charmer.

"Jee-zus Christ," Ben hollered, coming on. "Took you long enough to get here."

"Good morning, Ben."

"Is it?" the old man asked tartly. "Might be for you. Still last night to me. Why I haven't slept a wink. The carrying on from that goddam island was ridiculous, Carter. And I'm telling you right now, I'm not putting up with those park campers or another summer like last. Jee-suz Christ!"

The teeth were precious when he ranted. To change the view, Cross looked down the channel to where it joined the Mississippi proper, and to a green speck in the distance, the portion of the Rock Island visible from there. As for noise, he heard nothing whatever out of the ordinary. "There are folks partying all night up and down the river, Santa Fe Beach, Crappy's," Cross said. "Makes no sense to blame the camp."

"Now you're telling me what I'm hearing and where from?"

"I didn't say a thing about you, Ben. Not a thing. I was reminding you of a fact, of which you are already well aware, in regards to the river. It's a busy place, night and day, especially in spring and summer. As for the island, I don't even know if they're open for the season yet over there."

"Christ on a crutch! I didn't say it was Cub Scouts. Anybody with a boat can get over there and raise hell. And they do! Disturbing the public peace. Worse, disturbing my peace. Now, you going to do something? Or are you leaving it up to me?"

"If I was you, Ben… I'm not but, if I was, I'd turn her down to a slow simmer." Cross brought his hands up to his hips. "Patrolling that island is police business. You stick your nose in police business, you're going to wind up with a bruised nose."

"Son of a bitch," Ben growled. He wasn't calling the officer a name, merely starting a sentence. "You ain't threatening me, chief, are you?"

"I don't need to threaten anyone. I'm telling you exactly how it is. Now, as long as you've known me, have I ever left a complaint unchecked?"

"I didn't say you had."

"Same goes for this complaint. I'll see if there's anything to it. And I'll get back to you."

"Well, there's plenty to it. See that you do."

Cross longed to ask, "Ben, don't you ever smile," and maybe return the "you son of a bitch" as a postscript, but he didn't. Enough had been said already. He made do with a sigh, turned, and started back for his squad. He didn't know why he'd bothered to come all the way out there. The man was always inhospitable and unreasonable. It had been a waste of time.

Ben, meanwhile, fumed and blasphemed, watching with one eye as the police chief disappeared into the trees. The old hermit didn't know why he'd bothered to call the cops. They were lazy and stupid. It had been a waste of time.

"You looked just like Lon Chaney," Angela told her guide as they stepped from the theater.

As was becoming their norm, Paul had no clue what she was talking about and looked a question.

"From The Phantom of the Opera," Angela said in answer. "Well, sort of. Your color scheme was wrong. The robe and cloak were right but the feather should have been red too." Paul continued to stare. "And your rod of Asclepius should have been black."

"My what?"

"The staff, the big walking stick, it was brown; should have been black, with a serpent entwined around it biting the skull. Uh, there should have been a skull at the top." She made what she must have imagined was a skull face. The young professor pulled the theater door closed, continuing to stare as if the girl were nuts, which she obviously was.

"Otherwise," Angela went on, ignoring him. "You looked a lot like Lon Chaney. You'll have to forgive me, I'm a horror fanatic. Not a fan; a fanatic. I love scary movies."

Paul nodded. "Lon Chaney," he said, stretching his memory. "*The Wolf Man*, right?"

"No. Lon Chaney Junior was the Wolf Man. I'm talking about his father; who was not, by the way, Lon Chaney Senior. You see, Chaney Junior, whose real name was Creighton, didn't become Junior until 20$^{th}$ Century Fox blackmailed him into it in 1939. They offered him a contract, when he was all but starving, but made it conditional on his changing his name to take advantage of his father, who was one of the great stars of the silent era. His dad, who was never Senior, and never wanted Creighton to have anything to do with the film business, had been dead eight years by then. So there was just Lon Chaney and his son, Lon Chaney Junior." Paul's mouth hung open. "You don't care about any of this, do you?"

"No," he said. "Not at all."

"Well, that was fun." She inhaled, stretched, and strode into the campus. "It's beautiful here. So quiet."

"It's louder in the evening. Come to think of it, and at the risk of a cliché, it's too quiet."

"I noticed that when I stepped on the island," Angela agreed. "No critter noises. Except for–" She stopped herself.

"Except for… what?"

She shook her head, deciding then and there to keep the great bird escape, and the imaginary howl she'd heard after, to herself. "Nothing."

Paul shrugged, looking around. The campus was not only quiet but strangely vacant. He'd seen Harry Towers go off with his guest, the Reverend Snow, touring. Who knew when they'd be back? Hilda was inside cleaning and puttering around. Where Arthur had gotten to was anybody's guess. There were no visitors from either mainland and, though he hated to admit the ditzy new girl was right, the usual chirp of birds and the padding and slithering of the island's crawling beasts were all oddly absent. "I wonder where everyone… Where everything is?"

"Are there other guests right now?"

"Huh? Oh, no, not at the moment. Still…" He let the thought fade, keeping the details of the oddity to himself, then shook the notion from his head. "Any idea of the time?"

"You don't have a cell phone?"

Paul raised a brow. "Why do I need a cell phone? I want to know what time it is."

"They have a clock."

Unable to help himself, Paul stared again. He'd never met anyone whose mind always drove in a circle regardless of how straight the road. Angela, for her part, returned his stare as if she were dealing with a child. "Cell phones," she explained, "they have a clock on them."

"Fascinating. No, I don't have a cell phone. Do you happen to have the time?"

"You don't wear a watch?"

Paul inhaled deeply, held it, then exhaled slowly. He smiled, proud of his display of patience. "I usually wear a watch, but not when I'm on vacation."

"Vacation? You mean you don't work here?"

"Yes. I don't work here. I never said I did."

"You mean you're not Harry Towers?"

Paul laughed. "God, no!" He turned and headed for the picnic tables and his gear still resting there. Angela followed, complaining, "You mean... you just let me think you were Harry Towers?"

"I'm not responsible for your thoughts. Hard enough being responsible for my own."

"You gave me a tour."

"You asked for one," Paul said. He smiled again. "And you're welcome."

Angela frowned and reddened with embarrassment. She began violently digging through her coat pockets. Paul stopped, amused and curious. "What are you doing?"

"Looking for my cell phone," she said, spitting the words. "You said you wanted the time."

"You mean, you don't wear a watch?"

She glared. "Why would I? I have a cell phone." She returned to her search and angrily extracted a billfold, keys, a pen, a wad of tissue, a root beer barrel candy, and her phone. She returned the junk, flipped the cover of the phone, and tapped at the key pad. Her lips became a mean straight line. She snapped the cover closed and returned the device to her pocket without comment.

Paul waited, counting 'One Mississippi, two Mississippi...' in his head. Ten Old Man Rivers later, he had to ask, "No cell signal?" Angela shook her head without looking at him. "So you can't tell me what time it is?" Her lips remained pinched. "All right, then."

Paul had had it. His colleague and climbing partner, yet to arrive, was surely now not coming. None of the usual suspects were around. And the goofy girl who loved horror films, as yummy as she was to look at, was rubbing his rhubarb the wrong way. Raspberries to all of them. It was an absolute no-no to rappel alone. But his vacation was an ass-aching bust and he'd had it. He grabbed his helmet and rope bags in one hand, and his duffel in the other, and loudly announced, "I don't know where the others are, but they ain't here. You've seen all this tourist trap has to offer. Now I'm going rock climbing. Have a nice life."

"You're not even going to tell me your real name?"

"I never gave you a false name. You assumed I was Harry Towers."

"Okay. You're not even going to tell me your name?"

"As you probably won't be here when I get back, what's the point?" Paul started away.

Angela watched until he reached a trail head, to the right of the theater, at the edge of the clearing, then she hollered, "Wait!" and hurried after him. "When you say rock climbing, with all that stuff, you mean rappelling, don't you? I mean, you're not going to climb up a sheer cliff like real rock climbers do, are you? You're just going down the side of a cliff, right?"

Paul stopped to face her. He would have counted ten again but was plumb out of Mississippis. "I meant what I said. You see, having spent your entire life alone watching *King Kong* or *The Mummy* at 3 a.m. on television, or in the oh-so-real world of the theater, you wouldn't know, but it's possible to both climb up something or to climb down something, like the face of a cliff."

"Sounds like I climbed on your last nerve."

Paul chuckled his amusement. "Getting back to my point. The technical term for what I intend to do is *abseiling* from the German *abseilen* meaning "to rope down." Rappelling, or rapping in American English, depelling in Canadian slang, abbing in Britain, and rappling in Hindi, is a means of controlled descent down a rock face using a rope when a situation is dangerous, a method to access difficult to reach areas at height, and a terrific way to escape difficult to deal with individuals on the ground. I'm just saying."

"Okay," Angela said, nodding pleasantly. "I'll watch you."

"Watch? What fun would that be?"

"Well, I'm not rappelling."

"You mean you're not abseiling," Paul corrected, starting away. "I didn't ask you to come."

"Well, I'm coming," she replied, starting after him. "But I'm not rappelling."

"Do you want to bet?"

They disappeared together up the trail.

# NINE

*"Are Ben's knickers all a-twist?"*

"Easy," Chief Cross told his microphone and, with it, his sergeant, who knew better. There was a day, once upon a time, when you could ask tactless questions over the radio. But, thanks to too many nosy folks, too many scanners, and too many bottom-feeding lawyers, that day was gone. Though, in Ben Nath's case, he had a hard time working up a lather. Still he'd have to have a talk with Lester. For the scanner fans, he keyed his mic and added, "If you're listening, Ben..." He paused, fought the urge to say 'Don't bother calling because you know it's true' but instead said, "Everything is under control." He could hear old Ben covering the walls of his shack with bouncing blasphemies and Lester laughing himself silly in the radio room.

Cross had by then reached the opposite side of Savanna, and was pulling his squad into the parking lot at Miller's Landing, when he remembered something he wanted done. "Say, sergeant," he told the mic, "Give them a call over there at the island."

"*I already have. Just to see who was about.*" The radio haze crackled. "*I couldn't get any answer. If she's there, Mrs. Aaron probably has her radio blaring.*"

Cross parked, facing the river, called on more brains cells than he'd planned on using at that hour, and decided. "Well, as long as everything's quiet here," he said, "I might as well run down; see who's up and what they're up to. The island's due for a patrol anyhow. Might as well wipe out as many birds as I can with the same rock."

"*You mean, kill two birds with one stone?*"

"S'what I said."

Dead air followed. Lester was, no doubt, laughing again. Finally, *"Do you want me to bring the boat down, chief?"*

Cross stared out the squad window at a river that, by that time of the morning, was usually bustling with barge traffic and boaters. Today there was little happening and not much expected to happen, not with the south lock closed. There were Iowa County boys and State Troopers on the bridge but, until his Department was called, that was none of his business. There were a few fishermen about. One boat in particular caught his attention, racing upriver. The operator was too far away to identify but the boat was unmistakable and, to his good fortune, looked to be on a bee-line for the landing.

"No to the Department boat," Cross told the mic. "I don't think I'll need it." He signed off, stepped from the squad, and headed down onto the concrete ramp. He reached the water as the boat he'd been watching drew near. Cross was glad to see he'd been right. He waved and called to the operator at the wheel, "Morning, John P."

"Morning, chief," John shouted back, slowly bringing his vessel in. "How are you?"

"That's yet to be determined."

"Oh? Why's that?" A sneaking suspicion was building in the fisherman's mind. Still he had to ask, "What's going on?"

"I need a lift down to the Rock Island."

John's face fell. His idling motor died and Cross put out a hand to stop his drift before the boat bumped the ramp. "I'd like to help, chief," John said, without sounding helpful. "But I just got back from the island and I'm running late."

"Sorry," Cross said. "But you're just going to have to run late. I'm on official business and I am requesting your assistance. Now, please, give me a ride down to the island."

"Damn, Carter, this isn't right," John said. Cross ignored him, wetting the toe of his boot as he stepped aboard. "I got fresh fish need to be cleaned."

The uninvited guest lifted the seat on the boat's fish keeper and examined John's morning catch. "Yeah, couple of beauties there." Cross dropped the lid. "They'll keep."

"They will," John said. "But my wife won't."

"You married that little dollop of pretty poison, brother. Blame the fool in the mirror." That ended the conversation for the police chief. When the fisherman started to whine again, Cross cut him off. "John, take me to the island or I'll cite you for interfering with the law."

"Aren't you the sadist? This is a heck of a way to treat a citizen in good standing."

"I couldn't agree more." The chief grabbed an oar and pushed into the river, shoving the boat away from the concrete ramp. Frustrated but helpless, and committed in spite of himself, John restarted the motor, cranked the wheel, and guided the craft back into the current.

Not a lot was said on the trip down. Both had their minds on future troubles; the chief with the unknown each time his portable radio squawked, and John P with the chewing out he expected from his better, if darker, half. If that wasn't worry enough, two-thirds of the way to the island, John started tapping on one of the dials on his boat's control panel; the same gauge that had vexed him earlier. Cross ignored his antics at first but, when the pilot continued his tapping, finally felt compelled to ask. "Is there a problem, John P?" he called over the growl of the motor.

"I noticed earlier. My compass wasn't working."

"What do you mean *wasn't* working?"

"Just that. It wasn't working when I was down here earlier. Then, when I picked you up, it was working fine. Now, the compass isn't working again."

Cross nodded silently and pointed downriver. "That's south."

John glared. "You're a big help."

Cross nodded again. "Civil service is my life."

Silence reclaimed the boat as they approached the island. John took the left river branch and slowed as they moved in on the dock on the northeastern shore. Arthur's small boat was still there, tied to the pier, and all appeared quiet. John reduced the motor to an idle as they inched up beside it. Cross was on his feet before they bumped and out immediately after. The pier dipped with his weight. He turned to catch the rope to moor the boat, but there was nothing to catch. No sooner had the chief cleared the gunwale than John had shoved off, idled up, and was backing away. "Get back here, John P."

"I can't, chief. I'm late."

"I won't be but a few minutes."

"I can't wait. You asked for a ride to the island and I give it. You're on the island. Now I got to get back."

"Damn it, John. You're leaving me stranded."

"I know and I'm sorry, Carter. But all you can do is arrest me. My wife's a spinning dust devil when she's mad and she'll do a lot worse. I'm sorry, I got to go." John gave the motor fuel and headed back upriver.

Almost as annoyed as he was embarrassed, but unable to do anything about either, Chief Cross stood rocking on the pier as he watched him go. He'd need to find a ride back; Arthur he imagined. But he'd hurdle that bridge when he got to it. For now, he was on a mission to shut Ben Nath up. He might as well get to it. He stepped to the shore and headed inland.

Angela spoke zero French, but she knew the meaning of *deja vu* and was overwhelmed by the feeling. She'd followed Paul through the timber, up the step hill, yakking and teasing him all the way, to the top of the rock for which the park island had been named; the rock from which Paul intended to rappel. She stood on the brink of the sheer cliff, dropping nearly a hundred feet to the river below, and knew that despite never having been there before, she had been there before. That very morning – in her dream. This *was* the clearing on the cliff as she'd dreamed it. What did it mean? What could it mean? If she had any powers of precognition, it was news to her. But here she was, and here was the cliff from her nightmare, and she knew darn well she'd never been on the island before.

Somewhere a boat motor buzzed, though none could be seen on the river below. In the distance, a long way off, she could see a monstrous machine on the water pitching muck toward the shore. It was the dredger of which the radio DJs had spoken. Beyond that was what must have been the iron lock and concrete dam. It was too tiny, from her vantage point, to see clearly. None of that had been in her dream. But the river most certainly had been, and the cliff, and the clearing behind her.

"Quite a view, huh?"

The question came from Paul, who'd paused in the middle of rigging his rappelling gear, to ask. For a moment, Angela considered telling him about the cliff and the dream. Then sense took over. He already thought she was nuts. Why give him ammo? She turned from the expansive view to watch him finish off his anchor, webbing he called it, wrapped around two trees on the inland side of the clearing. He connected the colored belts with two locking carabiners in-line with the cliff.

"So other than dangle from cliffs and tell humongous lies," Angela asked, "what do you really do?"

"I didn't tell you a lie."

"Whatever. Since you don't work for the park, what do you do?"

"I'm a professor."

"Of what?"

"I teach Geology."

"Oh."

Her disappointment was audible. Paul couldn't help but stop what he was doing and look at Angela. "I'm just wowing you, aren't I?"

"Sorry. When you said professor, I thought you meant you were a scientist or something."

"Geology *is* a science."

Angela smiled, humoring him. "If you say so."

Hilda carried a box of rags and cleaning sprays, with her good ol' boom box balanced on top, and a broom and mop pinched under her arm, down from the upstairs dorm, through the swinging double doors, and into the community house kitchen. She leaned the broom and mop, set the box on the counter, plugged in her radio, and raised the antenna. The work never ended but she'd found a way to make it all bearable; more than bearable. This was her favorite time of day.

She turned the radio on, to her beloved jazz channel, and was startled by a burst of static. That had never… Oh, well, the radio like everything else had seen better days. A moment of playing with the tuning knob did the trick. Lovely jazz! Hilda paused to look out the window. The door to Arthur's shed was closed and all seemed quiet. She turned away, back to work, and missed seeing the flash of two dark figures as they appeared from the woods and quickly vanished behind the shed.

Inside the shed, Arthur stared at his empty boat trailer and scratched his head. Wasn't he supposed to go somewhere? And do something? He was almost certain he was, but danged if he could remember just where, to do what. He pulled out his flask, sipped, got nothing, and shook the empty container in disappointment. Arthur's melancholy was short-lived. He may not have remembered all his chores but he sure as heck remembered where he'd stashed the nearest *other* flask. He found it, hidden behind a shelf of life vests and boat seat cushions. They belonged to the park's pontoon boat, still over at the marina, waiting to be got out now the dead season had passed. One more thing

Arthur would have to tend to soon. Wasn't there something he was supposed to tend to now? He opened the new flask, took that badly needed nip and, when he heard the door creak open behind him, whacked the blue blazes out of his knuckles hurrying to push it out of sight. "You needn't check up on me, Hilda," he barked, sucking on his throbbing fingers. "I don't spy on you."

Arthur turned to see it wasn't Hilda at all. It was the young one from the other side of the island. What was his name? Caleb, that was it. Caleb Harper – standing in the doorway. It took another look, another moment, for him to realize there was something dreadfully wrong with the little boy. If it was the little boy. "Caleb? That you, son?"

The door moved again and something filled the doorway behind the child. Arthur gasped. It was Ellis Harper, the boy's father. At least it seemed to be from the size and shape. But he'd never have guessed had he not seen the boy first. Arthur blinked, trying to focus. But it wasn't him and it wasn't his old eyes. It was them. What in the name of the good God had happened to them?

Fifty yards away, inside the house, Hilda's boom box filled the kitchen with Big Band swing; the only music there was in her opinion. She cherished them all; Benny Goodman, Count Basie, Tommy and Jimmy Dorsey. Don't even suggest Glenn Miller had died. He was missing in action – period. Gliding to her music, Hilda went about her chores. She was sweeping around the center island when Duke Ellington and his orchestra came on with their *Sophisticated Lady*. Enraptured, Hilda clutched her broomstick (twice the dancer Arthur was) to her slight bosom and turned the radio up. The sweeping could wait. She danced, smiling at, swaying with, being dipped by her not-Arthur. Nothing existed but the sweet romance of that sexy saxophone leading her around the floor. As the song wound down, and the romantic smoke cleared, Hilda danced past the window looking out on Arthur's shed and paused to study the scene.

The shed door was closed. All was quiet. Her husband had apparently, finally, gotten on his way. She could imagine that poor teacher, Angela *Something* waiting all morning at Miller's Landing for the boat that never came. Why in God's name had she ever married poor Arthur, Hilda couldn't say. She stole a final look at the shed and allowed herself the fleeting thought, '*Lord, I hope he's on his way*'.

Hilda returned to her kitchen cleaning – and her music. Rex Stewart led with the trumpet. Illinois Jacquet stayed right with him on the tenor sax. Together, they laid their *C Jam Blues* at the happy cook's tapping feet. She swept as she danced and the community house floor never had it so good.

Despite Hilda's silent prayer Arthur wasn't, of course, on his way. At least not on his way to the landing. He was still inside his shed, with Ellis and Caleb Harper advancing on him. Arthur threw tools and gardening implements at the pair as they came, but he may as well have been spitting in the wind. They attacked, irradiating him, burning him, biting him, and eating what pieces of the old boy they managed to tear off.

Arthur screamed while his blood spurted and the monstrous pair groaned in satisfaction as they drank. Finally, thankfully, Arthur died. Ellis and Caleb let him drop to the floor like a sack of garbage.

# TEN

Unaware of the dance of death just ended in Arthur's shed, Hilda had the community house kitchen in full swing. Occasional bursts of static from her radio jarred and infuriated her, but she was determined to ignore them and dance on. The volume had been high all along but, now, the music could only be described as blaring. She'd tossed away her broom and taken up with a randy mop that whirled her wildly about the room. Over the airwaves, Gene Krupa moved from his manic drums to the string bass, providing the frenetic *pizzicato* with his sticks, as he flooded the commons with his *Big Noise From Winnetka*. Hilda was moppin' and boppin'.

Then, out of nowhere, her back *cricked.*

Hilda all but fell on her face. Her mop, the instant before a rousing dance partner, was suddenly just a crutch – and a haphazard one at that. The fun was over. Holding her aching back, leaning heavily on the mop, Hilda struggled to the counter to turn the boom box down and then to the nearest chair.

Feeling old and tired, she was too wrapped up in her pain and her plight for another glance out the window. Had she the strength, Hilda would have seen death in the shadows; two figures, both blood spattered, the larger of them with smoke rolling off of his shoulders, exit and round the far corner of the small building. But Hilda was hurt and didn't see them. Neither did she see the door on the tool shed slip quietly closed.

Paul had his rappelling harness on and secured. He connected his personal lanyard. He eased the middle of the climbing rope into the anchor carabiners and secured the gate clips. He lifted the rope that remained, flaked on the ground with its ends knotted, and stepped to the cliff edge. He shouted, "Rope!" and threw the bundle over the side. The rope played out down the face of the cliff to the small beach below. Paul studied the results, happy with the straight and unobstructed line of the climb. The professor stepped away from the edge, back toward the anchor, and fed the rope into the ATC at his waist. "This is the descender," he said. "Your belay device. Fight the urge to remove it from the harness when you feed the rope through. It might seem easier to handle but you could drop it."

"Right over the edge, huh?" Angela asked with a smirk. She leaned, peering over, to button what she thought was a joke.

Paul wasn't laughing. "Possibly, yes." Then he warned, "It would be no picnic if you did. You don't have any spare parts up here."

"You have a whole bag full."

"Yes, *I* do. Leave it on the harness. The descender allows you to control the rope pay out on the way down."

"It allows *you* to control it," Angela said.

"Why do I have more confidence in you than you do? You're perfectly secure."

"I know," she agreed. "Because my dimpled bottom isn't leaving the perfectly secure cliff."

"Leave your dimpled bottom out of it, for now," Paul suggested. "Challenges are good for you. They reveal character."

Angela fanned her face with her hand. "I can almost hear the fife and drums."

"I was being serious. Without knowing you at all, I know for a fact you would go over the side of this cliff if the situation demanded."

"You would have to shove me over."

Paul paused and stared with laughing eyes. "Stop. You're making my mouth water."

Fate was conspiring with Destiny. They'd picked Hilda as their target and she was being tormented. At least that's how she saw it. As if her back going out wasn't bad enough, now the old girl's radio had gone out too. Growling in frustration, groaning in anger, she adjusted the tuning knob, the volume, the tuning knob again. Nothing. Her Big Bands were gone; her swing replaced by white noise and bursts of static. It wasn't right but her radio was dead. Annoyed, but darned curious if the technological disease had spread, she held her aching back, lamely shuffled across the kitchen, and tried the phone. No sooner did the receiver reach her ear than she jerked it away. The phone screamed with static as well. "What in the world?" Hilda cried.

She stared out the window and got another nasty surprise. The door to Arthur's shed was banging in the breeze. Wasn't it like her husband to leave it unsecured? Or, she wondered, could he still be there? No. That wasn't possible. Arthur had to be gone to fetch that theater woman. Come to think of it, where in the world was he? Then again, his whereabouts didn't matter. What mattered was he'd left the door ajar. Now the breeze was knocking the shed down one tap at a time.

Riled by her inconsiderate husband, annoyed by her malfunctioning radio, pained by her injured back, moving like a broken automaton, growling like a disturbed grizzly, Hilda left the kitchen by the back door, headed for the shed to – once again – mend one of Arthur's messes. "How I'm supposed to get ready for the season when nothing around here works, including my husband, is completely beyond me." She stopped short of the shed.

At her feet in the grass lay one of Arthur's garden trowels. She studied it, surprised to see it laying about, shocked to find it covered in dark red splotches that, on her sweet mother's soul, looked like blood. Oh, for the love of Pete, had he managed to hurt himself? She lifted it, stared at the mess, and turned to the shed. "Arthur. Arthur?"

With a sense of rising fear, something she hadn't felt in Arthur's name for a very long time, she stepped slowly toward the shed. Still carrying the gore-covered trowel, she reached for the door with her trembling free hand. It creaked open and Hilda stepped through the gates of hell.

Near the cliff edge, harnessed, attached to the rope, anchored to the trees, Paul was raring to go. Angela was close by simply being rare. She scooped up his helmet, dropped his leather gloves inside, and tossed them to him. "The gloves are for rope burns, I assume. But what's the helmet for?"

"To protect my–" The professor shook his head and grinned. "Thank you." He tucked the gloves under his arm and donned the helmet. "While I slip these on, you can start around."

"I can start around what?"

"Down and around." She stared back, nobody home. "*Tscha*," Paul said. (Not a word, just a frustrated sound.) He lifted the helmet off and pointed behind her. "Down the big hill and around to the little beach. I need you to second me, my belay back up. You do that from below."

"But I wanted to see you fall from up here. You know, sort of a Martin Balsam backwards down the stairs thing."

"Another horror film? You are, without exception, the weirdest sane person I have ever met."

Where, if anywhere, that particular conversation was headed was anyone's guess. And no one's to know. Because, just then, a scream reached their ears. It was female, difficult to hear clearly for the distance, but absolutely real. Paul, so startled all he could do was stare, stupidly asked Angela. "What the hell was that?"

"That," she replied, "was a scream. And you call yourself a scientist?"

Paul scrambled away from the cliff edge, pulling his harness as he moved. "Help me with this."

She did, loosening the loop straps on his thighs while he shrugged off the shoulder loops. Moving, Paul dropped the harness on the ground. The scream came again, as distant, but louder and rife with terror. Paul took off; the absentminded professor letting his helmet drop as he ran onto the path. Angela, on his heels, jumped over the helmet as it bounced. Her "Hey, watch it," and his "Sorry," were lost in the trees as they raced down the trail.

"Arthur. Arthur?"

Traumatized, bludgeoned by what she'd seen, Hilda, mumbling in terror, her knuckles white from her grip on the bloody garden trowel still in her hand, staggered back out of the shed.

"Arthur!"

She threw the shed door closed blocking out the vision of hell on earth. Yet the action gave her no time to catch her breath or collect herself for, in swinging it shut, she revealed an all new hell waiting beyond the door. The badly burned Caleb and the horribly melting Ellis, both covered in blood, stood behind it at the corner of the shed. Ellis opened his mouth, gargled a noise, then managed the words, "You're next." He nudged the child forward like a grown bird shoving a baby from the nest and told Hilda again, "You're next."

Hilda's eyes grew wide as she backed away. Her mouth fell open issuing a silent scream. Her fear quickly worked itself into a stutter. Then, finally, the real thing exploded; a full-fledged cry of horror that could shatter the world. She turned, despite the grinding pain in her back and, still carrying the bloody trowel, ran for the corner of the community building and into the front campus. The radiation possessed creatures, that once had been young Caleb and his daddy, started after her.

Hilda ran, her mind reeling, past the commons porch, picnic tables, fire ring, and into the timber. She frantically raced through the woods, breathing too hard to scream further, knowing those two things – they could not have been who they seemed to be, they could not have been people – were behind her in murderous pursuit. She ran in blind terror.

She'd been so frightened she had haphazardly run into the brush. Now, by either luck or instinct, she burst from the timber onto a trail. Stumbling, she turned from the island center and, taking a well-worn path, hurried in the direction of the east boat dock. Ahead, the trail turned sharply to her left around a huge tree. Mind fogged, horrified, and half-blinded by tears, Hilda took the bend and, on the other side, slammed head-on into the police chief coming the other way. Chief Cross yelled, falling back. Hilda screamed, freaking out. And, unseen by either, the chief's radio flew from his belt and disappeared in the wooded brush.

On the ground, flat on his back, Cross took an instant to recover, to get his bearings and figure out what had happened. The surprise of the meeting, the shock of the collision, had passed. Now intense pain made itself known. The chief looked down, stunned to see a garden trowel protruding from his stomach below his ribs on his left side. The keenly sharpened implement, as all of Arthur's yard tools were had, in their accidental impact, been plunged into his abdomen as if it were a knife. Seeing, and recognizing it for what it was, suddenly made it hurt like blazes. Without thinking, he clutched the handle and pulled. The triangle-shaped blade slid free, glistening with his blood and (though Cross had no idea) with the blood that had already been on it. The chief yelled in pain and anger, threw the trowel into the trees, and tamped the wound with his hand. Only then did he hear the camp cook shrieking.

"Hilda, it's all right!" He waved a bloody hand in her direction. She seemed not to recognize him. "Hilda, it's Carter Cross, the chief of police."

"Cross! Chief Cross!" She stopped screaming and the silence was suddenly overwhelming. Her eyes focused on him. "Chief Cross. Arthur. My God, blood. He's dead." She was screaming again. "They killed him!" Suddenly remembering her pursuers, Hilda turned back, pointing and screaming. "They killed him. Them. Them. Them!"

Bewildered, Cross followed her gaze into the woods. With the thick brush and the bend in the trail, he saw nothing and had no clue what she was on about. He rose to his feet, grunting at the pain, showing a growing blood stain on his uniform shirt, beneath his badge, left of the gig line. He pressed on the shirt and the wound again. "I don't see anything, Hilda. There's nothing there."

"They killed Arthur."

"All right. All right, we'll find them," Cross said. "Let's go back to the campus."

"No," she shrieked. "I won't go back there. I won't!"

"All right." He took a deep breath. God, his guts were burning. "Hilda, listen to me. If there's someone back there that's after you, someone who hurt Arthur, I have to check. I can't fight you and I can't leave you here in the middle of the woods. I'll take you to the east dock. You can wait by the river until I get back." That quieted her. Cross took her in hand and, with another glance over his shoulder to the empty trail behind, led her in the direction from which he'd come, toward the island dock.

They arrived a few minutes later without incident. They stepped from the trail into the clearing and Hilda, like a lost puppy found, went immediately onto the pier and climbed over into Arthur's boat. Cross made a move to stop her, then changed his mind and let her go. She didn't appear to be making an escape, merely taking a seat in the one place she felt comfortable. That's what she did, sat down in the boat, folded her shaking hands in her lap, and stared out to the river without any indication she was seeing it.

"All right, Hilda," Cross said, biting his lip for the pain in his guts. "Wait for me in Arthur's boat. I'm going to go take a look. You sit quiet and collect yourself. I'll be right back and, I promise, we'll get off this island." She neither responded nor looked at him, but seemed willing enough to wait. He'd have to hope she did. There was no evidence Hilda knew what she was talking about, but something had scared the old girl. He had to take a look. But he'd need to do it quickly. With the injury she'd done him, Cross knew, he was going to need medical attention soon. He returned to the shore already having made up his mind to contact Vance and get him over there. He reached for his radio, only to find his hip holster empty and the portable missing. Cross looked around and realized it was not on the ground nearby. He turned to stare back into the woods and down the trail. Damn it, his radio was back there... somewhere.

He turned to check Hilda again. She was still sitting, staring, unmoving. "I'll be back and we'll go," he repeated. Holding his belly and watching the ground for his radio as he went, Cross started away, headed inland.

Paul and Angela arrived at the campus clearing on the run, passed the theater, and came to a stop between the community house and the fire ring.

The professor was puffing his lungs out. Angela barely looked winded. Both turned in circles searching for the source of the screams.

"Mrs. Aaron?" Paul shouted between gasps for breath. He shared a nervous look with Angela and called again. "Mrs. Aaron!"

Not a sound. They split up to look, Paul headed for the community house, Angela around the side to see what she could see.

What Angela saw was a shed that called for investigation. She approached slowly, surprised to find her breathing speeding up. Okay, if asked, she'd admit it, she was nervous. She took the handle in her shaking hand and slowly pulled the creaking door open. She peered into the shed. Her mouth fell open and Angela whispered, "We have such sights to show you." She pushed the door closed and stared at the shed from outside trying to wrap her mind around what she'd witnessed. "P-P-P-aul. Paul!"

On the other side of the community house, at the big window on the porch, hands cupped, straining like a 'Peeping Tom' to see in, Paul heard Angela's shout. He took off like a shot around the building. He reached the back, saw Angela alone beside the shed, and raced to her side. "What is it? What's the matter?" She looked stunned. "What is it?"

"Death. I've just seen death."

"What?"

Paul took hold of the door and pulled it wide open. Sunshine reached past them lighting the inside of the shed. "Whoa," he said, taking a breath as he took in the scene.

It was an ordinary shed, tools, racks of junk, paint cans, fertilizer, gardening equipment, a boat trailer, and assorted boating equipment. But all of it, including the walls and floor, were spattered in a maroon spray of drying blood. Driven by curiosity, ignoring his instincts for self-preservation, Paul stepped slowly forward. Angela, holding her breath, her hand on his shoulder, followed. They entered and the door creaked closed behind them.

"Good gravy," Paul said. "What went on here?"

Catching a breath, her goofy defense mechanism in full gear, Angela whispered, "Yet who would have thought the old man to have had so much blood in him."

Paul turned from the red horror around them to glare at the girl. "Would you please stop that?" He had no time to finish the complaint. Behind them, without warning, the shed door was yanked open.

# ELEVEN.

John Henry Pucket was a pitiful sight, his hair matted, his drenched clothes plastered to his voluminous body, river water running from his pockets and being flung about in great droplets as he wildly gesticulated with his massive arms. Add his high-pitched whine as he complained about the theft of his beautiful new power boat and you have the pathetic image as witnessed by the sheriff and his favorite deputy. John Henry was tragedy, no doubt. But Rough Nelson and Melissa, at his side on the empty dock, were biting their lips to prevent it becoming a comedy. Not that robbery, vandalism, grand theft, and use of a deadly weapon in the commission were funny. Rough had every intention of hooking the bastards responsible and hanging them up by their nose rings. But, at the risk of showing bad taste, it should be noted poor John Henry was a sight.

"There was four of 'em, Rough," John Henry said. "All black!"

"Black? What do you mean black? You mean like The Four Tops?"

"The who?"

"Not The Who, The Four… Let it go. I'm not getting dragged into an Abbott and Costello routine."

John Henry was lost and looked it. "Huh?" he asked, wiping river water from his dripping chin.

"You said they were 'all black'. What did you–"

"Their clothes, goddam it. Black leather, black t-shirts, long coats, gloves without no fingers in 'em. Big silver buckles and studs, one had a chicken leg hanging around his neck, but everything else was black. I'm talking about their clothes. How could I see their skin? They were covered with makeup, tattoos, eyes like cat people, looked like death warmed over, like the revolt of the zombies!"

"Ghosts on the loose," Rough said. "I got it."

"Ghosts hell! They were the devil's nightmare, if you ask me. Ear-rings, lip-rings, nose-rings. Hell, them sluts prob-ly had rings in their titties! S'cuse me, Melissa. Looked like a goddam traveling Halloween party."

"I got it! Now… wait a minute. How many were women?"

"Not all. At least one, maybe two."

"What do you mean maybe two? There were four of them, you said. Now think, John Henry, how many of the four were women? And while you're at it, try again on the skin color, and their height, their weight. Damn, son, give me something to start with."

"I can give you one hell of a lead. The little bastards are in my stole boat and they're headed south as fast as the devil rides out."

"You got *devils* on the brain."

"You didn't see 'em, Rough. And, at this rate, you ain't gonna.

"They won't get far, you can be sure of that." Rough considered laying the whole situation out again; the lock and dam being closed above the Quad Cities with nothing moving to the south save fish, the dredger holding everything up, the units he had blocking the roads. But, to hell with it, let him read it in the paper. "We'll get them," was all he said.

"You might want to put some effort into it. They were moving fast, like they were headed out of hell looking for ice. They're going to wreck my boat!"

Rough rolled the ever-present toothpick with his tongue, considered putting effort into slapping John Henry upside his head, but decided instead on a meaningful grin. "That's why I don't commit armed robbery, John Henry." He tugged his gun belt up under his gut. "Moving fast is for felons."

"Well," the big man said, throwing out his ample chest. "I tried to stop 'em."

Rough looked the wet mountain over, from his muddy hair to his soggy boots leaking river water in a puddle on the dock. "Yeah," the sheriff said. "Pretty damned stupid, John Henry."

"Don't add up to much," Rough told his deputy, a minute later, as they stepped from the pier back onto *terra firma*. "But it's something. Get on the horn, Melissa. Update our 'all-points'. There's four of 'em for sure, at least one a female, maybe two, dressed like a motorcycle gang of creatures the world forgot. They were headed south when they left here too."

Rough disappeared around the corner of the house. Melissa followed, starting a transmission on her portable radio. John Henry was left to drip-dry in the sun on his empty dock.

Inside Arthur's shed, splashed with buckets of blood, Paul and Angela were already aghast. They couldn't help but grab for each other when the door was yanked open from outside. There was no time to think or prepare. Neither knew what to expect. But it certainly wasn't what they got; a gravelly shout of, "Police." Their instant relief was quickly replaced by a new fear. "Don't move." The stranger in the doorway was indeed a cop – with a cold blue gun in his upraised hand pointed at them.

Carter Cross examined the pair quickly but minutely. In less time than it takes to say, he decided they were no immediate threat and turned to the shed. His face gave nothing away, as he took in what was obviously the scene of a violent crime, but his voice momentarily faltered, "What is… going on here?" No answer. The couple looked at least as stunned as Cross felt. He couldn't blame them, it had been a stupid and unprofessional question. He scanned the shed again. "Are the two of you alone in here?"

Both nodded and Paul said, "Just us."

"Are either of you armed? Any guns?" That got him a 'No' from each. "Any weapons," he asked, "knives, clubs, hand grenades?" 'No' and 'No' again. "Are either of you injured?"

"No," Paul said.

"We don't know where the blood came from," Angela added.

"I'm Chief Cross of the Savanna Police Department. Without touching anything, I want you to step, single-file, out of the shed." He lifted his weapon to ensure they understood the threat and backed a step out of the doorway. Both complied with hands raised.

Only then, as they moved carefully and somewhat fearfully past him, did Angela notice the police officer's free hand on the side of his stomach and, showing beneath it, his shirt stained dark with blood. "Chief," she said, "you're hurt."

"Forget it," Cross barked. He looked over the area outside the shed. Satisfied it was clear, he waved his pistol forward. "Lead the way, folks. Out front."

He ushered them around the community house to the picnic tables beside the fire ring and ordered them to sit. "Now," he said, catching his breath, "who are you people and what's going on?"

"I'm a guest, a camper, whatever you call it," Paul said. "Paul Regas."

"And I was a potential guest, Angela Roskowic." She pointed at the growing stain on his shirt. "That needs looking at."

"It's not life-threatening."

"You've never heard of peritonitis?" she asked.

Cross looked at her, not unkindly, then regained his practiced hard features. "Never mind. Let's get back to the subject at hand. Where did all that blood come from?"

"We don't know," Paul said. "We were up on the cliff when we heard a scream."

"What scream?"

"I assumed it was Mrs. Aaron. We came running and found this. Where Mr. and Mrs. Aaron are, I don't know."

"I've got Mrs. Aaron waiting back at the dock. She's in a hell of a state; half out of her mind with fright."

"Hilda Aaron?" Paul asked.

"Yes," the cop said. Then, pressing on his stomach, he added, "She's the one who stabbed me."

"Hilda stabbed you?" Paul asked, aghast. "I mean, I don't know her, but it seems a little *out there* for a middle-aged camp cook."

"It was an accident," Cross said. "Apparently, she never learned not to run with scissors. She rounded a blind corner on the path holding a sharp garden trowel. She said she was being chased, and folks, you're the only ones here."

"It wasn't us," Paul said. "Where's her husband?"

The chief stared, trying to determine if the guy meant it or was trying to pull one over. He seemed in earnest. "I don't know. According to Hilda, he's dead."

"Well, we haven't seen him. If we had, we would have said so by now. As for her guess that he's dead... From the look of his shed," Angela said, "I'd say she's right."

Cross couldn't argue with her assessment; the shed was a blood bath. But the situation left plenty unanswered and he couldn't help but voice his foremost question.

"If Arthur's dead, where's his body?"

Hilda sat numb in Arthur's boat where Chief Cross had left her. She hadn't moved an inch. But the jostled boat had left the pier and drifted with the current. It bobbed, eight feet downriver, held in check only by the taunt mooring rope. Hilda, lost in thought, or beyond thought, stared at the racing water without appearing to see it.

"Mrs. Aaron. Mrs. Aaron."

The cry came from a child in a strained and desperate voice. Hilda seemed not to notice.

"Mrs. Aaron. Mrs. Aaron."

That time the call reached her, wherever Hilda had been, and returned her to the boat and the present. Slowly, she turned, found the overgrown bank and the little clearing beyond. Slowly, she focused. Her gray eyes glinted with a spark of life – then grew wide with terror.

Not ten feet from the pier, in the tall grass off the path, stood a burned and bleeding Caleb Harper. It had been weeks since she'd seen the boy, but it was him no doubt at all. But, good heavens, what had happened to him? His clothing was torn and burned. His throat was a torn mess and he was covered in blood. The child was suffering. His skin looked, dear God, to be sagging as if he were an old man.

Hilda gasped.

Something moved behind Caleb, bigger and looming. It stepped from the shadows of the trees into the sunlight and even then, though Hilda knew him well, it took a moment to recognize the boy's father. Ellis was an explosion of horror and gore, burned and bleeding like his son, but far worse. He was disfigured. His skin looked to be falling off like some incredible melting man. Hilda could not believe her eyes as she stared at the uninvited pair.

"Mrs. Aaron," Caleb called again, drawing her attention from his monstrous father.

No sooner had Hilda returned her focus to the boy than a volcanic eruption took place within his head. His face split down the middle. Caleb cried in agony. Blood and ooze poured from his bifurcated nose. His front teeth gleamed behind his opened upper lip. Hilda watched, her eyes saucers, her tongue a lump of meat in her mouth.

Behind the boy, Ellis emitted a freakish gurgle. His many wounds were bleeding, seeping, and smoke billowed off of him as if he were a stirred campfire. A glob of flesh, hanging from his elbow like a huge bloody tear, plopped to the ground as he shoved Caleb toward the pier – and toward Hilda.

Hilda's mouth fell open in horror but no sound came out.

"We're sorry 'bout yer husband," Caleb blurted, his gravelly voice failing him. "Since the space rocks come, it's the only way to cool the heat, to stop the pain." He stepped onto the pier. "We just cain't get enough." Caleb cried great yellow tears yet, at the same time, licked his bloody lips in hunger. "We're sorry we hadda do that to Mr. Aaron. An' we real sorry… 'bout you."

He caught the mooring line in his swollen hand and began to drag her boat back toward the pier. Hilda, in her first voluntary action since opening the door to Arthur's shed, nearly tipped the boat as she crabbed to the stern-most seat in the craft. Her attempt to put distance between herself and the Harpers was pointless; the boat was nearly to the pier.

Caleb grabbed the gunwale, yanked the boat awkwardly toward him, and reached for Hilda. She screamed and, out of room, fell back over the stern into the river. Caleb let loose with the cry of a banshee. Ellis joined him, sounding like a wounded animal.

Behind them, someone shrieked, "He who is not with me is against me!"

The shout came like a trumpet blare from the trees. Reverend Snow, wide-eyed and mad as a hatter, leaped from the brush swinging a chunk of heavy tree limb like an ancient barbarian. Caleb and Ellis turned from Hilda, flailing in the river, to the raging man of God. The melting Harper creatures, it seemed, couldn't believe their red eyes. Caleb hissed and ran at the reverend. Snow swung his club and batted the boy to the ground.

"And he who does not gather with me scatters!"

The reverend swung the limb again, a roaring roundhouse. He hit Ellis square in the side, waist-high, and drove the club through him, cutting him completely in half. Ellis howled. Muck splattered. His legs plopped to the trail in a writhing and decomposing pool of goo. His upper torso cartwheeled through the air and landed like a shovel load of pudding in Arthur's boat. Ellis' shrieking head hit the gunwale and splattered. The shriek stopped. Beneath the irradiated gore, the boat caught fire. On the shore, the grass under the pool that had been Ellis' legs browned and began to smoke. Exultant, the reverend turned on Caleb. The boy jumped to his feet and ran into the brush. Snow shouted after him, "The Lord said, You of little faith, why are you so afraid?"

During the chaos, Hilda had bobbed up in the river, soaked and slapping the water. Sputtering, she'd gained her footing on the muddy bottom and, stunned, had trudged to shore. Now, with no energy and little force of will left, she dragged herself from the river. The reverend saw her, threw the branch down, and reached for her, saying, "Then he got up and rebuked the winds and the waves, and it was completely calm." He helped her to level ground and lifted her to her feet. Then he squeezed Hilda's shoulders and yanked her to him. Wide-eyed he exclaimed, "Do not fear, for I am with you. Do not be afraid, for I am your God."

Hilda, overwhelmed by his mad eyes and contorted face, screamed. Oblivious to her terror, the reverend ranted on. "I will strengthen and guide you. I will uphold you with my righteous right hand."

# TWELVE

Cross holstered his gun. Whoever they were, this Paul and Angela, it seemed unlikely they were responsible for turning Arthur's shed into a charnel house. And it was gratifying, the chief found, that without the threat of being shot, the pair even relaxed a bit and did their best to answer his questions.

"We'll do what we can to help," Angela said. "But first you need that wound patched up."

Cross frowned. He didn't like being mothered when he had a mother. He liked it less from a *person of interest* in a crime. He would have told her so again had they not been interrupted. But suddenly, distantly, another scream filled the air and thoughts of the chief's wound vanished. All three looked up and toward the east path, while Paul and Cross complained in unison, "Not again."

Pressing his hand firmly on his abdomen, Cross took off running in the direction of the scream. Paul followed, hot on his heels, shouting, "Wait there," to Angela over his shoulder.

"Not very likely," she yelled back, starting after them.

The chief stopped and turned, backing Paul up. "Wait there."

Paul could go climb a tree as far as Angela was concerned. But there was no mistaking the police chief's order. Cross had made it official. She pulled up and stopped, but didn't like it and didn't pretend to. "This is crap!"

Ignoring her complaint, the chief and Paul continued onto the path and into the woods.

The reverend had his hands full with the struggling Hilda. Still, in his freshly mad way, he was trying to get through to her. "Have I not commanded you?" he asked as they wrestled. "Be strong and of good courage. Be not afraid, neither be dismayed, for the Lord your God is with you wherever you go."

Hilda answered with another scream.

On the path, Paul had taken the lead over the injured chief and, on the run, arrived first at the small clearing beside the island dock. The scene before him was such a bizarre circus of horrors, Paul had to pause and decipher what he saw. The motor boat, Arthur's boat, on the river near the pier, was on fire. Hilda, the camp's cook and house mother, was soaking wet as if she'd gone for a swim and looked to be in the clutches of – of all people – the minister he'd met only that morning. Both were shouting for their lives. Hilda was in terror. While something about the reverend's demeanor, even more than his actions, made him seem darkly sinister.

Paul joined the fray coming to Hilda's rescue. He grabbed Reverend Snow, pulling him off the hysterical woman. Cross arrived a moment later, out of breath, with pain etched across his face. He too had to take the scene in before he could react.

Paul was thrown off and nearly landed in the puddle that once had been Ellis' legs. He had no idea what it was but the stench invaded his nostrils and the smoke stung his eyes. Sickened and half blinded, Paul got back to his feet, found Hilda, and pulled her out of the tussle as Cross grabbed the reverend.

"I will instruct you and teach you in the way you should go," the minister screamed. "I will counsel you and watch over you."

It was short work for Cross, once he had him, to throw the reverend face down on the ground. He leaped atop him and, despite his own injury, expertly cuffed Snow's hands behind his back. Then and only then, with the suspect secured, did the chief allow his own condition to slow him. With his head swimming, sweating in waves, with the bleeding from his stomach flowing anew, he rolled and sat up beside the trussed up minister. "I might have known," Cross said, puffing. "A religious wacko."

Paul eyed the chief in surprise. "The nuns used to whack your knuckles, did they?"

Cross would normally have apologized. For that matter, normally, he wouldn't have said it in the first place. But things were looking less and less normal. He gripped his stomach, winced at the pain, then caught sight of the goo puddle on the ground, the smoking and bubbling mess into which Paul had nearly landed. "What the hell is that?"

"Don't know," Paul said, holding the spent Hilda on her feet. "Whatever it is, I nearly bathed in it." The high dry grass around the puddle caught fire. Paul did his best to stamp the flames out without touching the red and green slime and without dropping the stunned camp cook.

Arthur's boat, cushions, oars, and motor were toast, burnt offerings to the river gods. With the port gunwale turned to scattered ash, she shipped more river then she could hold and the shell went under. The burned bow popped briefly to the surface as the weight of the blackened outboard took the stern to the bottom then, despite the shallow depth, she disappeared. It took a good eye looking in the right spot to see that old Arthur had ever had a boat.

"I don't know what's going on here, but I think we've found the cause." Cross indicated his wide-eyed captive and asked Paul, "You know this guy?"

"His name's Snow."

"Where did he come from?"

"I don't know another thing about him. We were introduced when the park superintendent toured the place with him this morning. If you know Mr. Towers, you know neither of us got a word in."

Cross knew Towers well and could only nod. If anyone had ever been a prime candidate for wearing a choke pear, it was Harry *diarrhea of the mouth* Towers.

The reverend, still face-down on the ground, suddenly joined the conversation, mumbling, "God presented him as a sacrifice of atonement through faith in his blood."

Cross examined him with a frown, then turned from his prisoner to Paul. "I assume the reverend wasn't… like this… when you met him this morning?"

Paul shrugged. "Like I said, I didn't hear him say five words. He looked normal enough."

"Well, he isn't normal now."

"He did this to demonstrate his justice," Snow told the grass, "because in his forbearance he left the sins committed beforehand unpunished."

Cross rolled his eyes and stood. Then he took a breath and closed his eyes tightly, looking inside to deal with the pain in his guts. When he opened them, he turned from the mumbling reverend to Hilda, who was again staring into oblivion. "Did you see her this morning?"

"Hilda?" Paul nodded. "Friendly and normal."

"Well, something's happened to unscrew their hinges."

"We all go a little mad sometimes."

The chief studied Paul suspiciously, then shrugged and said, "I imagine. But… *Geez.*" He peered into the river, giving Arthur's sunken boat a last look, decided against the comment he was going to make, and turned inland. "Let's get back to the campus, figure out what's going on here, and what in hell we're going to do about it."

"No," Hilda shouted. "No!"

"Hilda, that's enough," Cross said. "I know you're scared and I'm sorry. I don't blame you." He took another breath, finding it difficult to get air, and returned his hand to his aching stomach. "I don't blame you for what's happened. But, I've lost a lot of blood and I'm not feeling well. We need to find what's going on here. For the moment, we can't get any help from the mainland. Until we can, we have to go where we can rest, get something to eat." He indicated his wound. "And I can tend to this."

Though Hilda did not acknowledge the chief, she did halt the squabbling. She seemed to shut down, vacated her head, as if the whole shooting match went on automatic. She offered no resistance when Paul turned her inland like a lost six-year-old and ushered her down the path.

"You are under arrest," Cross told the reverend as he lifted the man to his feet. Guiding him by the arm, the police chief started after Paul and Hilda. The minister, too, went without fighting, though he continued his speechifying as they moved. "Cast your burden on the Lord and he will sustain you; he will never permit the righteous to be moved."

"Reverend," Cross said over top of him, "You have the right to remain silent. Feel free to use it."

Ben Nath burst from the door of his wetland shack in an explosion of blue blasphemy. He pulled on a straw hat as dilapidated as its wearer, stared into the trees down the channel (envisioning the shadowy offenders on the Rock Island in his mind's eye), and shook his disbelieving head. He'd heard it again, screaming coming from the island, and he'd had enough. He jangled his boat key on the pinky of his crab hand, exclaimed, "Bastards," to the suddenly clouding heavens, and stormed as only a truly bull-legged man can across his yard and onto his waiting dock.

"I guess a little bit of quiet's too damned much to ask for?" he muttered as he untied his boat. "Boat motors and hollering all the damned night, screaming all morning." He angrily hopped the gunwale and threw the line down. "Jee-suz Christ. I warned Carter. Do something about the noise on that goddam island, I said, or I will." He grabbed the wheel and slid into his seat at the cramped helm.

"Well, he can spend the day sitting on his ass. That's fine by me." He stabbed the dashboard with the key, turned it, and fired up the motor. "I'll handle this."

Ben hooked the throttle in his claw and threw the shift lever down. The motor growled, the stern sank as an arc of water kicked up behind, the bow lifted and danced a yaw to port as the boat moved away, then headed south – down the channel and through the trees.

"The Sheriff and I are heading south towards the dredger," Melissa told her portable radio. She stood on a slanted concrete boat landing, like the one at Miller's, this one in Iowa outside the Sabula town line. Rough stood below her, nearer the water watching J.D. Morales, the Department's part-time mechanic, knee-deep to his waders, ratchet the County's boat off its trailer and into the river.

"Melissa," Rough yelled past his toothpick and over his shoulder. "Tell him to keep watch… in case they double back on the far side of the island."

"We haven't seen them yet," she told the squawk box. "So they're still south of us. We expect to either find them or meet them coming back. But Sheriff Nelson wants to know if you boys will keep an eye peeled in case they slip over to Illinois?"

On the other end of the radio signal, on the opposite side of the river, Lester Vance paced the southern-most pier of the Savanna marina dock. He'd come down amid the houseboats, binoculars in hand, to gaze to the southwest and see what he could see of the police scientists at the scene of the robbery in Sabula. What he'd been able to see, beyond the flickering reds and blues, was squat. Their City Hall was in the way. "I've got everyone from Bellevue to Clinton watching; have had since your first call," Vance told Melissa, via his portable. "The way they was described, dressed all crazy-like, someone will spot them soon. But, just between you and me, I'd loved to have seen John Henry's face when they skedaddled with his boat."

"*He wasn't happy,*" the radio replied in a hazy version of Melissa's voice. "*Jumped right into the drink after them.*"

Vance laughed, picturing it. "Well, we're watching, for sure."

"*Thanks, Lester.*"

"Hey, Missy," Vance asked the radio. "What about tomorrow night's dance?" The volunteer EMTs and firefighters were hosting their annual charity hoe-down, with grills roaring, kegs gurgling, and a couple of live bands (local kids, pretty good) playing until 2:00 am. He'd asked Melissa, more than once, to cross the river and shake a leg with him. So far she'd turned him down every time but that meant nothing to Vance. He knew eventually she'd grease his squeaky wheel. "What about it?" he asked. "Did you give any more thought to going with me?"

His radio crackled and Melissa's voice came loud and clear. "*Nope. Not one bit.*"

Back in Iowa, on their side of the river, Rough was already aboard the County's boat. Melissa climbed in beside him, telling her portable, "The sheriff is much obliged, Lester. Out." She holstered the radio with a smile. She'd most likely give it up to ol' Lester one of these days, she knew. Why not? He was a hunk. But it was gold, by God, and he was going to have to mine for it.

Safely outside of his deputy's randy thoughts, Rough Nelson had his mind on a quartet of gun-toting weirdos who would soon be entering a very unpleasant period in their worthless lives. He fired up the motor and turned the boat downriver.

Two miles away, on the marina dock, put in his place by the gorgeous little deputy, Vance tried to get the town dance out of his mind and get back to work. To that end, he changed the frequency on his portable. "Savanna Two. Savanna One." He gave it a second and repeated the call. "Savanna Two. Savanna One." He stared at the radio in mute surprise. Chief Cross was renowned for answering his portable in a timely fashion. The silence was strange to say the least.

Vance had no way of knowing that Carter Cross' radio lay, half buried in high grass and loose foliage, off a trail in the woods of the Rock Island. No way of knowing, beneath the fallen leaves, the portable emitted an unheard burst of static – and then went silent. All he knew was Cross wasn't answering. Dismayed, Vance holstered his radio and looked out to the river wondering what he should do next.

The answer to his unspoken question appeared in the distance, buzzing like a mad dragonfly, fast approaching from the south.

# Thirteen

His wife was going to be as mad as all get out. And, as John P motored upriver, he decided he didn't care. Because he wasn't going home; least ways, not without putting on armor. He wasn't having any luck getting out of the water at Miller's Landing and, if it held, he wouldn't be surprised if someone else wasn't waiting there now for another ride. He'd fool 'em, and his dear wife too. He'd put off the trip back to his trailer and truck and, instead, tie up at the town marina. Then he'd stroll up the street to Crappy's bar. Late was late and there'd be music to face no matter when he got home, so he might as well strike a blow for liberty first. His mind made up, John turned for the marina.

He didn't know, and never could have guessed, Sergeant Lester Vance was out and about.

On the marina dock, as the distance closed, Vance saw it was John P and, more importantly, John's boat heading his way. Strange the fisherman would be on the river so late in the morning. Mind you, it was understandable, with that acid-tongued bridge troll of a wife he had at home; just hard to believe she let him out to play. Stranger still he was headed for the marina. But, as Chief Cross would say, "*Don't sock a gift horse in the teeth.*" As the boat drew near, Vance waved to attract his attention and signal him in. John returned the wave, without enthusiasm, nodded, and slowly turned the boat.

"Hey, John P," Vance shouted as the vessel drew within shouting distance. "I'm going to need your help."

John turned from Vance, to stare upriver in the direction of the landing, not *even* believing his luck. Then he turned back, raised a palm, and replied, "Don't even think about it. I gotta get home."

"I'm talking police business." The boat, drawing nearer, made the disgruntled look on the fisherman's face easier to see. Vance decided not to care. "I need a ride to the island."

"That's what I thought. The answer is 'no'. I already give one to the chief."

"Did you? Well, I know he appreciated it. Then what'd you do? Just leave him there?"

John moved to speak but nothing came out. He looked like a landed trout.

"Never mind," Vance said. "I can't get a hold of him now, for whatever reason, and I need to. So, now I need a ride."

"Damn, Lester, the chief's got a boat. I mean your department. I know you do. I knocked the dent out of it and painted it back up after you run it into the wall up at the Bellevue lock and dam."

Vance twisted his lips and rested his hand on his holstered handgun. He started a ten-count, working on his patience, and got all the way up to three. "You won't believe this, John, but opening that wound back up isn't going to help your argument one bit. Yes, we have a boat. What I don't have is time to get it. Nor do I have the time to debate it anymore."

"You don't understand," John said as his vessel finally bumped the dock. "My wife ain't going to stand for this."

"Now don't bring your charming wife into this, John. If you're still trying to talk your way out of giving me a hand, you're missing by the width of your wife's big ass. If you're trying to make me angry, well then, your aim's perfect."

"Damn, Lester, I've already been to the island twice."

Vance sighed. He unsnapped the hammer strap on his holster, drew his gun, and pointed the weapon at the bottom of the fisherman's boat. "Give me a ride, John P," Vance said, "or I'll shoot holes in your boat."

"Are you out of your mind?"

Vance chambered a round.

"All right. All right. Fine! I'll give you a gall-darned ride. But I'm filing a complaint on you when I get back. I'm reporting you to the town board."

"So you should," Vance said. "I would if I were you. Pitch a great big bitch… when we get back." Vance stepped for the boat.

"Wait," John P demanded. He pointed to the stern. "Let me change these tanks out first. I already told you I've run down to the island twice already. I'm running low on fuel. I don't need to run out of gas and be stranded on the river with a damned crazy man."

In no time at all, John P and his refueled boat, with Lester Vance aboard, were headed downriver again. John, at the wheel feeling sorry for himself, was glum and looked it. The sergeant had too much on his mind to worry about the fisherman's trouble. Still, he couldn't help but be amused. "Cheer up, John. Your help is appreciated."

"Shouldn't even be out here without my equipment working."

"Your equipment? You never heard of Viagra?"

"To hell with you. That equipment works fine."

Vance laughed. "Calm down." He cocked his head, listened, and was satisfied with the hum of the motor. "What isn't working? What are you talking about?"

"The compass." The fisherman tapped the plastic face on the control panel, showing the badge-wearing village idiot. "I'm talking about the compass. It works, then it don't. Works, then it don't. On and off, just this morning."

"Where is it now?"

"Just went back to don't," John grumbled, staring at the gauge. "It happened earlier, when the chief was aboard."

"Froze up?"

"Nah, ain't froze, it's all haywire. Pointing south 'stead of north. I told Carter about it when he kidnapped me."

"When someone abducts you on the water, you're shanghaied, not kidnapped."

"I care. Point is, I told the chief about the compass going insane, but he wasn't interested."

Despite his teasing laughter, Vance was interested. He leaned over, gave the panel gauge a look, and tapped it himself. Sure enough the needle was pointing bass-ackwards. "Is it doing that erratically or when the boat reaches a certain spot on the river?"

John ogled him, confused. "I didn't think of it like that. Now you ask, I guess it started at about this same spot this morning."

"This spot on the river? As you draw near the island?" Vance asked, suddenly grim. He stared ahead, giving the matter thought. "And the phones are out. And I can't raise Chief Cross on his radio."

"What's the radios and phones have to do with my boat equipment?"

"What?" Vance turned, looking startled to find John there. "Oh. I don't know that it does. It's just strange they all fall off the perch at the same time." He forced a smile. "Haven't you heard, John P, cops don't like coincidences."

## The Melting Dead

When Angela could no longer stand waiting near the picnic tables, she moved to the mouth of the path where Paul and the police chief had disappeared. She didn't know what she'd expected, but the move did her no good at all. Her anxious curiosity continued to grow. The woods should have been alive with the sounds of creatures skittering, slithering, flitting, but there was nothing, not a peep. They looked empty and felt foreboding surrounded by the maddening silence. The young director's nerves were tight as a drawn bow string and thoughts of hockey masks and machetes danced in her head. If the men didn't show back up, she told herself, in the next couple of minutes...

Angela gasped, startled. Fifty yards away something in shadow burst round the bend; a wide thing with two heads. It passed through a spot where the dwindling sunlight reached through the trees... and revealed itself to be Paul with Hilda in his arms. The cook was a sight, leaning heavily on the professor and staring ahead as if in a catatonic daze. Angela realized she was holding her breath. She remedied the situation, sucking in a chest full of air, then hurried up the trail. "Are you all right?" she called, drawing near. "Is she all right?"

Paul rolled his eyes, nodded at the cook, and shook his head. Angela took the other side and helped the poor lady back down the trail and into the campus clearing. So alarming was Hilda's appearance, so intent were they on getting the old girl somewhere safe, Paul and Angela ignored the chief lagging behind, until they heard the unmistakable sounds of someone being sick. Both turned to see Cross had pulled the handcuffed minister to a stop at the trail head and was vomiting into the bushes. Angela started his direction, but the chief waved her off. "I'm all right," he managed, spitting. She got the message and, torn, returned to help with the cook. Cross took several deep breaths to collect himself, made a face at the taste in his mouth, and ushered the reverend from the path onto the campus.

The police chief now took the lead, pushing his prisoner past the others and toward the community house. As they passed the silent trembling Hilda, in the arms of Paul and Angela, the reverend vented, "If we claim to have fellowship with Him yet walk in the darkness, we lie and do not live by the truth."

Angela's eyes widened and she whispered to Paul, "Should I ask?"

He merely shook his head. "It wouldn't do any good. I don't know."

Angela took charge of Hilda inside the main hall of the community house. She led the poor thing to a quiet corner near a stack of plastic chairs, pulled one off the pile and helped her to sit. Hilda offered no resistance. Paul gave

Cross a hand getting the cuffed minister onto the floor near a row of stacked and leaning folding tables.

"Do you want a chair for him?" the professor asked.

"This is good," Cross insisted. Though he didn't feel at all like it, he answered Paul's frown. "It will be harder for him to get up, cuffed, if he has to rise from the floor."

"Seems a little harsh."

"It isn't going to hurt him a bit." When that answer didn't satisfy Paul, the chief stood tall and froze him with steel blue eyes. "We may as well get this straight, right now, Professor Regas. This island is a crime scene, every inch, until we know differently." He poked a thumb toward the minister at their feet. "This is probably our criminal – whatever the crime. I don't know that, I merely suspect. But I do so with grounds. Until we know something, until I have help, I am declaring a state of emergency here; a martial law. Unfortunately, that requires everybody's civil rights be curtailed temporarily, his and yours. I'm sure none of you will like that. You don't have to. You also do not have to like the way I treat the prisoner. You have every right to your opinions. But I would appreciate it if you would keep them to yourself." His frown remained fixed, but Paul nodded his understanding. For the moment, that was all Carter Cross cared about. "I would also appreciate it if you would call my office for me. The phone is in the kitchen. Make certain my dispatcher knows we're here. Tell him to call in as many officers as he can reach, but to have them 'stand-by' until they hear from us again."

Paul stepped away without another word, waved to Angela, and disappeared through the swinging doors into the kitchen. Angela whispered a soothing word to Hilda, rose, and followed the professor.

Cross pulled a chair up in front of his prisoner. Exhausted and nauseated, he eased himself onto it, holding his stomach, breathing deeply. "Reverend," he said, his voice a pained whisper. "I need to know what happened here. Where's Harry Towers, boy? Where is Arthur Aaron?"

Angela entered the kitchen to find Paul in a snit. He stood near the large center island, hands on his hips, lips a thin angry line, staring into nothingness. "What's up?" she asked.

"Did you hear that?" he demanded in a whisper.

"How could I not?"

"No. Did you hear that? Martial law. Who does he think he is? Well, if he thinks he's going to order me around, he's got another think coming." He turned, looking for her, but Angela had walked away in the middle of his sentence. She'd crossed the room and was searching the cupboards. "What are you doing?"

"Unlike you," she said, without looking back, "I'm trying to be useful." She paused to smile. "But don't let me interrupt your hysterics, if they make you feel better."

"He's a fascist," Paul said. She was ignoring him. "You think I'm wrong?"

"The whole college professor '*enraged at the man*' thing is a little dated for me. When was that, the sixties? I'm for civil rights, and being down for the struggle, but I also saw the inside of that shed. And my eyes work. That means I have no choice but to agree with his premise; a crime has been committed here. Just what, when, by who, I don't know either. Luckily, it isn't my job to find out. It's his. Who am I to tell him how to do it? *Aha!*" She pulled out a First Aid kit and waved it triumphantly.

"So you think he can just declare a so-called state of emergency?"

"What difference does it make what I think?" She grabbed several plastic tumblers from the drying rack, ran the tap until the water was cold, and filled them. Armed with her bandages and water she gave the professor her full attention. "What I know is he has a badge and a gun. I don't know about you, but I don't have a badge and a gun." Angela, kit under her arm, water in hand, headed for the doors. "I have a couple of patients that need tending. I'm not a nurse, but I played one on cable access. Were you going to make that call for the chief?" She pushed through.

"I'm calling," Paul grumbled as he lifted the receiver on the wall phone. "I'm calling." At least he tried. But the phone was a riot of deafening static. He held the receiver away from his ear and tapped the cradle like they did in the old movies. It was no go; the phone was kaput.

## FOURTEEN

Angela tried, with little success, to get Hilda to take a drink. Finally, defeated, she gave up. She left the poor old thing to herself and joined Paul, instead, loitering by the kitchen doors.

On the opposite side of the room, the chief's luck was no better. He hovered over the handcuffed minister demanding answers, through gritted teeth, to his many questions. The demented man seemed willing to cooperate. But his vehement responses reached Cross as nothing but incongruous biblical claptrap; no answers at all.

"Can you understand me?" Cross asked. "What happened here?"

"The people walking in darkness have seen a great light," the reverend replied in wide-eyed sincerity. "On those living in the land of the shadow of death a light has dawned."

The chief shook his head wearily. "What did you do to Arthur? Where is he?"

At the sound of her husband's name, Hilda turned to stare across the room. It seemed for a moment she would speak but, in the end, she merely stared. Then she silently turned away. With the chief busy and Angela and Paul whispering to one-another, her brief return to earth, like an alien stopping to take a pee, went unnoticed.

"Where is he? Where's Arthur?"

"The people walking in darkness have seen a great light."

"All right, reverend," the chief said. "Just relax and stay put."

The chief moved his chair out of the prisoner's reach, sat heavily, and sighed in frustration, pain, and exhaustion. Angela and Paul joined him. "Thanks," Cross said, gratefully accepting a tumbler of water from the director. He drank half in one go. "I'm dry as dirt."

"Did you learn anything?" Paul asked.

"Yes. The people have seen a great light," Cross said. He finished the glass in a second gulp. "Did you get hold of anyone?"

"No," Paul said. "The phone is dead."

"Even the phone is dead," Angela whispered.

Cross ignored her contribution and nodded at Paul as if he'd expected nothing else. "And my radio is missing." He checked his wrist and frowned. "Hell, my watch isn't even working."

Angela opened the First Aid kit and began pulling at the chief's uniform shirt. He complained he was, "All right." She took a turn ignoring him. She exposed the wide stab wound in his abdomen; a vicious grin with a dark beard of dried blood. "Yeah, you're all right," she said, with sarcasm. "This needs to be cleaned." Stealing herself to his yelps, she went at it with gauze and alcohol.

Paul took the room in, from Angela tending the wounded cop, to the disheveled minister mumbling to unseen listeners, to the old lady staring into space with her mouth hanging open. "We've got to signal the mainland," he declared in agitation. "We've got to get help over here."

Cross howled at Angela's ministrations, took in air, and turned to Paul, shaking his head. "That's exactly what we don't need. I'm all for alerting someone to our situation. I'm certainly for getting back to the mainland. But, as for the island, we need to keep people off. It's a crime scene; and we don't even know for sure what crime. We've got to find out what our holy friend here has been up to. We've got to find Arthur – dead or alive."

"There's more at stake than Arthur and your crime scene," Paul said. "Harry Towers, the park super, where is he? And the homesteaders, the squatters Towers was always battling, the Harpers, where are they? Or do they have something to do with whatever happened here?" He pointed from Hilda to the reverend on the opposite side of the hall. "These two need care we can't provide. And you, chief, you need a doctor. We need help here."

"What we need is… to control this situation." Cross drew a breath, riding a wave of pain. "Nobody, absolutely no one, comes onto this island until I say so."

Gar throttled down and he and his gang, in their stolen boat, rode the momentum toward a clear spot on the western shore of the Rock Island. Falcon leaped up with a mooring line in hand.

"Forget the line," Gar told her. "I'm just dropping you guys off. The boat's too exposed here."

"So what are you going to do?"

"I'm going to hide this thing," he said, smacking the steering wheel. "Everybody out, with the loot. Hide the stuff somewhere around here for the time being."

Falcon scooped up an arm-load of stolen goods and jumped the gunwale. She dropped them in the high grass on the shore, turned, and grabbed the bow, steadying the boat. She walked her way down the shore, pulling the boat flat against the bank. "Come on," she barked at the other two. "Need a special invitation?"

Limping and favoring his injured knee, keeping pressure on his wounded forehead, Dex climbed up and over the gunwale. Norene helped him as she was able, then grabbed a couple of bags and followed him ashore. Gar chucked them the last of the loot, boxes of smokes, bottles of booze, that had fallen into the bottom of the boat, while warning, "Stay out of sight."

"Wait for me," Falcon cried. "I'm not staying with these losers." Dex and Norene both began to protest. Ignoring them, she moved back to the boat.

"No, babe," Gar said. "You're staying here."

"I don't want to stay here."

"Falcon."

"Well, where are you going?"

"Just around the shoreline. I need to find some thick cover, hide the boat till things calm down. It will be quicker if I go alone." Falcon pouted but Gar cut her off. "Just do as you're told, please."

She grabbed the gunwale, lifted herself, and pushed her nose into Gar's. "I hate doing what I'm told."

"I know. Do it this one time." Gar slid his hand inside her top and squeezed what he found. "I'll make it up to you." They locked lips and traded tongues. It wasn't romantic but got the job done. Coming up for air, Gar pushed Falcon back to the shore.

"All right," she said. "But next time I see you, I want a big surprise."

Gar grinned mischievously, winked as she stepped back on the bank, and idled the motor up. With her push, he backed the boat away from the island. Clear, he turned the wheel and revved the motor. Falcon watched him disappear around the bend of the shore, then watched his wake die down on the river. She turned to take in the two losers, history's worst armed bandits, with whom she'd been temporarily stranded. Dex and Norene; a love story... for geeks.

Ben Nath swung wide toward the Illinois side finishing his second lap of the north end of the Rock Island. (No reason to go south. Everybody knew them squatters kept the tourists off.) He'd made up his mind the best approach was to sneak up on the trouble making sons of bitches and catch them red-handed. But he needed to find them first. He'd made the crescent twice to the west cliff and back again without seeing shit. That left him no choice but to land and take his search inland. But, to catch the bastards by stealth, he had to avoid the main island dock and campus trails. He needed to come ashore elsewhere to keep from giving them a heads-up. He'd creep up on 'em, catch them fuckers in the act of raising hell, and put a stop to the noise, the rowdiness, and the tomfoolery. He'd see to that, by God. Ben finished the wide arc and brought his boat back past mid-isle out of sight. He killed the motor and let her drift toward a clear spot on the eastern shore.

Ben climbed out, grabbed the bow line, and tied her to a tree well-onto dry ground. He wiped his hands (one hand and one claw) on his pant legs and faced the wooded depths searching (with one eye and one squint) for his bearings. He'd been there, on the island, a few times; everyone who lived in that part of the river had. But he didn't know it well. Je-suz Christ, he had better things to do than spend his time in recreation. Not like these noisy inconsiderate bastards.

The campus was to the north, he knew. He could tell north easy enough. "Now we'll stop this goddamn nonsense," Ben said aloud, fuming, as he headed into the trees.

John P took the river's left branch, again, and a stone's throw after, slowed the motor and brought his boat in at the Rock Island dock – for the third time that day. Lester Vance was already on his feet, line in hand, when the boat shuddered. "We hit something," Vance said, over the hum of the idling motor. "What lies beneath?"

"Don't know," John replied with a frown. "Whatever it is, it wasn't there this morning."

The boat eased into contact with the dock and Vance stepped onto the pier. "Shut her down," he shouted over his shoulder. "I'll need your help."

The outboard revved and Vance turned to see that no sooner had he cleared the bulwark then John had thrown the motor into reverse and was backing his boat away. The fisherman was already out of reach and quickly widening the distance between them. "Get back here," the police sergeant barked. "I just said I'm going to need your help."

"I just helped," John squeaked, afraid but determined. "That's all I can do."

"You can't strand me here, you jackass."

"I got no choice, really Vance. You ever looked into the mouth of madness? My life ain't worth a damn when my wife's upset. It's more'n a man can take." John turned the boat and revved the motor throwing up an arc of water. "Good luck," he shouted back toward the dock. "I mean that."

Vance exhaled his frustration, motor-boating his lips, as he watched John P motoring away. The little jerk had put one over on him. "This will not look good on my resume," he said, shaking his head. Vance caught sight of the thing under the surface of the river that they'd hit on their approach. It was a small sunken boat only a few feet away. Arthur Aaron's boat, if he didn't know better. He leaned to the water. It was, Arthur's boat. And danged if it didn't look like it had caught fire and burned.

The small cove looked like anything but when approached from the river. Gar had been nursing his stolen boat against the current, idling for quiet, hugging the island to stay unobtrusive, warily watching for any sign of the authorities, and on the lookout for some place along the shore to ditch and cover his hot vessel, when he spotted the inlet. It was perfect; little more than a notch cut into the southeast corner of the island and all but invisible from the north. The mouth was framed by cattails and lily pads. Inside, out of the current, the edges were choked by weeds. The body of the cove was deep and dark and the bank fell sharply away at the point where a carelessly constructed and, from the looks forgotten, pier jutted over the water. It floated, without stilt supports, on three rusted barrels that had taken on so much water the tip of the pier sagged below the surface. A lone rowboat lay moored there like a miner's pony hitched outside a ghost town saloon. The whole was overgrown from the still water below and trees above. A handmade sign reading, Harper's Cove, dangled from one of the branches looking far more like a warning than an invitation. Where better to hide a stolen boat?

The coast was clear. Gar saw no one on the river, or the island shore, and trolled carefully in. He lifted the low-hanging branches, guided the boat against the upriver side of the bobbing pier, and shut the motor down. The limb drooped back in place throwing the boat into gloom like clouds hiding a full moon. A ridiculous notion, Gar knew, as it was the middle of the day. Spookiness aside, the hanging foliage did a fair job of covering the craft. A few loose branches, some brush borrowed from the bank and hung on the rails, he thought, would do the rest.

Gar grabbed a mooring line and got as far as the gunwale when, with seemingly no provocation, a shiver raced down his spine. He stopped and held his breath as the little hairs rose on the back of his neck. He was overwhelmed with the sense of another's presence, the feeling he was being watched from the dense shore and, in answer, he quietly found the grip of his handgun.

"Hello," he croaked. He cleared his throat and tried again. "Hello?" Nothing but silence and the stirring of the river. "I was having trouble with my boat," he told the trees. He scanned the shore for signs of life. "Is it all right if I stop here for a moment?"

He dropped the rope and carefully, though he hated to do it there, popped out his lizard's eye contact and slipped it into his coat pocket. It was dirty, unwise, and a risk to the expensive lens, but he couldn't see a damn thing with it in. Just then, he needed to see. Besides, Gar wore it to startle and creep people out. Who was there to annoy in this godforsaken black lagoon? "Is anybody there?"

There was – in the brush off to his right. He heard it now; a deep-throated animal's growl that stretched into a rattle. Gar scanned the bank. He saw it; something shook the bushes and moved within the high grass down the shoreline. Whatever it was came to a stop and, apparently, turned because the shimmy repeated itself in the opposite direction. Something low to the ground was walking sentinel.

But that was stupid. He swallowed hard and renewed his stare. What could be standing guard– Then, of course, the answer struck. It was a fucking dog. Gar sagged with relief and laughed, feeling the fool. He'd scared the shit out of himself, for nothing. "Pooch," he called out, his twisted nerves unwinding. "Here pooch. You scared the crap out of me, you little bastard." He pulled his pistol. "Come here, you mutt." He waved it toward the shore. "Bet my bite is worse than your bark."

The brush went still. The animal, Gar heard, padded away from the clearing and into the thicket. "Don't want any?" he asked after it. "Can't say I blame you, pooch."

It was just as well. Gar didn't want any either. He wanted nothing more than to lay low until they found an opening in whatever dragnet the cops were laying and got out of there. That meant not drawing attention to themselves. That meant, if he could help it, not shooting a dog. That thought led to another.

He was lucky Falcon hadn't been along. She'd have shot the pooch deader than hell with a smile on her face. Certified 'Grade A' psycho, that's what his old lady was. Still, Gar couldn't resist her; the sex was not of this earth.

He stashed his gun, grabbed the mooring line again, and got a leg up on the gunwale of the boat to make land. But he never made land. A hair-raising noise out of nowhere, part gasp, part gurgle, split the air and froze Gar in place.

He fought it and jerked up to see something, on two legs but growling like an animal, racing from the gloom in his direction. It passed through a single shaft of sunlight as it came on but the fleeting glimpse failed to answer any of Gar's questions. Smoke rolled off of it, globs of liquid dripped from it, it was round and dark; that was all. It hit the dock running, dripped flaming ooze onto the pier and into the Harper's rowboat, bounced and rebounded with the splash of the barrels, and launched itself as if from a diving board. In a swirl of smoke, the flying thing landed, tackling Gar in John Henry's boat.

Gar had never heard of Harry Towers. Even if he had, he wouldn't have recognized him. Transformed by Ellis Harper's bite and the space rock radiations, Towers was the bleeding, dripping thing on top of the Goth gang leader. They struggled in the bottom of the boat, Towers groaning in agony and hunger, Gar screaming in agony and terror. As they fought, the melting creature was burning up, burning Gar and, at the same time, setting the boat on fire; the ropes, cushions, seats. The creature raised his head through the smoke and, slobbering through the hole in his neck, sank his teeth into Gar's throat. They struggled to the sounds of their own screams and growls, Gar fighting helplessly, Towers consuming Gar's flesh and blood, while the flames grew beyond control and consumed the craft around them. Oblivious to the fire, Towers fed, Gar died, and the boat sank. In short order, all vanished beneath the surface in Harper's Cove.

The steaming water churned, slowed, then settled with a few final bubbles. Two spot fires had burned themselves out on the sagging pier. The fire in the rowboat had burned through its bottom. The vessel settled to its gunwales as it shipped water, then it gurgled and went under. The stillness of the tomb blanketed the cove. The quiet lasted a moment, perhaps two, then the inlet waters began to bubble, churn, and stir. The Towers-thing burst to the surface and bellowed like a collapsing bagpipe. Dripping water and burning flesh in equal amounts, he trudged toward the shore. He reached the bank, set the branches of a bush afire pulling himself from the river, and staggered onto land.

There the Towers creature stood, black and dripping clods of flesh, with steam rolling off his head and shoulders. He took another step up the bank and, with an otherworldly cry, collapsed and disintegrated into a puddle of steaming glop.

A moment passed. Harper's Cove stirred again. Up from the depths, the burned, bitten, and now undead Gar surfaced, sending shock waves of black water toward the shore. With eyes glowing like red coals, he howled, slapped the surface, and moved toward land. He climbed from the river, stumbled gaining his footing on the ground and, dripping water and blood, shambled into the woods.

# Fifteen

The river valley on both the Iowa and Illinois sides of the Mississippi were, outside of the Palisades, predominantly low lands. In seasons of high water, like that spring, much of the land took a bath, becoming twisted, tree-filled back channels and, in the open clearings, temporary lakes. It abandoned its usual look of monotonous stereo corn and became something beautiful and mysterious. But, in so doing, it also created uncounted miles of blind waterways in which the Pucket boat bandits could run and hide. Searching those channels required more volunteers, with boats, than the authorities had on hand. If that weren't enough, the Jackson County Sheriff's Department had to work without the help of the Savanna Police. Strangely, Savanna couldn't locate their senior officers. Neither Chief Cross nor Sergeant Vance were answering their radios. Worse, the sky was growing dark over the valley and the predicted rain would soon be upon them. Despite these hurdles, a handful of volunteers were rounded up and, by late morning, a search of the back channels was on.

Rough and Melissa motored down the main river channel, headed for the Rock Island, but taking their time with eyes peeled in all directions. Compared to normal the Mississippi was quiet and, so far, neither the leather-clad thieves nor their purloined vessel were anywhere in sight. That didn't mean there was nothing to see. John P was on the water, Rough saw, and motoring at them from the south. The sheriff lifted a ham hand to wave and, even at that distance, saw the fisherman frown. When he signaled John over, his scowl deepened. Something was biting him. Sadly for John, the sheriff wasn't interested in his mood.

At sight of Rough Nelson, the thought reverberating in John P's head amounted to little more than, "Damn, damn, damn." He'd used up his chivalry giving that young lady a lift to the island. He'd done his duty helping out the chief of the Savanna police. And he'd suffered the threats of the *big deal sergeant* Vance and delivered him. Now all John wanted was to get off the river and home. But, sure as shit, there stood the Jackson County Sheriff waving from his boat. John knew better than to pretend he didn't see him. He slowed his motor and brought his craft near the County vessel – but not too near. John idled the motor and nervously called, "Sheriff, what's the good word in Iowa?"

"None. No good word at all. We have fugitives on the river, John P," Rough said. "They stole John Henry Pucket's new boat."

"You don't say? That's a beautiful boat. I bet John Henry's mad as all–"

"He ain't happy. They're a gang of hippies right out of the Rocky Horror Show, dressed all in black leather, tattoos, piercings, for all I know they got snakes in their hair like the Gorgon. They're probably headed south. Have you seen anything?"

"In John Henry's boat?"

"Yeah, John. I thought we'd got past that? They're in John Henry Pucket's motor boat. Have you seen 'em or anything like?"

"No, sir. Not hide nor hair. I know the boat, but I ain't seen it. And I sure ain't seen anyone fitting the description you give. Sure they didn't go north?"

"John Henry says not. Lock operators up at Bellevue say not too. They haven't shown up there and they won't get through if they do. Savanna's quiet. We've got folks teaspooning the back channels on both sides for what good it'll do us. No one has positively identified them since they left Sabula on the hop. They could have gone anywhere; that's why the search parties and road blocks. But I'm thinking they went south. They couldn't have got past the dredger or the Clinton lock and dam, so I'm guessing they're hold up on the Rock Island."

A look of terror crossed John P's face. He turned to his wheel and grabbed the throttle, ready to rev, shouting, "Well, good luck catching them, sheriff."

"Hold your boat, John," Rough said. "That's a big island over there. We're going to need a hand searching."

"I already dropped the Savanna chief and the sergeant off on the Rock Island in two different trips this morning. They got the island surrounded."

"That so?" the sheriff asked. "Mighty strange. Neither one is answering a radio. We're still going to have to take a look. You can give us a hand."

"The dark clouds are moving in. Looks like the devil's rain is coming on."

The sheriff examined the sky for nearly a full second. "Yes. Yes, it does."

"I ain't no policeman," the fisherman whined.

Rough waved it away. "You will be in a second. We need help and I'm going to deputize you. Raise your right hand and say, I do."

"This ain't funny."

"I ain't laughing," the sheriff said. He wasn't, not at all.

"I gotta get home, Rough. I'll be lucky if my wife only wants a divorce. She's probably planning my murder."

"Oh," the sheriff said, feigning concern. "I'm sorry. I didn't realize, John."

"Thanks, Rough. I appreciate it."

"Think nothing of it. Melissa."

As if her boss had flipped a switch, the deputy reached back and pulled out her handcuffs. "John P," she said, "you are under arrest for obstruction of justice."

His jaw fell slack and it took John several tries to get it working again. When he did, he stammered, "Y-Y-You can't do that!"

"The hell she can't." Rough stared, unblinking. "We need your help, boy. But it's entirely your choice. You can wear a badge or this shiny pair of bracelets?" He waited a full second before adding, "I'm not kidding, John. Either raise your right hand all by its lonesome or stick 'em both out together."

John was disgusted and made the noises to prove it. But what choice did he have? He shook his head and raised his hand in frustrated surrender.

Rough smiled past his toothpick. "Deputy, you want to see if he solemnly swears?"

"Son of a bitch," John grumbled in his boat.

"Ooh," Melissa said, "I guess he does."

The daylight began quickly to disappear behind the promised storm clouds. The busy afternoon, for the law, the volunteer searchers, the victims of recent crime, and the victims of cosmic calamity, came and went without anyone being aware of the time, on the river or on the island.

It wasn't a pool party by any stretch, but Falcon, Norene, and Dex, owing to their disastrous adventure at the Sabula convenience store, and its explosive conclusion, were forced to go for a fully-clothed swim in the river. Even the mighty Mississippi had its work cut out trying to wash away that horrendous mess and odor. Norene and Dex took the opportunity to rid themselves of their black and white Goth makeup proving that, while both were still peppered with myriad piercings and tattoos, they had actual skin beneath. Falcon washed her clothes but left her Goth face in place. In public, whether she was trapped on a deserted island with weenies or not, it was part of who she was. As they scrubbed, Falcon entertained the others with creative complaining. "Wasn't enough to wreck the van and screw the gig," she said, splashing her leathers. "The Georgia peach here had to ram into a pile of discount, Iowa Grade D cow shit." She ran her hands over the leather, adding, "Too bad you didn't steal any soap, home boy," then disappeared beneath the surface.

Dex and Norene shared a look of camaraderie, and matching thoughts of holding Falcon under until she drowned, but neither acted on them. It was, after all, just Falcon bitching; as normal as Falcon breathing. A few more splashes for good measure and the couple threw their clean clothes back to the shore. They followed with their clean selves soon after. Norene, a red head all over with skin as white as milk, looked whiter still beside Dex's dark chocolate brown.

The couple had met only six weeks earlier.

Norene Gayle hailed from Valdosta, Georgia; the world's *'Best Adventure Town'* if you believed the National Geographic. It had been an adventure for her. Norene had just turned nineteen and already the Feds had taken her man, the state her son, and the mill her job. She could have gone home, her momma would have let her without batting an eye, but home wasn't home anymore. Momma pretty much had a little farm going, what with the two Pit Bulls (and the girl Pit just having had pups) and the pet house pig they'd all fell in love with. It was a cutie, and Norene loved animals, but it wasn't her home no more. She liked hunting, fishing, and mud bogging, but didn't she wonder if there wasn't something else out there? There was only one way to know. She stuck out her thumb, hitched her way up Highway 75, and never looked back. She wouldn't have seen much anyway what with the tears in her eyes. She met Dex near the napkins at a *Tastee Snack* in Joliet. She dropped a twist cone in her lap at the same time he spilled a cherry soda down his shirt. He was a sculpted ebony god, a little clumsy like her, and smiled with ever so much charm as he suggested they sop up each other's messes. His true name was Charles Ward but everybody called him Dex, though he wouldn't say why. He was from the south side of Chicago. Otherwise, Norene knew little about him as he didn't like to talk about himself. That was all right. In less time than she ought to admit, she found out Dex was darn fine in the backseat of a borrowed automobile and, later, even better in the sack.

They sat now, hidden in the brush at the edge of the island woods, lost in the woods really (they certainly were not from around there). Norene tended to Dex's now clean wounds, first his knee and then his head, while the breeze and what little sun that could eke its way through the late afternoon storm clouds dried them.

As for the third in their small stranded group… Once upon a time, in a different lifetime, Falcon was a blonde, blue-eyed little girl named Alice Fallon. But blonde hair goes away with jet black dye, blue eyes vanish behind colored contacts, and horrendously painful childhoods are no more once you turn your back on them. At least that's what she told herself and insisted she believe. Her ceaselessly drunk mother could have that stupid name *Alice* back. Life was no Wonderland and nothing worth a damn returned her stare through the looking glass. Come to think of it, the pervert the old bitch had married could take back his *Fallon* too. She kept only a piece and changed it to her liking. Alice Fallon died, and *Falcon* was born; brave, free, a predator… Yeah, she liked that.

Falcon splashed ashore, her black hair matted, her gray face running at the edges, impressive in her wet t-shirt, smelling her jacket. She was still bitching at Norene, but without notice. For Norene's ministrations to Dex's ailments had moved south again, stopped below the waist, and turned decidedly sexual in nature. Falcon got an eyeful, yelled, "Get a room, damn!" and stuck a finger down her throat to loudly gag herself.

"Wanna watch the stuff?" Dex asked, pointing at their piled bags, cigarettes, booze, lottery tickets with his half-erect member. Then he jabbed a thumb toward the woods. "We're gonna–"

Falcon held up a hand, "Spare me the details."

"You don't mind?"

"Have at it, stud," she told him, not bothering to hide her critical look at Norene's scrawny, naked behind. "If screwing stupid is your idea of a good time, who am I to judge?"

Norene flashed Falcon her middle finger then let Dex lead her into the woods.

Falcon opened a carton of smokes, removed a pack. and tucked the rest away. She lit one and stared at the river, trying not to hear the lovebirds getting their freak on nearby. She wondered where Gar had gotten to and when he would get back. It all turned painfully dull even faster than Falcon imagined. Bored to tears, she flicked the cigarette away, picked up her handgun, tucked it into her waistband, and headed into the woods in the other direction.

Barely had Falcon gotten out of earshot of Frick and Frack bumping uglies, found her own trail, and moved into the woods, than she heard something she hadn't heard since they'd reached the island; the sound of an animal. The death-like quiet had, until then, been weird as hell and made Falcon realize how much she'd taken the usual *outside* noises for granted. Now, she heard something moving in the brush – before her and to the right. Something moving, finally, along the ground through the high grass, the ferns, the low brush at the base of the trees. She wasn't a nature lover. It could have been anything from a bear to a wolverine for all she knew. But it sounded like a dog – and a big one at that.

Falcon didn't like dogs. Strike that, dogs didn't like her and she returned the favor. Still, everything being relative, she hoped it was a dog. Of all the things it might be, the least nerve-wracking would be a dog. Especially now… Because the damned thing had moved and was suddenly behind her.

She couldn't see it, but Falcon felt it sure enough. How or when it had come around, she didn't know, but she heard it now in the brush. It serenaded her, with a low and vicious growl, somewhere off the trail. Falcon drew her gun, flicked the safety off, and panned the timber. "Here, Cujo," she called. "Come and get it."

A twig snapped to her left. She adjusted. But she was guessing as the growling had stopped. She whispered under her breath, words best left to the imagination, but held the gun steady. Then Gar's order rang in her head; no shooting. No shooting! They didn't need the noise, didn't want to draw attention. Besides, with her shitty luck, she'd probably send a cap wide, over the river and through the woods, into the upraised ass of either the ebony dick or the ivory dork doing the horizontal mambo back where she'd left them. How would she explain that to her old man?

She couldn't see the dog anyway. If it was a dog? If there was only one? Maybe she heard more than one? If they were there, they weren't coming any closer at present. Falcon sighed and tucked the gun away. Okay, she wouldn't shoot the damn thing, or things. But, as that was the case, it made no sense to hang around waiting for the rabid bastards to bite her either. She got the hell out of there.

Falcon hated it, hurrying away like a frightened kid, and hated herself for doing it. She didn't like it any better when, fifty yards further down the trail, she stopped dead in her tracks again. Another noise had scared her stiff; a completely different sound. Falcon could hear a little girl.

The voice was faint, distant, but it was definitely a girl – and she was crying.

Falcon didn't know what a siren was, and didn't care. Still, she felt compelled to follow that mournful cry. Why wouldn't she? She drew her gun again and headed stealthily that direction. She left the trail and, moving through the trees and brush, soon came upon what looked to be a teenaged girl sitting balled up at the base of a tree. Her arms were crossed atop her raised knees, her head draped on her arms. The girl's tied top and shorts, what Falcon could see of them, were torn, filthy, and spotted with blood. Her blonde hair looked mouse brown with dirt. She shook as she cried.

"Hey," Falcon called. "Where'd you come from?"

The girl turned quickly away, facing the tree. She rose slowly to her feet and her crying supped to a stop. Sniffing, the girl asked, "Can you help me?"

"What's the matter with you?"

*Sniff.* "I need help."

"Yeah, you said." Falcon approached slowly, flexing her fingers nervously on the grip of the gun. She felt for the kid, who wouldn't? But something about her was making Falcon uneasy. "What's your problem?"

"I'm hungry," the girl said. Crystal Harper turned. She stared with glowing eyes, the same color as her bloody grin, in a burned face just beginning to show signs of melt.

In the last few hours, the middle Harper child had been through a lot. She'd gotten her baby brother away with an order that he get help. She'd stayed behind. She'd played cat and mouse with the park superintendent, the thing that once had been Mr. Towers, darting through the woods ahead of him and the hunger that possessed him. Over and over again, she hid in the bushes, or behind a tree, or in the grass, waiting and holding her breath, while the gurgling Towers creature staggered by. Each time, for a long time, he'd missed her. But nothing lasts forever and their murderous game didn't either. Soon he'd gotten a hold of her and satisfied his primitive desires. Falcon was seeing the results.

Few things startled Falcon but that did. She didn't know Crystal, and didn't know what to do when the burning, bleeding teen-thing lurched at her. Crystal knocked the gun from the startled Falcon's hand and grabbed both fists full of her T-shirt. Despite her shock, Falcon recovered her wits in time to keep Crystal's hungry mouth away. She threw the girl off and ran, without her gun, into the trees. With a growl, Crystal scrambled up and took chase.

Falcon ran, cutting this way, turning that, found a trail and started down it as fast as her legs would carry her. She left the timber, entered a clearing gray with lingering smoke, dodged a wrecked little building and pulled up, gasping, in a junk-filled yard.

She couldn't believe her eyes or her good luck. There, across the clearing, standing in the shadows at the mouth of another trail, was her man. What the hell he was doing there she didn't know or care. She was just delighted to see him. She cried out, "Gar, baby," and ran to him. Half-way there, she pointed to the woods behind her, adding, "This crazy bitch is–" By then she was to him, in her lover's arms, and getting a glimpse of his condition. Falcon had made it plain, when Gar left to hide the boat, that the next time she saw him she wanted a big surprise. He delivered now, in spades. Falcon screamed, trying to pull away, but he held fast. Gar bit deeply into his girlfriend's shoulder.

Crystal entered the clearing on the run. She pulled up in horror, watching Gar nosh Falcon's flesh and drink her blood. She angrily shouted, "Mine! Mine!" Crying, Crystal fell against what, a lifetime ago, had been her favorite tree and slid to the ground in disappointment. "She was mine!"

Falcon, the former Alice Fallow, sagged dying against Gar. Nobody on the island was in the know, or keeping count, but she was already the ninth victim of the meteorite's vile and violent contagion.

# SIXTEEN

The afternoon passed slowly in the community house. Chief Cross, looking sicker and more pallid each moment, was still on his feet, moving back and forth between the Reverend Snow and Hilda, questioning each repeatedly, but gaining no ground. The minister was eager to talk, but only in frenetic bursts of biblical verse that may or may not have meant anything to anyone. Paul considered it all to be babbled fiction. Angela, not a disbeliever, still found it fairly scattered and unintelligible. Cross thought it all crap. Captured perps shoveling crap was nothing new to him. Hilda, for her part, offered nothing at all. She merely stared. Paul's repeated offers to venture out and look for Arthur and or check on the Harpers (though he'd never met one and wouldn't know one if they bit him) were refused without discussion. Apparently, the chief's 'no' meant 'no', enough said. So, while Cross interrogated in vain, Paul and Angela talked quietly about nothing in particular, doing their best to pass the time, to get to know each other under the odd circumstances, and to stay out of the cop's way.

Time did pass and Angela, up for a stretch, stole a look out of the hall's large main window. She paused, staring. In the distance, she saw a child wander into the main campus from one of the southern trails. "Look," she told the others. "A little boy."

"Sons are a heritage from the Lord," the reverend said, "children a reward from him."

Paul and the chief stood. They followed Angela's gaze out the window and saw what she'd reported, a young boy wandering aimlessly in the open.

"That's Caleb," Cross said. "He's the youngest of the Harpers, the squatters on the south side of the island."

"Harry Towers talked about them all the time," Paul said.

"Yeah, they were under his skin. At the same time, they scared the living daylights out of him. I have an eviction notice for them but haven't had the heart to serve it." Cross watched intently, bothered by what he was seeing. There was something strange, unnatural, about the way the boy was moving. So entranced was he by the oddity of the child's appearance, the chief let go his stomach, momentarily forgetting his own pain. "There's something wrong with him."

"He looks like he's hurt," Angela said, starting for the front door. "I'll get him."

She was through the door and off the porch before any of them could say a word. Any but the reverend, that is. Like a Greek chorus, the minister declared, "And whoever welcomes a little child like this in my name welcomes me."

Outside, Angela crossed the campus clearing headed for the ambling child. "Hey, little boy."

She didn't know for sure if Paul and the police chief were watching. She had no idea the holy man, handcuffed on the floor, was muttering. ("See that you do not look down on one of these little ones.") She had no time to think about it. "Caleb," she said, approaching him. "I'm Angela." Only then did she see that the front of his clothes were splashed with blood. And, on a closer look, that the child was injured. "Oh, goodness, are you all right?"

Though she couldn't hear it from that distance, the reverend continued. "For I tell you that their angels in heaven always see the face of my Father."

The boy looked up with eyes glowing like hot coals and a face torn down the middle. He licked his swollen blue lips and charged at Angela with a howl. Wide-eyed, she screamed and backed away. She turned and bolted for the house. She leaped for the porch, which Caleb was simply too small to do, and made it inside. Paul slammed the door closed as the child hit it on the run.

Paul struggled, holding the door, while Caleb savagely tried to open it from the outside. The breathless Angela joined him, grabbed the door, and helped to hold it closed.

"Got a movie quote for this one?" he asked her.

"No!" Angela shouted.

Caleb screamed in anger and hunger, rattling the door.

The stunned chief looked on. "What's wrong with him?"

"He's insane," Paul said, shouting to be heard over the child's screams. "That's what's wrong with him." Holding the fiercely shaking door, Paul looked up and through the window to see someone else entering the clearing from the woods. "Hey, isn't that–"

"It's Arthur," Cross said, following his gaze. "That's Arthur right there."

Behind them, Hilda raised her head and, for the first time in a long time, recognition dawned in her eyes. She rose from her chair. Busy as the others were with Caleb, as the child growled and pushed, struggling to open the door, no one paid Hilda any mind.

The chief took Angela's place to give Paul a hand. Angela moved from the door to the window to get a better look, past the little monster on the campus, at the old man. So that was Arthur. No wonder he hadn't picked her up. The old boy was staggering about and had obviously been drinking. But it was more than that. As he made his way nearer she could see that, like the crazed little boy, there was something desperately wrong with him. The caretaker was bloody, badly burned, and acting oddly.

"We've got to warn him about Caleb," Paul said. "We've got to get to him."

"No! Paul," Angela screamed. "Look at him. Whatever sickness Caleb has, Arthur has it too."

"These aren't the people I know," Cross said. "They're all messed up."

"Arthur." It came in a whisper; Hilda calling to her husband. But nobody paid attention. "Arthur." An instant later, Hilda bulled her way across the room, past a startled Angela, between Paul and the chief. She grabbed at the door, struggling for the handle and screaming, "Arthur. Got to see Arthur!" Caleb was still outside fiercely trying to push the door. Hilda was inside trying to pull it. Paul and the chief had hell on their hands. "Arthur. Arthur!"

Paul ducked, putting his shoulder to the door for a brace and himself between it and Hilda. Angela grabbed the hysterical woman from behind. The chief pulled away and grabbed a folded table from the wall behind the reverend, sliding it toward the door. Cross shouted for Paul and, when he moved, shoved the table between them and the door setting up a blockade. Caleb couldn't get in. Hilda couldn't get out. Cross fell against the door, beside Paul, holding his stomach in pain.

Angela yanked Hilda back into the room away from the door and, to end the matter, tackled the old woman to the floor. Angela straddled her, trying to keep her from hurting either of them, while Hilda screamed, "He can't stay out there with the space rocks! He can't stay out there!"

"What are you talking about?" Angela demanded.

"Nothing's the same since they came. Caleb said. Caleb said. Nothing's the same since the space rocks came. Arthur!"

"They will bring you down to the pit," the minister screamed. With all that was happening, the man of God had quite been forgotten. His shout, out of nowhere, scared the hell out of everybody. "They will bring you down to the pit!"

Caleb had given up pushing, rapping, scratching on the outside of the door. He moved across the porch to the large picture window. Chief Cross left the door, following the child-thing. Caleb paused and drew back his fist as if to strike the window. Cross drew his sidearm, cocked it, and pointed at Caleb through the glass. Blowing bubbles in the blood on his lips, Caleb turned and stared. He lowered his fist and backed off of the porch. Behind him, Arthur was halfway across the campus, approaching at a stagger, suddenly interested in what Caleb had found in the community house.

Hilda was crying. Angela was still awkwardly straddling her on the floor, trying to calm her without success. Paul, at the door, sank to the floor against the table blockade. Nearby, the chief leaned on the picture window frame. Paul tried to control his breathing, the chief tried to control his pain.

Reverend Snow's voice had dropped to a whisper. "And you will die... a violent death..."

Darkness had fallen. Not because the sun had gone down but because the storm clouds had entirely rolled in. The rain threatened but was still holding back while a damp murkiness settled over all. Sheriff Nelson and John P maneuvered their boats out of the strengthening river current, whitecaps bursting on the surface of the black water, into the still waters of Harper's Cove. They slowly crossed the small secluded inlet, killed their motors, and drifted both vessels toward the sagging dock.

"There's nothing, Rough," John said, gaping at the overgrown shoreline. "John Henry's boat ain't here. Heck, the Harper's boat ain't even here."

The sheriff ignored him. He'd seen the scorched patches on the dock and was now staring into the water beneath.

"D'ya hear me?" John asked. "I said John Henry's boat ain't here."

"I heard you. And you're wrong. It's here all right."

"You're crazy, Rough. There ain't nothing–"

"Pluck your head out of your ass," the sheriff barked, interrupting the fisherman. He pointed into the shadowy depths of the cove. "Look down there."

John followed his gaze, leaned over his gunwale, and peered below the surface. It took a moment to make the image out but, sure enough, there was a boat, or part of one, under the water. It lay below the surface, just off the dock.

Melissa rolled up her sleeve and reached into the water. She grabbed the sunken boat by the windshield frame above the bridge and held on to stop the drift of their own vessel. The piece snapped off in her hand and the deputy pulled the melted and scorched chuck from the drink. "It is. It's the *Sabula Pride*. But, wow, someone had a barbeque. What'd they do, scuttle her?"

Rough grunted. "John Henry only thought he was pissed before. Wait until he sees this."

"Can I go now?" John whined.

"No, John," Rough growled in annoyance. "Ask again and I'll shoot you. Now, you got a short memory, son. You *are* a Jackson County deputy until further notice. Melissa swore you in, I already congratulated you, and you 'So helped you God'. Now you're going to help, so you might as well be helpful about it." John made to protest. Rough snatched his 12 Gauge from its bracket on the side of the control panel and, *chik-schik,* worked the action.

"All right," John screamed. "I do. I will!"

"I knew you would." Rough turned his attention to the shore and the Harper's lonely dock. "Now let's bring these turds to justice."

The sheriff snagged the dock with the butt of the shotgun and dragged the police boat in. Melissa tied it up then, as he pulled near, tied John's as well. All three disembarked and, with Rough Nelson in the lead, headed up the trail. In the deepening dark beneath the trees, none noticed the bizarre puddle on the grassy bank that once had been Harry Towers or saw it dripping downhill into the river.

Rough, Melissa, and John P (their pouting temporary deputy), emerged from the trail leading from Harper's Cove to the clearing the clan had claimed as their homestead. They came to a stop, startled as one, and took in the unbelievable sight. Even the sheriff gasped, and absolutely nothing alarmed Rough Nelson. The shack was blasted to the ground, completely destroyed. The tin roof was twisted and most of the plywood and barn board broken or burned. There were spot fires among the piles of tarp covered junk. The air was heavy with smoke.

"What in Sam Hell happened here?" John asked.

"Someone threw a shivaree," Rough said. He handed the fisherman his shotgun. He knew John could shoot, they'd been duck hunting. Then he drew his own sidearm; a .357 Magnum, because what else would someone named Rough carry? Melissa drew her Compact 9mm. (She also had a 6 shot Kahr P.380, in '*ladies pink*', strapped to her ankle. But that was no one's business but hers.) Rough started to the north and pointed for her to head west around the far side of the shack. John remained behind in the debris-filled yard. He poked around the scattered junk, timidly calling the names of Ellis Harper and his children. Then he froze, stood quiet, and pricked his ears. He thought he heard… something.

He listened harder. Nothing. Maybe he hadn't really heard anything at all? John turned, straining in the gloom to checked the others' progress. It was dark but he could still make them out in the distance. Rough, having reached the outhouse, took a breath (for several reasons, John imagined) and yanked the door open. It must have been empty because the sheriff breathed a big sigh of relief. (And probably wished he'd waited till he'd closed the door again.) Rough moved beyond the outhouse, still searching. On the other side of the clearing, Melissa was matching him stride for stride. Neither one looked back toward John P and neither showed any sign of having heard… whatever it was he'd heard.

Hell, John thought, spooky as this scene was, it was no wonder he was hearing things. He returned to poking through the junk. "Hello," he called in a whisper. "Anyone there?" Then he heard it again, louder this time, an answer in a desperately weak voice.

A pained voice calling, "Help… me…"

# SEVENTEEN.

Chief Cross, Angela, and Paul had been busy in the commons hall. With the crazed and vicious Caleb, and the untried but untrusted Arthur, pacing with menace outside and with the inability to keep an eye on them in the deepening gloom of the coming storm, a decision was reached to fortify the community house. The front door, already blocked as a result of Caleb's rampage, received a second table for a batten and an added layer of stacked chairs. The inside door, under the stairs on the room's east side (communicating with the nature museum) was blocked in a like fashion. That door had been locked throughout, as had the outside door beyond, but the museum was surrounded by windows. No sense dealing with those; there were plenty of tables. The kitchen door, to the back yard, got the same treatment. And several of the tables were lifted to the counter to cover the windows above the kitchen sink. The upstairs dorm was, at least temporarily, left untouched. The island was densely wooded, but there were no trees near the building and no way for anyone, or anything, to reach the roof. "If something comes up," Cross told them, ignorant of his pun, "we'll adapt."

Three openings remained in the main hall. Two small windows in the west wall they also chose not to bother with, for roughly the same reason. They were too high for Caleb, and Arthur – whatever was eating him – didn't look up to lifting the boy. That left the large picture window looking onto the porch. It was heaped with several layers of stacked folded tables and looked, upon completion, like one side of a Mayan pyramid. Stacked chairs buttressed the bottom. The top few inches of the window, all the way across, remained uncovered; a happy accident that worked in their favor. By standing on chairs, they could see out, but those outside could not see in. Caleb or Arthur might still break the glass, but that wouldn't get them anywhere.

Hilda, calmed and back in her silent world, was again in her chair. The Reverend Snow remained handcuffed on the floor. Paul was likewise on the floor, against the tables blocking the door. The police chief, looking poorly and feeling worse, had excused himself and gone upstairs. They heard him being sick, running water, and being sick again, but had left him alone by request. Angela stood on a chair watching out the top of the picture window. She'd hoped for insight into their situation by reporting Caleb's and Arthur's activities. But there was nothing to report. The pair were still there, but off the porch now, standing together near the picnic tables, just staring at the community house.

Frustrated, and not a little unnerved, Angela said, "They're just waiting out there."

The reverend replied, "During those days men will seek death, but will not find it; they will long to die, but death will elude them."

Paul ogled the reverend silently and rolled his eyes. He stood, moved a chair, and joined Angela's vigil. To the professor, Caleb and Arthur looked like bad topiary; misshapen statues in the grass.

"It's like Night of the Living Dead," Angela said.

"Like what?" Paul asked.

"It's a classic," she said. "It's *the* classic. You never saw it?"

Paul shook his head. Then he smiled, content to have never seen it.

A sinister *creak* startled them, and the heartbreaking sight of Chief Cross inching down the stairs returned them to earth and captured their sympathies. The policeman, ghost pale and sweating, had a wet towel draped heavily around his neck, his grip on the bannister all that stood between him and collapse. Yet Cross did his best to hide his infirmity, to look indestructible. "Is that… the one… in the underground bunker?"

"I'm sorry?" Angela asked.

"Night…" Cross caught his breath, "of the Living Dead. Is that the one in the army bunker?"

"No. You're thinking of the second sequel. Or, more likely, the remake of the second sequel," Angela said. "This was the classic original. The black and white one. Flesh-eating zombies, a bunch of them surrounding a few people… and a little girl… All trapped in a remote farm house."

"Stop it!" Hilda screamed. "Stop it! Who cares!"

Angela and Paul looked down from their perches; she in embarrassment, he in surprise at the woman who had been so far gone they'd all but forgotten her. Cross went to her, took her flailing hands, and calmed her. "It's all right." He pulled up a chair and, feeling suddenly dizzy, collapsed into it beside her. "Listen, Hilda." He fought for breath. "Hilda, think. What was it you said about space rocks?"

"Space rocks?" Angela asked, something dawning. "The meteorites. We saw those!"

"Who's we?" the chief asked.

"Me and the guy who brought me, John something, one of the local fishermen. Gave me a ride in his boat when Arthur didn't show."

"John P. I know him. He gave me a ride too."

"We were nearly here, on the river, when we saw the meteorites fall. They went right over us."

"Did you see where they landed?" Paul asked.

Angela shook her head. "No. I mean, not for certain. John thought they landed in the river. But they could have landed here on the island. Couldn't they? Wouldn't those be space rocks?"

The chief returned to the cook. "Hilda, what did Caleb tell you?" He paused, fielded a wave of pain, then went on. "What did this to them?" He was too late. Whatever had happened to shake Hilda from her coma had passed and she'd returned to staring blankly ahead. Cross patted her arm as his voice fell to a whisper. "You poor thing."

Paul and Angela stepped down from their chairs and sat.

Cross left Hilda. He moved to the minister and crouched beside him. "I'm going to uncuff you, reverend," the chief told him. "I'm going to move your arms in front, then cuff you back up again. Do you understand me? It's against the rules. It's not safe for us but... You can't sit there with your arms behind you all night." He stopped to catch his breath and balance himself against the tables. He felt like baked hell. "Now, while I do that," Cross said, getting back to work. "And afterward, I don't want any trouble out of you. Do you understand? I'm trying to make you more comfortable. Don't make me regret this."

The minister nodded minutely. "Blessed are the meek... for they shall inherit the earth."

The chief made the switch, bringing relief to the put-upon man of God. Then, looking decidedly ill, Cross moved to the corner of the room and slumped on a makeshift bed roll. He ran fingers through his hair and, quietly, hurriedly, tucked away a clump of hair that came out in his hand. Looking about, to ensure nobody had seen, he came face to face with the reverend's knowing stare.

"How suddenly are they destroyed," the minister whispered, "completely swept away by terrors."

Cross turned away, fighting the pain, fighting not to cry, and fighting the terror.

Paul, ignorant of the chief's newest symptom, was well aware of the reverend's continued muttering. He saw the pop-eyed minister staring at the wounded officer. He leaned toward Angela and whirled his finger around his ear. "Poor guy's lost it," he told her. "Completely bananas."

Angela said nothing.

"Speaking of losing it," Paul said, suddenly grinning. "What *was* that all about earlier?"

"You ask questions like a girl. I can't read your mind. What was *what* all about?"

"The quotes. When we looked into the shed and saw all that blood, and then again later, you quoted something. I didn't know it, but it was clearly a quote. Why? What's that about?"

"I already told you. I like horror movies – and I'm a theater major." She sealed her lips, ending the matter. Paul's infuriating grin grew wider. To wipe it off his face, Angela growled, "Lines of dialogue pop into an actor's head all the time. It's an occupational hazard. When you're into horror, you get horror movie quotes. It's not funny. It helps. It's grounding."

"I couldn't help noticing," Paul went on, refusing to let it drop. "You slipped a little Shakespeare in while you were at it. They might love you in New York but, in Transylvania, they're going to take away your monster card."

"Show's what you know. I quoted *Macbeth*. A ghost, witches, murder. It counts."

Paul folded his arms, still grinning, and crooked his head at the reverend. "You two have a lot in common."

She smiled a threat. "Don't make fun of our coping mechanisms."

She looked the room over, the better not to see Paul, and took in sad Hilda. The poor thing had vanished back into her mental haze. Angela rose, whispered, "Speaking of coping," and headed to the old girl's side. After all, she had to do something, didn't she? "Hilda. Do you remember me? Angela. Listen, we could use some food. I'm not much of a cook, but I wouldn't trust these guys to boil water. I guess it's up to us. What say you help me in the kitchen? It's your kitchen, after all."

She waited what seemed a long time, wondering whether to repeat herself or just give up, when Hilda slowly turned and focused her eyes.

"Will you help me?"

Hilda nodded. Angela smiled, helped the lady up and, leading, pushed through the swinging doors to the kitchen.

Beneath the rolling clouds of a storm that threatened, but had yet to produce, the community house kitchen had fallen into a soul-stealing gloom. With no working radio, phone, watches (or cell phones), there was no way to tell the time or to know day from night.

Hilda seemed not to notice the darkness. She stood near the kitchen's center island looking, Angela thought, like the weird tailor's dummy waiting for his new suit in *Asylum*. The image made her shiver. She found the string for the fluorescent fixture over the double-sink and pulled it into flickering life. The usual kitchen 'reflections' were absent, with the tables covering the windows, but the room glowed and Angela couldn't help but blink in the amber nimbus. When sight returned, she found the fridge and, inside, a cold cooked roast, a couple of tomatoes, an impressive chunk from a cheddar wheel, and a bowl of shelled fava beans (fate had a nasty, but delicious, sense of humor). The only decent knife Angela could find was an outsized weapon that would have made Kane Hodder green with envy. She hesitated in handing it over. But, when she did, the mannequin came to life and, despite her condition, Hilda went to work slicing cheese like an expert. Outside of her mechanical duty, the old girl gave no indication she was aware of her surroundings.

With Hilda hard at it, Angela set to exploring cupboards, drawers, and behind doors for whatever she might find. She discovered a walk-in pantry and walked in to commercial cans of vegetables, potatoes, meats, and condiments; more than enough to eliminate starvation as a worry. There were also paper products; plates, napkins, cups, and plastic utensils. Angela had as much conceit as the next person but, with more than enough worries already, decided to leave saving the planet for another day. They'd use the paper. Food, and no clean up.

Were it not for the marauding killers outside, the place could have passed for heaven. The things you think, Angela thought, when you're too scared to think.

In a corner in the back of the pantry, half-hidden beneath hanging aprons, Angela found a rifle (a 'gun' to her) and several boxes of bullets. She wasn't a gun person, didn't like them, was half-afraid of them, but she wasn't an idiot either. She knew the terrible moment might arise when they would be needed. She scooped them up like the prize they were.

A moment later, Hilda looked up from her work to see Angela step from the pantry. She saw the weapon in Angela's hands. She went crazy. "That's Arthur's!" she screamed in a voice to shatter glass. She ran at the startled theatrical director with the gargantuan carving knife raised for business.

Angela dropped the ammunition (the burst boxes scattering bullets beneath their feet) and lifted the rifle to defend herself. They struggled, with Hilda crying Arthur's name and Angela demanding the old woman "Stop it!" She slapped the knife from Hilda's hand, then slapped her face. Stunned, Hilda gave up the fight and walked away crying. Angela caught her breath and, with a firm grip on the gun, went after her. "I'm so sorry," she said, wrapping her arm around the poor old woman. "But we're going to come out of this alive. You need to help us. Or you need to stay out of our way."

Ben Nath moved through the woods and down a park trail, grumbling, building up more steam with each bull-legged step. "Either take care of business," he barked at the trees, the air, the sky, "or get outta the way and let me." He jumped over a fallen branch, nearly fell in the gloom, recovered, and continued on. "That's what I told him." A turn in the path made him angrier yet. "Jee-suz Christ. It's ridiculous." Now he was shouting, so loudly that, were he home, he'd have complained about the noise from the island. He ducked a low-hanging branch and collected a knot of burrs for his troubles. He was livid, and at the end of the trail, and he burst into the clearing shouting, "But where in hell are the police when you need 'em? Son of a bitch!"

Ben stopped, getting his bearings with his good eye. He rarely got to the island but not much seemed to have changed; commode shack there, theater barn beyond it to his left, picnic tables and fire ring in the distance and, beyond that, the community house. Not far from the main building, by the look of it just staring at the main building with their thumbs up their asses, Ben saw two fellas; an adult and a young one.

"Do you two work here?" he demanded, starting for them. "Or are you part of the problem? Damn it, I wanna talk with you and it can't wait. The noise and carrying-on on this island are outta hand. If you people think I'm going to put up with it this year again, you're crazier than a shit-house rat."

Paul didn't know what, but something bad had happened in the kitchen. Whatever it was it sounded as if somebody needed a hand. Headed that way, he pulled up in time to avoid being smacked by the swing of the double doors. His exclamation was interrupted by his gasp when the business end of a rifle went nearly up his nose. He jerked back to see Angela on the other end of the weapon. "Geez!"

"Look what I found," she said, stepping fully through the door.

"Where did you get that?" The question, weakly, breathlessly asked, came from Chief Cross, looking up from his makeshift bed in the corner of the floor. From across the room the reverend added an indecipherable mumble.

"It was in the pantry," Angela said. She added in a whisper, "It must have belonged to Arthur. Hilda put up a fuss." She gave the kitchen doors a sympathetic look. "She's okay."

"You'd better bring that here," the chief said, raising a trembling hand.

She did as instructed, while Paul returned to his window perch atop a chair. She handed the weapon to Cross, then knelt to feel his forehead. It was a paradox; his skin was pale, cool, and clammy to touch, but the man was sweating like a whore in church.

"It's an old squirrel rifle; a twenty-two." Cross checked, found the rifle unloaded, and smiled weakly at Angela. "You didn't happen to find any ammunition?"

"I did. It's scattered all over the kitchen floor. I wanted to get the gun out here before Hilda made another grab for it."

"Good idea. Oh, I should have asked," the chief said. "Do you know how to handle a weapon?"

"I'm in the theater. I know stagecraft, props, and blanks. I don't know anything about guns." Cross leaned the rifle against the wall. It did not escape Angela's notice that he was shaking his head at her. "If it were my world," she said, "nobody would have guns."

"It's a nice thought," the chief said. "Maybe we can all visit your world sometime."

The professor laughed hardily. Still laughing, he returned his attention to his window. He strained to see over their blockade and out into the campus – and the laughing stopped. "Back in the real world," Paul said. "I don't know if it's good or bad, but we've got another visitor."

# EIGHTEEN

"Who's this?" Paul asked.

He watched through the top of the window as the newcomer made his way across the campus, headed straight for Caleb and Arthur. He was a mean-looking older man in a straw hat and appeared to be shouting, though Paul could make out none of his words. He was waving a hand, missing most of its fingers, to highlight whatever point he was making. Caleb and Arthur, who's attention had been devoted to the community house, turned in unison at the stranger's approach.

"He's an old fart but he looks relatively normal, whoever he is," Paul reported. "Seriously ticked off, if I don't miss my guess, but normal. And... now Caleb and Arthur are looking at him."

Angela moved toward the door with her eye on the table blockade. She was reaching for it when Paul jumped down from his chair, barking, "Don't open the door!"

"We've got to warn him."

"Wait!" He grabbed Angela's arm. "Warn him? You mean by opening a door we just got secured? I don't think so."

"Well, we've got to do something." Angela hopped on a chair, reached over the blockade, and rapped sharply and repeatedly on the window.

Despite the effort, she failed to draw the man's attention. Worse, she failed to divert mad Caleb or the monster that had once been Arthur. Her fears exploded, and her hopes were buried alive, as a collision of the living and dead seemed inevitable. She gave up rapping on the window. The hall fell into silence. Even Reverend Snow ceased his mumbling. Maybe he'd gone into silent prayer, Angela thought. She hoped so. Whoever the man out there was, he needed it.

All Angela could do was watch. Her eyes grew wide. She screamed.

Outside, the man who'd just arrived had stopped shouting. Now he was screaming too.

Lester Vance, on the path, making his way to the park facility from the island dock, heard two unique sounds simultaneously. The first was rain falling, finally, after a long afternoon of threatening black clouds, that *tick-ticked* on the umbrella of trees above the trail. The second was a blood-chilling scream. Vance took off running in the direction from which he was sure the cry had come. A moment later, impetuously breaking the rules regarding scene safety, he burst into the campus clearing. He spotted the cause of the disturbance – and could not believe his eyes.

Two men were attacking a third and it wasn't just a 'closing time' street brawl. It was an all-out feral assault, two carnivores on warm prey. They were scratching, biting, tearing his flesh. The victim was screaming his head off, awash in his own spurting blood. Vance, closing in, froze in place as the assault moved from atop a picnic table to the ground and from the vicious to the incredible. The attackers, not merely ripping the man apart, looked to be drinking his blood and eating his flesh. The victim wasn't fighting back or trying to defend himself. He was simply trying to escape. Never having seen the like, it took all of his strength to accept what he saw and all of his courage to do anything about it. "Hold it," Vance shouted. "Police. Let him go!"

The attackers ignored the officer and continued – their activity.

"I said let him go!"

This time they stopped and turned with blood dripping from their maws. Vance got a good look and, to his horror, recognized both. They were Arthur Aaron and Caleb Harper, or some semblance of them, and outside of their obvious animal viciousness there was something horribly wrong with them. Their features were distorted, their eyes seemed to blaze. Arthur stood and took a threatening step toward Vance. Caleb, seeing an advantage, returned his attention to the victim.

A victim that, in that instant, Vance recognized too. It was Ben Nath, bitten, bleeding, and crying for help. But what in hell was Ben even doing there? Vance interrupted his own thought, knowing it made no difference. What mattered was, why in hell was he being eaten? Arthur took another step. Vance drew his sidearm, demonstrating – as earlier on the river that day – he meant business. He didn't carry granny's .38 like his chief. His .45 delivered the goods like a brick through a window. He pointed it with a steady hand and told Arthur, "I'm not even going to mess with you." The gory groundskeeper took a third step and Vance fired two rounds into the old boy's chest.

The bullets disappeared like pebbles into pudding.

Arthur paused with a startled expression on his twisted face and looked down at the holes in his new work shirt, one in the middle of his left breast pocket, one dead center below his third button. Both quickly disappeared beneath growing pools of deep red. For a second, somewhere inside his burning brain, it occurred to Arthur that Hilda would be angry. He stepped toward Vance again, to explain that Hilda would be mad – and to fulfill an aching uncontrollable need.

Mouth agape, Vance heard Arthur groan but saw him still coming. It wasn't possible, of course. The two rounds he'd fired should have turned his target from an old man into food for the conqueror worm. But they'd done no such thing. Arthur was still on his wobbly feet. Vance's brain raced wondering what he was going to do about it. To his right, he heard Ben screaming again (weakly, almost finished). Then distantly, behind Arthur another voice, a strong male voice, yelling, "Over here!"

Vance looked past the dripping, smoking caricature of the groundskeeper, through the rain coming harder now, to see a man (normal looking compared to the blood-soaked horrors around him) shouting from the door of the community house. "Over here!" The officer understood none of it, but knew in an instant he'd rather discuss the situation with the fellow in the doorway, whoever the hell he was, than with the two at hand.

There was nothing he could do for Ben, Vance knew. Caleb was still on top of him and the old hermit had quit making noises altogether. He was done. Resigned, Vance realized it was time to look out for number one. With a nod to his old 'halfback' days, the sergeant beat feet. He darted left around the groundskeeper, juked around the feral child and his victim, then turned for the community house. It wasn't as easy as it looked in the movies; running in the rain, on slippery grass, his balance thrown off by the heavy gun in his hand (add being shocked, appalled, and terrified).

Caleb was too busy feeding to care. Arthur, on the other hand, turned clumsily on his heels and took chase. Not that he had a chance of catching the cop; he was well-behind, old, and dead, but that didn't prevent his making an effort. Still, with long strides and terror for fuel, Vance was to the community house and on the porch in seconds.

Vance reached Paul, waiting for him in the doorway, spun back on the campus, took aim and fired his handgun. Paul threw his arms up and fell back against the jamb, blinded by the muzzle flash, his ears ringing with the explosive report, acrid smoke stinging his nose. Vance snatched Paul's shirt-front and jumped through the door, yanking the disoriented professor – his rescuer – inside with him.

The shot hit Arthur dead-on; smack in the forehead like a marble, and out the back like a softball. The caretaker went down in front of the steps like a ton of falling bricks.

As quickly as they piled in past her, Angela blocked the door closed again, sliding the tables back in place and following with the stacks of chairs.

The police officer still had Paul by the front of his shirt – and was still waving the smoking gun in his hand. "That was Ben Nath," the cop shouted into the geologist's face. "They've killed him." He paused to gather himself, to catch his breath, and to try to make sense of what he'd seen. He released Paul and lowered the pistol. "They killed him," he said again, his volume lower, stunned but back under control. "They ripped his throat out with their teeth."

"Yeah," Paul said, straightening his shirt. "We know." He extended his hand and introduced himself.

Still reeling, the cop shook the hand. "Vance. Eh, Sergeant Lester Vance. Savanna Police."

"I'm Angela," the director put in.

"Lester Vance," he said again. "I'm with the Savanna Police."

"You said. Welcome to the house by the cemetery."

"There isn't any cemetery here."

"When dead men walk," Paul said, "the whole place is a cemetery."

The officer darted his eyes between the two as if he feared they were nuts.

"We're lucky you found us." Angela spread her arms, making the room *us*, and for the first time Vance took notice of Hilda Aaron in one corner and a disheveled and not at all well-looking priest, he didn't know, in another. Hilda was staring into nothingness. The priest was…

"He's in handcuffs!"

"Must be the training," Paul said, examining the cop with a raised brow. "You notice everything, don't you."

"What in hell is going on here?"

"It's a long story."

"And we only know a little piece of it," Angela added.

"I'm looking for my chief," Vance said. "His name's Carter Cross. He came out here to the island earlier this–"

He paused, following the young woman's hand as she pointed to another corner of the room. There, under a blanket, barely visible, and hardly recognizable, lay his Chief Cross stretched out on another blanket on the floor. Vance hurried over, while Angela told him, "I've done what I could for him."

Vance crouched over his superior officer, and friend, and for the umpteenth time that day, his mouth fell open in shock. "Did those… things get him?" he asked over his shoulder.

"No. No, it wasn't them. He was stabbed."

"Stabbed?" Vance took in a third shock in five minutes. He turned from his wounded superior to stare the couple down.

"Oh, not by us," the girl said. "It was an accident. He collided with Hilda and…" Angela threw her hands into the air in surrender, then pointed back to the chief. "He's lost blood." She approached and kneeled beside the sergeant. "But he doesn't act hurt, he acts like he's sick." She removed the dried cloth from her patient's forehead, told the sergeant she'd be right back, and disappeared with it into the kitchen.

Vance leaned over his boss and whispered, "Chief. Chief."

Cross slowly opened his eyes, saw Lester's mug hovering, and frowned. "What are you doing here?" he asked weakly.

"Jackson County has been updating their all-points bulletin. They're still looking for the four that held up the convenience store in Sabula this morning. Search parties are out. Blasko's goose egg is bigger than his brain, by the sound of it, but he'll recover. I've been trying to get hold of you. Haven't had any luck."

"Lost my radio," Cross said, licking his dry lips. "Dropped it somewhere in the woods here. I've had quite a morning."

"What's happened, chief? These folks say Hilda stabbed you. That right?"

"It was an… accident. She was running scared. Didn't see me. Lester, there's something wrong here. Something… very wrong."

"How much blood have you lost?"

"Some. Yeah, some. It's not… I'm sick, Lester. Something… making me sick." He closed his eyes as if holding them open took more strength than he had. "I lost my radio." He shook his head slowly. "I've lost… everything."

"You rest, Carter. Rest awhile. Get your strength back. Then you and I can figure what to do."

Angela returned and handed the dampened washcloth to Vance. He passed it gently over the chief's forehead tamping the sweat. To his horror, a clump of Cross' hair came out and dropped to the blanket. He passed his fingers through the chief's scalp and, in disbelief, brought them away with another clump of hair. "You're right," he told Angela. "This isn't from his being stabbed."

He cocked his head taking in the cuffed figure on the floor against the tables on the opposite wall. "Fill me in," Vance said, rising to stand. "Who's the priest?"

"He's not a priest, he's a minister."

"He's your prisoner," Paul put in.

Vance screwed up his lips and looked a question.

"The chief," Angela said, "when he was still upright, thought the minister, eh, Reverend Snow, was responsible for killing Arthur. So he arrested him."

Vance grimaced and turned to Angela. "For killing Arthur? But…" He pointed beyond the window. "Arthur is… out… I just killed Arthur."

Paul shook his head, strangely amused. "Let us know when you're caught up."

# NINETEEN

Vance did catch up. His problem thereafter, despite the shrieks of the mutilated still ringing in his ears, was believing the situation. With a delusional prisoner in cuffs, the chief incapacitated, two dead out in the yard, and the vicious Caleb-thing roaming somewhere free, he recognized he would have to take charge. He proceeded to issue orders that the others might see it that way too. Paul was asked to collect the ammunition spilled in the kitchen. He did so, without complaint, and stacked the re-boxed cartridges on the floor beside the leaning rifle. Angela, this time without Hilda, was asked to return to the kitchen and finish cobbling together their pantry smorgasbord. Vance, meanwhile, made a circuit of the doors and windows making certain of their security. In so doing, he learned a determined ten year-old with a plastic hammer could eventually force his way through their defenses. The sergeant kept that knowledge to himself and, further, resolved himself to a keen watch.

Through it all the rain fell. Then, beyond the black clouds, as the night truly arrived and real country dark overtook the island, the rain came harder, drubbing the roof and windows. The yard lights, on the porch, on the tall wooden pole at the trail head to the island dock, above the entrance to the theater and, distantly, over the small building that housed the toilets, all on timers, flickered to life. But these added little comfort. In the rain, and under the circumstances, they threw more shadows than light. The picnic tables and fire ring faded in the darkness. The shambling monsters lost what little human definition they had, becoming phantoms. The thunder rolled and boomed. White-hot lightning split the heavens. The stroboscopic effect of the storm, through the top of the blocked window, gave those inside the community house the eerie feeling the undead creatures had taken up cameras outside and, with old-style flash photography, were recording their bizarre siege for posterity.

"He made darkness his canopy around him," Snow mumbled. "The dark rain clouds of the sky."

Though it was becoming a habit, Vance couldn't help but look another question from the incoherent reverend to Paul. The geologist, collecting the plates from their ended (but barely touched) meal, rolled his eyes and nodded in reply. The policeman and the professor agreed, the poor man's mind was gone for good.

"You need a hand?" Angela asked as Paul reached for her plate.

"No. You made the grub, I'll do the dishes."

"You probably haven't noticed," she said. "Those as paper plates."

"Yeah. See how that works." He ferried the trash to the kitchen.

Vance moved to a window for another look outside. Caleb had finished with Ben. The corpse lay where he'd left it, in a pool of spilled blood quickly washing away in the rain. Meanwhile, blood and rain-soaked, Caleb went roaming the campus periphery from one trail head to another tramping through the puddles as little boys did. Refreshed, and looking better than he had all day, he now seemed bored with it all. He made his way toward the house, leaped over Arthur's body, and climbed to the porch. He moved slowly back and forth between the entrance and the window pausing periodically to scratch the glass or test the door before resuming his patrol.

Caleb's 'playing' continued even after Ben's corpse stirred and sat back up. The eyes of the Ben-thing now glowed as the boy's did and, once he regained his feet, he shambled in a like fashion; though even in death the old hermit remained as bull-legged as ever. He spotted Arthur on the ground and Caleb on the porch and stumbled toward them as if to attack. As he drew near, however, Ben realized the caretaker was dead and Caleb as undead as he was. He halted, cocked his head as if to formulate a thought, and turned away. Vance turned from the window. "What in God's name is going on?"

Paul and Angela met his incredulous stare. Paul sighed but said nothing. Another debate about what could *not* be happening seemed pointless. Angela, on the other hand, did what she always did, she said the first thing that popped into her mind. "How about this for an episode of *Cops*?"

Outside of those trapped in the community house, there were other visitors on the Rock Island. While Sergeant Vance and company were seeing to their security, tending to injuries, picking at meals, and watching the return of the living dead, they were busy themselves.

The storm, making itself so well-known at the main campus was, with the exception of the wind, bypassing the southern tip of the island. The trees rattled, the boughs bent around the Harper's clearing and occasional drops of cold rain, scattered outliers from the northern deluge, slipped through the shaking umbrella of branches and thwacked the ground with a strange dysrhythmic beat. But the real storm merely showed its teeth as it passed.

Beneath the trees, straining to hear in the blow, the already tense Sheriff Nelson was caught off guard and startled by something moving in the brush. He trained his massive handgun on the spot and, over his ever-present toothpick, told the bushes and the dark, "I've dealt with punks like you my whole life. Time after time I tell 'em, You're in one hell of a deep hole. You might wanna drop the shovel." He added slightly to the pressure on the trigger. "Come out. You folks have made a few mistakes today. But I'm warning you, messing with me is going to be your last."

He nearly blasted away when something, some things, scampered out.

But Rough caught his breath and held his fire. Then he saw his attackers and roared with relieved laughter. Puppies, two of them, cuter than hell; German Shepherd puppies. The sheriff holstered his sidearm and scooped up the furry little nothings. "Well," he said, still chuckling. "At least nobody threw a cat."

At the opposite end of the clearing, Melissa rounded the corner of the collapsed shack and headed beyond, intent in her search of the grounds and near edges of the woods. Someone may have escaped the cabin carnage and, if so, could be hurt nearby. For that matter, a perp (if there was one) could still be around. Scene safety and all that. If there was someone in the cabin wreck, they'd been there long enough she wouldn't be any help to them. Besides, she wasn't all that interested in digging through charred lumber and torn metal, by the light of flashing lightning, looking for violently traumatized bodies. So sue her. She'd start with nature and work back to the destruction.

Besides too, she could hear the sheriff laughing his big ass off over something behind her. She loved ol' Rough but also knew him pretty well. Whatever it was making him laugh that hard, she most likely didn't want to know about it. Putting space between them sounded like a plan. Melissa snapped on her pocket light and headed for the woods.

John hadn't gone as far as either of the cops. Why the heck should he? 'Deputy P,' he thought, 'don't make me laugh'. He watched the real cops disappear into the dark, Rough to one side of the cabin clearing, Melissa to the other, with no intention of following either. He'd hang right there, where he couldn't get into any trouble. He was in trouble enough. His wife was going to wring his neck.

It was during his silent, pitiful musings, John P first thought he heard the sound. A voice really, a weak and tortured voice, calling for help. But it was his imagination, wasn't it? He paused, listening intently. But the rising wind wasn't helping a bit. Then, despite his sincere hope he'd been mistaken, he heard it again. Someone, very nearby, was crying for help.

John started forward, slowly, with Rough's borrowed shotgun raised in his trembling hands. He passed junk and smoking wreckage unsure which piles were part of the Harper's regular landscape and which parts were new devastation. He was near the cabin when he heard it again.

"Help me," the voice called weakly.

So weakly, in such pain, the fisherman couldn't tell for sure whether the caller was a man or a woman. "Ellis?" John whispered. He slowed his approach to the collapsed cabin, swallowed hard, and strained his eyes. He heard the voice again. He spun on his heels as it sounded now to be behind him. John took another hesitant step, and another, to a pile of wood slats, junk, and tin. "Good God," he whispered. "Is someone under there?"

"Help me, please..."

Had whoever it was been buried in the disaster? Had they moved into that crawlspace to escape the flames? The rain? To hide in the dark? What the hell? John reached with a tremulous hand, threw off some loose debris, and lifted a dented sheet of tin. Whatever was under the metal growled, struck like a cobra, and sank its teeth into the flesh of John's calf.

John P screamed and tried to shake it off. The vicious thing held on like a Rat Terrier.

John didn't know, of course, the creature biting him was the eldest Harper boy, Jay. Crippled with a broken back, slithering on his belly like a reptile from hell, fighting for breath and life, Jay had lost the battle. As his late father had, he now suffered the cosmic horror. He'd made the trip from human being, through death's door and out the other side, transforming into one of those zombie things. Now, the blood hunger consumed him and forced him to consume others. John, in Jay's clutches, screamed in agony, bitten, bleeding, and burned.

A startled Sheriff Nelson turned at his spine-chilling scream. "John P?"

Melissa turned too, on the opposite side of the cabin, aimed her pen light back into the clearing and strained to make out the cause of the commotion. That was as far as she got. Before she could respond further, the deputy heard a shriek in the night. Then Crystal Harper jumped from above, from a branch of what once had been her favorite tree, onto Melissa's back. The teen rode the deputy to the ground – fighting to bite her as they fell.

Rough, startled again, turned his light toward his deputy's screams. "Melissa. Melissa!" He could see nothing in the dark, less with the glow of his flashlight beam refracting off the swirling smoke rising from the wrecked cabin. "Missy!"

Now both were screaming, John P and Melissa. The sheriff didn't know which direction to go. The fisherman was closer but his deputy meant a hell of a lot more to him. He split the difference and started warily back on an angle between the two.

John fought, pulling at his leg, dragging Jay's broken body along the ground as he worked desperately for freedom.

Melissa and Crystal rolled on the ground, scratching and screaming, Crystal trying to bite the deputy, Melissa trying to keep the bitch from doing just that. Even as they struggled, the cynical cop couldn't help but imagine how much the pervs of the world would have loved a front row seat to their battle. Though, she knew, they'd have preferred a pool of jell-o or a mud pit for a venue. It wasn't funny or exciting. And there was nothing exciting about this bizarre scene. The teen was really trying to hurt her. Then she did. Crystal sank her teeth into Melissa's upper arm, deeply. The deputy screamed, drowning out the spurt of blood and the undead girl's squeals of delight.

It started to rain with conviction on the south end of the island, and in Harper's clearing, as Rough ran up on the screaming John and whatever had a hold of him. He came to a stop gasping for breath and, by his flashlight, took in the frightful sight. Something, someone, stretched out on the ground had a lip-lock on John's leg and was biting the living hell out of the struggling fisherman. Rough ordered the attacker to stop, several times, loud enough to be heard over the rain and John's screams. He was ignored each time.

The sheriff kicked at the thing and, for his trouble, got a snarl and a glare from the damnedest set of red eyes he'd ever seen, in a face that used to belong to the oldest Harper kid. Still it, he, would not release his prey. Convinced the beast must die in order to rescue John, Rough drew his sidearm and fired a shot, then two more, into the attacker's back. Three brilliant flashes. But, when the smoke cleared, Rough saw no effect at all.

Jay Harper, for finally Rough wrapped his mind around the identity of the thing, was still hanging on, still biting John P for all he was worth. Rough had never seen the like and was having a hell of a time believing his own eyes. He lifted a rod of rebar from a stack of junk and viciously brought it down, beating Jay's back. As the sheriff wailed away, John passed out and pitched forward, unconscious. Jay fed on the fallen man, oblivious to the whipping Rough delivered. Wide-eyed, mouth agape, the sheriff gave up and dropped the rebar with a clang. He turned and ran in blind terror.

On the edge of the clearing Rough Nelson pulled up again, flashlight shaking in one hand, gun shaking in the other. There on the ground before him, being soaked by the rain in his pool of light, lay his deputy and the Harper girl in a clinch. The savage girl rolled off Melissa and lay beside her in the grass; both splotched in blood and physically spent. Melissa was badly injured. Something worse than an injury, something indescribable, was wrong with Crystal. A section of Melissa's blue body armor showed through a tear in her uniform. Crystal's budding breasts showed through her torn top. The deputy cried in pain while the teen sighed in delight. Crystal laid back in the wet grass to catch her breath. Melissa laid back in the grass – and died.

Rough stared. His lips trembled but nothing escaped. A moment passed, then another, and all the sheriff could do was stare. Finally, Crystal opened her glowing eyes and smiled. Then Melissa opened her glowing eyes and hissed. Both women saw Rough at the same moment and, as the rain came harder, rolled onto their stomachs and began slowly to crawl toward the sheriff. As they moved, whatever was wrong with Crystal, the melting condition that owned her features, seemed to markedly improve. Her face gained a distinct element of normalcy, while the obviously dead and unbelievably resurrected Melissa, crawling beside her in the grass and mud, began to show clear signs of melt.

Rough dropped his gun. He dropped his light. On rubber legs, he stumbled running into the woods. Melissa leaped to her feet. She staggered and fell. Then slowly she rose again. She scanned the edge of the timber with her unique new eyes and started after her frightened boss.

Crystal, like an animated lover, like a boxer's second, jumped up and followed them into the woods, shouting, "Kill him, baby! Kill him!"

The desperately ill Savanna police chief had, for some time, been mumbling incoherently. Now he'd fallen silent and unresponsive. He was feverish and sweating profusely. Vance tamped the sweat on Cross' forehead then replaced the tepid cloth with a fresh cool one. "Hang in there, Carter," he told his boss and friend. "I'll have another blanket for you in a minute."

He wasn't cold, obviously, but Vance was almost certain the man was in shock. You covered someone in shock, didn't you? Hell, he didn't know. He'd taken a first responder course six years ago. Who was he fooling? But he was doing the best he could.

"A day of darkness and gloom," the reverend said, still relentlessly babbling. "A day of clouds and blackness. Like dawn spreading across the mountains a large and mighty army comes, such as never was of old nor ever will be in ages to come."

Vance looked from the ranting reverend to the silent Hilda and back again. *Good grief.* He climbed atop a chair and gazed outside while the minister mumbled on. "Before them the earth shakes, the sky trembles, the sun and moon are darkened, and the stars no longer shine."

Nice, Vance thought, a nice big finish. He looked out the window. Beyond the barricade, beyond Arthur's body, to where the bloody, melting Caleb and Ben things were still meandering in the rain. It was all enough to give a strong man the shivers.

# TWENTY

In the dorm upstairs Paul and Angela collected blankets and supplies, as much to keep busy as because they needed blankets and supplies. Angela searched the bathroom cabinets for anything, *anything*, that might help Chief Cross. Paul went through the single massive walk-in closet. There, in the corner farthest from the door, on a shelf behind several boxes, he found a Thermos container. Beneath the closet's bare hanging bulb its contents looked like water and smelled like nothing at all. The professor stepped into the dorm, poured a taste into the cup top, wet his tongue, and gagged.

"What is it?" Angela called out, coming from the lav at the sound.

"What it is," Paul said with a grimace, "is gin." He coughed, still tasting the juniper pine. "It's bad enough we have monsters in the woods. You didn't tell me the place was haunted too."

Angela shook her head. "I give up. Once again I'm not following you."

"Hey, hey, I beat you at your own game." Paul raised the container. "There are *spirits* in the closet."

Angela groaned. Then she laughed. "The rumors must have been true. You found one of Arthur's Easter eggs."

Paul shivered at the thought and, though there seemed precious little reason for it now, returned the Thermos to its hiding place. He stepped from the closet a moment later, with a stack of blankets, to see the loony (but undeniably attractive) theater director standing at one of the windows, looking from on high, at the same scene Vance was watching on the floor below.

Angela's amusement had vanished, chased away by the rain-soaked sight beneath the window. Arthur, the camp groundskeeper and legendary drunk, who'd provided her more giggles than any man she'd never met, lay dead in a puddle beside the porch. Caleb and Ben roamed aimlessly in the rain. Spirits; the word hung in her thoughts. *Spirits of the Dead.* The whole affair would have been pathetic had these monsters not been holding murderous siege on everyone in the building.

Still staring out, Angela asked, "Did you ever see *The Food of the Gods?*"

Paul signed heavily, but something in Angela's tone, something in her look told him she needed an ear. "No," he said. "What's Food of the Gods?"

"The characters in the film are trapped in a log cabin, on a secluded island in Canada, surrounded by gigantic rats." Paul snorted. "No. I mean big, like six feet long." Angela was serious and spread her arms wide to give him an idea. "Big… and relentless. The rats are gnawing the sides of the cabin, the roof, scratching at the windows, trying to get inside; ravenous. There are six people barricaded inside, waiting for the rats to break through, waiting to be eaten. And, out of nowhere, Pamela Franklin turns to Marjoe Gortner and says, 'This is going to sound crazy, but I really want you to make love to me right now.' "

Paul stared, absentmindedly letting the blankets drop. Angela stood as before, staring out the window at the moving things in the rain-soaked yard. "Make lo…" His voice cracked. He swallowed, wet his lips, cleared his throat, and tried again. "Make love to her?"

Angela nodded. "I want you to make love to me right now." She turned, green eyes glistening, and looked into Paul's deep browns. "That's what she said. With giant rats attacking. The stupidest thing I've ever seen in a movie. Written by a man, of course."

"Of course," Paul agreed. He grinned. "If you don't mind my asking, why this obsession with scary movies?"

Angela smiled weakly and turned to stare out the window again. "Blame my parents. It'll be hard, but picture me as an innocent child. I'm walking past the family room where mom is watching television. I stop, I look in, and see on the screen a stage full of actors, in period costume, singing their hearts out. Suddenly there's the sound of tearing fabric and a guy, hanging by his neck at the end of a rope, swings through the stage curtains right at the screen. And now the screaming starts! All the actors are suddenly in hysterics. Most little girls would probably have run from the room, traumatized. But not me. I'm bug-eyed with fascination. I don't know what I'm seeing but I'm going to see it all. Then my mother sees me and goes nuts. 'You can't watch this! Go out and play. You can't watch this!' So I went. But I was madder than heck and more curious than I was mad. From then on I swore I would find out what it was that I was *not* supposed to watch."

"Did you find out?"

"Oh, yes. She was watching a Hammer film. Phantom of the Opera."

Paul smiled. "With Lon Chaney?"

"No," Angela said, shaking her head. "Herbert Lom. But the point is, from then on, science fiction, fantasy, giant monster, or straight terror, it didn't matter; I had to know. By chasing me out, my poor mother, who hadn't the least insight into child psychology *created* a lifelong horror movie junkie. My dad became my co-conspirator, sneaking me in to watch them whenever mom wasn't around." Angela turned to look out the window again. Despair crept into her voice. "I never imagined I would wind up in one for real."

"Sorry I brought it up." He laid a hand on her shoulder. "Try to think about something else."

"Like what?"

"Like… Have you made up your mind?"

She looked a question at him.

"Have you decided? Are you going to recommend this place to your director's guild?"

"Yes." She nodded, fighting back the tears. "Of course. It's perfect."

Paul laughed and Angela began to cry. They embraced each other and, for a moment, lost track of the creatures below.

In the rain, on the campus grounds below, Caleb paused in his meandering to stare at the lighted windows in the second floor, and one window in particular. Two humans were there in a clinch. He vaguely remembered, a long time ago in, what seemed, a life far away, in a small, still-functioning portion of his brain his daddy and momma had hugged like that. He'd spied once and seen his brother do the same with a Thomson girl. That slice of Caleb's brain seemed now to understand that he would never grow up to hug a girl like that. The rain fell. The raindrops hit the window and ran down the glass in rivulets distorting the human images behind. From Caleb's perspective, it looked as if the couple inside were melting.

Dex and Norene stumbled, running for all they were worth. They were half dressed and carrying the rest of their clothes, hurrying as best they were able through the rain. Their tattoos and piercings, in and on their contrasting skins, lit by flashes of lightning, gave them the grotesque appearance of characters from a twisted Tod Browning film. Freaks racing through a circus of the absurd. Fighting for breath, independently darting glances behind, trying to stay together, in terror, they ran for their lives through the trees.

Behind them, cackling cries fought to reach them through the wind and rain. "Join us. Join us." The voices belonged to two horrid *things* that, notwithstanding their shouted invitations, were chasing them with murderous intent. Gar and Falcon, recent partners in crime, no longer human, now among the space children, the burning descendants of the meteorite, were in pursuit and closing.

Closing so quickly, Dex and Norene barely escaped the woods. They burst from the trees into the clearing surrounding the community house. Dex fell with a yell. His head was bleeding again and his already injured leg was wrenched horribly. Norene came back for him.

"My knee again," Dex told her. "I can't do it, baby."

She rubbed the rain water from his eyes, then her own. Both caught a breath looking furtively from the lighted house, to the woods they'd just escaped, and back again. Even through the storm they could hear that Gar and Falcon were right behind. If that wasn't enough, near the porch of the park building stood several others, a bull-legged man and a child, looking as bizarre as their former friends. The pair, Ben and Caleb, heard the newcomers and turned with more than a little interest.

In the commons, downstairs again, Angela spread another blanket over top of Chief Cross. He was sweating feverishly and she felt guilty for contributing to it, but Vance insisted. On the other side of the hall, Paul wrapped a blanket around Hilda's shoulders. She paid him no mind whatever.

The sergeant, on a chair watching the clearing outside the window, asked aloud, "Who the heck are they?"

Paul and Angela joined him. Sharing a chair, they stood and followed Vance's gaze. Their alarm matched his. The traffic in the campus yard had doubled and the new attendees were a sight in the lightning; a tall, muscled African-American man and a tall but scrawny and very red-headed white woman, both half naked, metal studs glittering in their noses, ears, and lips. Then the odd sights increased.

Gar and Falcon, their names unknown to the on-lookers, ran into the clearing. Like the others, this pair were pierced, tattooed, dressed in leather, torn, bloodied, and burned. They wore gray make-up streaked with rain and running down their faces; two more bizarre and frightening clowns in the lightning. They stopped on the far side of the campus to stare, through eyes as red as Caleb's and Ben's, at the terrified Dex and Norene. "Join us," Gar told them, lifting a swollen hand in their direction.

"And who in the world are they?" Paul asked, reacting to the newest arrivals.

As if the affair had been staged by Angela's titled guild, with lightning gobos being flashed from the booth and an entrance elaborately blocked, the grotesque and blood-spattered John P and Melissa ran into the clearing from the southern most walking trail. They too examined the situation through red-lamp eyes then, switching to improv, drifted in the direction of Gar and Falcon, and Ben and Caleb, taking their places in a haphazard circle around Dex and Norene.

"Okay," Angela said, seeing the newest arrivals and no longer able to suspend her disbelief. "My turn, I guess. Who in the name of–"

Angela, Paul, and Vance made an interesting club, all three standing on chairs, staring outside, taking in the scene beyond the windows. A club of the collected powerless, for they watched helplessly as the newly reinforced group of stumbling gore-soaked, blood-hungry monsters closed in on the just arrived and obviously frightened couple; Dex and Norene, to those in the know. Sometime around then the rain stopped (nobody remembered when, for certain, with their minds on other things). But the ambiance remained. The lightning continued to flash, the thunder to roll, and the melting dead to walk.

"Wait," Angela said, louder than she'd intended. "My God, I know him! That one there. The one with the lady policeman. That's the boat guy. That's John!"

"Lady policeman?" He hadn't seen her clearly from his angle. Now Vance stared where Angela pointed. He saw her, and something familiar in her movements, as she stumbled from the shadows into one of the yard's pools of light. She was a smallish figure in what remained of a torn blue uniform. A badge glinted as she turned and Vance recognized her for certain. His worst fear was realized; it was Melissa Renee. "Oh, hell," Vance groaned and, under his breath, without meaning to, added, "So much for tomorrow's dance."

"What?" Paul asked.

Vance reddened. He didn't, of course, mean anything so shallow. He liked Melissa very much, as a woman, as a person, as a cop. His brain was just dealing with yet another gross trauma. At least that's what he told himself. It's what he had to tell himself.

"What did you say?" Paul asked again.

"I know her," Vance said. "The deputy. She's a friend."

"What's she doing here?"

"Does it matter?"

Did anything matter anymore? What was it, Vance tried to recall, the reverend had said earlier? How had he phrased it? *'A large and mighty army comes.'* That's what he'd mumbled. Maybe the old boy wasn't as daft as they all thought. All right, it wasn't an army yet. Though it felt it, there weren't two thousand maniacs clamoring for their blood. But there had been two and, in minutes, those two became six. Now the brood looked ready to add two more to their ranks.

"We've got to help those people," Angela said, putting Vance's thoughts into words as she climbed down from her perch.

"How?" Paul asked. "It's a convention out there. A mad monster party!"

Vance jumped down too and pulled out his pistol. "We're going to do the only thing that works," he said, reloading the gun. "We're going to shoot them."

Paul, still on his chair, still watching outside, shouted, "Good goddam gravy!"

Angela and Vance gawked. Neither had heard the professor swear to any extent before and he'd caught them off guard. "What?" the startled pair asked together, knowing that whatever Paul had seen outside had to have been remarkable.

"You didn't see it. Arthur…" He looked at Hilda, shook his head, and lowered his voice. "I mean Arthur's corpse… It just sat up! It shook, and it shivered, and it sat back up; with the bullet hole leaking in his forehead where you shot him and a whole chunk missing from the back of his…" Paul took a deep breath. "He's alive, or undead, or whatever the hell it's called. Again!"

"You're supposed to be some kind of atomic brain," Angela screamed at Paul. "How do you explain this? How do you explain these incredibly strange creatures?"

"Who stopped living and became mixed-up zombies?" the professor asked, a defensive edge rising in his voice. "How am I supposed to know? How could anyone know?"

They all traded a round robin of looks, from startled, to disbelieving, to disgusted with the idea. What really was driving this madness? So caught up were they looking for an answer that none of the three paid any attention to Hilda. She'd come to again at the mention of her husband's name and, while they argued, without a word or sound, rose from her chair and edged herself to the kitchen doors.

Vance holstered his handgun and grabbed up and quickly began loading Arthur's rifle.

"They're moving again," Paul called out, jumping down from his lookout post. "They've ended the staring contest, those things, and they're moving toward that couple out there." He turned to confront the sergeant. "What are you going to do?"

"We," Vance said with a scowl, "are going to do exactly what I said."

"Bullets don't stop them," Angela said. "Didn't you hear Paul? Arthur is up again. Obviously, bullets don't work."

"They work for a while," Vance said. "Arthur is proof of that too. Bullets knock hell out of them for a short while. That's all those two out there need, time to get in the door. And they need it now." He pushed the rifle into Paul's hands. "It isn't much, but it'll go boom." The geologist took the weapon without enthusiasm. Vance ignored his reaction and drew his own sidearm again. He hurried to the door, pulled the chairs and table blockade away, and asked Angela, "You ready?"

"Wait." She waved her hands nervously. "What do you want?"

"I want to hear you scream," Vance said. "Scream your head off. Get the live people headed over here to safety. We'll clear the way." He smiled at Paul. "Ready?"

Without waiting for an answer, Vance threw the door open and stepped onto the porch. Paul followed with a death-grip on the squirrel gun. Angela stepped into the doorway, behind and between them, and shouted, "Over here! Hurry! Over here! Run!"

She had everyone's attention, the two terrified humans and the ring of slathering melters encircling them. "Run!" Angela screamed again. Dex grabbed Norene by the hand and jerked her with him as he darted between the ogling creatures. The race with the has-been humans, the devil's rejects, was on.

To the sounds of growls, grunts, screams, and hisses, Dex and Norene kept their lead. John P, the fisherman now very late in getting home, and a feral and angry looking Falcon, led the pursuit and were almost on the human pair when they leaped for the porch. Vance lifted his arm, his handgun barked, and the shot hit John in the head dropping him like a stone.

Paul followed the officer's example, leveled the rifle, and blinked as an explosion left the barrel. The bullet hit Falcon in the stomach. She slipped on the wet grass and fell down – and that made her very angry. The other monsters hurried as best their conditions allowed, past their fallen comrades and towards the community house. All of them, with the exception of the deputy-thing. Melissa had pulled up when the gun play began and now stood watching intently from the back of the pack.

Angela got the soaked Dex and Norene inside and was calling to her two heroes to follow suit when she spotted, and was appalled by, movement at the side of the building. It was Hilda, running from the darkness, across the front campus toward Arthur. "Hilda, no!" Paul grabbed Angela and pulled her back inside. Vance pushed in behind and quickly slammed the door as the melting dead at the front of the pack swarmed the porch.

Outside, beyond the growling carnivores, they could hear Hilda shouting. "Arthur! Arthur!"

Angela raced past the dripping newcomers to a chair, jumped up, looked out, and located Hilda in the crowd as the old girl fell into Arthur's arms. The groundskeeper immediately and without reservation bit his wife in the throat. Hilda struggled. Arthur did too (as much with his dentures slipping in his melting skull as with his flailing wife). But age had all but turned her skin to paper and her determined husband finally struck oil. Caleb moved in below and tried to bite Hilda's leg but Arthur was having none of it. The old man shoved the monster child away and kicked after him for good measure.

"Poor Hilda," Angela cried. "My God. Poor, poor Hilda."

"How the heck did she get out?" Paul asked aloud. A light shown in his eyes and, renewing his grip on the rifle, he hurried through the kitchen's swinging doors.

Too much was happening too soon for anyone to give a moment's thought to the couple they'd just risked their lives to rescue. Norene, still badly shaken, holding Dex tightly in her arms, both dripping rain water in a puddle on the floor, began breathlessly hurling praise to anyone who would listen. "How can we thank y'all? How evah can we thank y'all? Y'all saved our lives!"

Vance turned, pointed his gun at Norene and her boyfriend, and barked, "Don't move!"

# TWENTY-ONE

From her chair perch, Angela stood with her mouth hanging open watching the police sergeant wave his gun at the couple they'd just risked their lives to rescue. It was all she could do to find her voice. "What are you doing?"

"My job," Vance said. "Stay out of it."

The swinging doors opened and Paul, oblivious to the scene being played out, entered the hall from the kitchen. "She went out the back door," he called out. "Hilda. She left the kitchen standing wide open. I've got it blocked back–" He froze in his tracks, taken aback by the sight of the tight-lipped sergeant drawing down on the newcomers. "What's going on?"

Vance ignored Paul, speaking instead to the half-dressed Goth couple. "Drop everything in your hands." That amounted to the remainder of their clothes. They did. "Are either of you armed?" Both replied in the negative. Vance patted down the few clothes they wore with his free hand. "Any weapons? Guns? Knives? Bazookas? Anything that will hurt me?"

"Nothing," Dex said.

He eyed the tall slender black man severely. "Where's your weapon?"

"What are you doing?" Paul insisted, suddenly conscious of the rifle in his own hands.

"I said, stay out of it." Vance glared daggers at the geologist then returned his attention to the Goth couple. "I asked about your weapon?"

"I don't know," Dex said. "I dropped it in the woods somewhere. With those things chasing us... I was scared shitless, man."

"He did," Norene put in vigorously. "He surely did." Vance turned on her. Reading the question in his glare, she added, "I never had one, sir. I don't touch guns."

"You were the driver?"

The redhead lowered her eyes in embarrassment. "Yes, sir, I was."

Paul leaned the rifle against the wall. Angela came down from her chair and she and the professor drifted together, looking on in confusion and not a little disbelief. The cop was going out of his way to ignore them.

"You have the right to remain silent," Vance informed the pair. "If you give up this right, anything you say can, and will, be used against you in a court of law."

Paul had had enough. "What the hell is going on?"

Norene, looking as annoyed as Vance, wanting to get it over with, turned to Paul, and said, "We robbed a convenience store, if it's any of yore damn business."

"Shut up, babe!" Dex said.

"Why?" Norene asked, her angry drawl as thick as molasses on a cold morning. "What difference does it make now?"

"Hey," Vance shouted, taking the reins again. "Listen up. You have the right to speak with an attorney and to have one present during questioning."

Angela put in her two cents. "This is ridiculous."

"I'm not going to tell you again," Vance growled.

"Don't yell at her," Dex demanded. "She's got nothing to do with this."

"It's all right, sweetheart," Vance told Dex. "There's nothing to worry about. I'm your number one fan. You just zip it and I'll be back to you in a second." With Dex silenced, he turned hard on Angela. "You. This isn't any of your business. I have a duty here."

"You're kidding, right?"

He shot her a look to kill.

"It was poorly phrased, sergeant," Paul put in, trying to calm things. He laid a hand on the feisty director's shoulder. "But Angela's question is sound." The geologist was no idiot. A blind man could see that confrontation with a cop aiming a gun would get them nowhere. Diplomacy stood a much better chance. "I see your duty. I do." He waved at Norene. "Even the young lady admits you have them dead to rights. But, as it is, Chief Cross has already supplied you with one prisoner." He indicated the minister, seated against the wall, mumbling. "As long as we're surrounded by, whatever those things are, how many more handcuffed people do you want to be responsible for?"

"We want to stay alive," Dex told Vance. "We won't give you any trouble."

## The Melting Dead

It was four to one, among those present whose brains were functioning, but Vance didn't care. It wasn't after all a democracy. With the chief laid up, he was in charge and they needed to know it. Still he couldn't escape Paul's logic. What the hell would he do with three prisoners zip-tied together? He conceded the point with a nod and holstered the gun. "But let me be clear," he warned Dex and Norene. "You *are* under arrest. And I will have one eye on the both of you at all times."

Dex snorted and, with one hand on his bruised and seeping head wound and the other on his swollen knee, moved to sit on the floor. He paused mid-crouch. "May I?"

Vance waved.

"We're not goin' anywhere, off-cer," Norene said, giving her man a hand down. "That's plain enough."

"How about some introductions," Paul said and started them around. Once they were all old friends, he asked, "The two that were chasing you, when you first arrived, they were with you this morning?"

"When you robbed the gas station?" Vance added, crossing his arms over his chest.

"You want the story or a confession?" Dex demanded. The officer shrugged.

"I'd like the story," Angela said. "Maybe we can learn something about these things." She gave Vance the evil eye. "Or is gathering evidence more important than good old fashioned information?"

Vance shook his head. "Tell your story."

"To answer your last question," Dex said, "Yeah. Those two chasing us are – were – our friends. A few hours ago they were normal; like you or me. Now, I don't know, man, they're sick or something."

"They're not sick," Angela informed him. "They're dead."

"Dead?!" Dex asked.

Paul nodded. "They are not men. They are dead bodies. Here, apparently, the dead don't die." He pointed to the minister. "Some of us want to blame the prince of darkness." He pointed to Angela. "Some blame the cosmos." He threw his hands up. "For myself, I wear neither a cross nor a space helmet. I'm betting on science. Some sort of infection loosed here on the island kills and, soon after, resurrects those same corpses and makes them ambulatory and deadly."

Dex laughed uproariously. Norene didn't. She moved to the big window and, as she'd seen Angela do, stood on a chair to get a look outside. She stared aghast, rubbed her arms, started to squirm, and finally asked, "Y'all mean...? That they're...? I see dead people?"

"The Eagle has landed," Vance muttered.

Angela frowned, wishing Paul had said it. Paul she could have slapped.

Dex ended the conversation with a rousing shout of, "Bullshit!"

"You see," Angela whispered to Paul in mock sincerity, "they don't believe you're a scientist either."

"Yeah. Well, *science* covers many subjects but not, as far as I know, the study of melting zombies." He turned to the redhead on the chair. "I'm sorry, I forgot your name."

"Norene," she said, all Georgia peach and glad to meet him. "Norene Gayle."

"Can you see them, Norene? What are they doing now?"

"They're bein' ridiculous, if ya ask me." She pushed a fist into the air. "Go Bulldogs!" Norene caught their stares, smiled, and blushed as she pulled her arm down. "Well, they... They're in a huddle." When the collective stares turned to questions, she elaborated, "A huddle. Like they was playin' football."

Only the background noise of the mumbling minister would have prevented their hearing a pin drop. Otherwise the room was stone silent. Everyone moved at once, even the suffering Dex, stealing chairs for height or a sliver of open window through which to look. Unbelievably, each saw what Norene had described. The creatures, the things that once had been Gar and Falcon, Arthur, and Melissa, were gathered in a loose circle looking for all the world as if they were having a meeting.

"Damn," Dex exclaimed. "That's fuc –" He caught himself, what with ladies present and a badge-wearing pig that already had it out for him, and started again. "That is ridiculous. They're in a huddle."

"No," Vance said. "It would be ridiculous if it weren't real. This is happening. Those things are making a plan."

"Making a plan? You mean they're working together?" Angela exclaimed. "Live people don't even do that!"

The ring broke up and the melting dead spread out in a scene growing more unbelievable by the second. No ghost story ever told around that fire ring, or any other, could in the wildest imagination of the teller have compared. Gar and Falcon stood, together, watching the community house and campus like military commanders. The corpses of John and Hilda lay near, where they'd fallen, adding to the battlefield illusion. Melissa paced in the shadows as if with something weighty on her undead mind. Caleb and Ben, nasty creatures both, climbed up onto the porch. While Arthur, the shambling old caretaker, outside of human notice, disappeared from sight.

Outside, alone in the darkness at the side of the community house, Arthur stopped before the gray box holding the electrical service entrance and the protruding glass meter base. The groundskeeper stared through lamp-like red eyes, watching the tiny wheel spin slowly inside. He grabbed the heavy globe in both hands and yanked down and out at once. With a metallic *thunk* and a bright shower of sparks, the meter base came off. Arthur let it fall to the wet ground.

The community house was plunged into darkness.

The commons hall went black. Norene yelped. Dex and Vance swore. The creatures, vague outlines roaming beyond the windows, instantly became haunting silhouettes backlit by the still-functioning night lights dotted about the campus clearing. Following their initial shock, the occupants ceased all movement in the hall. No one spoke, moved, or breathed.

"He sent darkness and made the land dark – for had they not rebelled against his words?"

"The Reverend Snow, ladies and gentlemen," Paul called out. "He'll be here all week. Don't forget to tip your waitress."

Norene, despite her terror, perhaps because of it, giggled nervously. Everyone breathed again.

"If it was *my* power company," Angela said, "this would never happen." On the floor, she pushed a table a skosh to the side to steal a look out the big window. When she did, she gasped, for her reflection in the dark glass had red-searing eyes. Then, realizing it wasn't her reflection at all, but one of those things, the female creature in black leather looking in from outside, Angela screamed her head off. She didn't know Falcon, but she knew horrifying when she saw it. She slammed the table back in place.

"Are you all right?" Paul asked.

"There's one at the window," she squealed, grabbing his arm. "She's right outside the window with those glowing eyes. Those red eyes!"

"It's all right. It's okay," he said, trying to be reassure her. "I know it's disconcerting, but don't let the eyes freak you. It's just a mutation. Something about the disease alters the rod and cone light receptors in their eyes. Afterward, after they change, their eyes are able to collect higher UV levels than normal. Higher than ours."

"Are you're telling me they can see in the dark?"

Paul shrugged. "Well, eh… Yes."

She could have scratched his eyes out. "You have this amazing ability," she told him acidly, "to make even horrifying news boring."

Paul mouthed an *ouch* unseen in the Stygian surroundings then, struck with an idea, smiled (equally unseen). "At least you forgot your fear of the dark."

"I'm not afraid of the dark," Angela said. "My parents taught me before I could walk, *'Don't be afraid of the dark'*. I'm afraid of being fatally annoyed by fake scientists, using false names, giving boring lectures on why the eyes of these mutants glow with fire."

"Don't know how y'all could be bored." Norene's voice trembled on the verge of hysteria. "I *am* afraid of the dark. *And* blood-drinking mutants that see in the dark."

"Zip it," Vance barked in an aggravated whisper.

Norene began to cry and moved from the window into the dark room, away from the cop with the attitude. Dex followed the sound, found her, and wrapped her in his arms. Angela sidled up next to the sergeant, close enough to make out his outline in the gloom, and whispered, "You're not too terribly compassionate for a peace officer, are you?"

"Besides my incapacitated boss," Vance said through gritted teeth, "I've got a hopeless basket case, two scofflaws, you, and the geologist. As for you, you can close the vault of horror anytime, sister. In fact, you might want to start thinking about westerns instead. We're in *The Alamo*. The chief is out of it, which makes me John Wayne." He pointed at the pair of Goths. "I don't need those two urging Joan O'Brien and Ward Bond to go to pieces on me. You and the prof are all I've got."

Vance walked away. Paul took his place, brushing up to Angela to ask, "Who's Joan O'Brien?"

"Work it out, professor."

"Huh?"

"She was the female lead in The Alamo." Paul stared, not getting it. Angela sighed. "I'm Joan O'Brien."

"Okay," Paul said. "So? What? That makes me Ward Bond?"

"Count your blessings. Ward Bond wasn't in The Alamo. So, I guess, you're not here."

## TWENTY-TWO

Angela sat, rewriting *The Legend of Hell House* in her head, under siege in the dark in that house of horrors. Those trapped with her, all afternoon and into the night, no doubt felt it too. Ravenous eyes, hungry gaping mouths, hands melted into claws threatening, waiting for them. Their survival lay in keeping the creatures out. While their sanity hung on the hope that one among them could somehow conjure an escape. The situation, a nightmare from the *Outer Limits*, was horrible and damned near hopeless. Amazingly, it was also horribly dull.

That was the awful dichotomy, at least in Angela's mind. The doors were locked, windows blocked, and they were as secure as could be in that setting. Nothing remained for her, or her compatriots, to do but simply go numb. It was an Irish wake, without the booze, and with the dear departed already returned from their eternal slumber. But the waiting went on – and it was boring.

Not that there wasn't plenty going on. For starters, the police chief, Carter Cross, all alone on his makeshift bed in the corner of the room, gave up the ghost and died. And nobody knew it. They weren't ignoring their patient. Everyone believed they were providing badly needed rest and took pains not to disturb him. Besides, at the exact moment he passed, the others *were* busy. The squinting Ben-thing was pounding on the door with his pink crab claw, Falcon scratched playfully at the window, Arthur (out front again now he'd killed the lights) rapped the outer walls, all three leaving scorch marks behind. It was nerve-racking and diverting. And because of it, in a room full of people, Chief Cross died alone in the dark.

Then came the other little incident. Beyond the irritating creatures pecking away at the building, from her resting place in the cold wet grass, touched by whatever re-animating agent was at work, poor dead Hilda sat up. Like those who'd risen before, her eyes glowed as if she was a jack-o-lantern. Paul, watching from atop a chair, dryly reported, "Hilda is back on her feet."

Insisting she wanted a look, Angela switched places with the professor. She saw the former camp cook, as described, up and about, and wandering toward the undead groundskeeper. Arthur and his corpse bride met, stared blankly at one another, turned to face the house and took hold of each other's hand like a pair of kids discovering love on a walk home from school. Angela turned away and climbed down. "That's just... messed up."

"What?" Paul asked. "What's wrong?"

She couldn't answer, couldn't even speak. She just shook her head.

"Have you noticed these..." Paul hesitated, struggling for a word. "What do we call them? Burning Dead? Melting Dead?"

"What's the difference?" Angela asked. "They're insane and unbelievable. Anything you call them will be insane and unbelievable."

Paul couldn't argue with that. "Okay. These... melters... They go through stages. Three, I think. First, the newly dead return to life."

"You call this life?" Vance asked.

"I'm neither a linguist nor a philosopher. They're condemned to a semblance, a parody, of life." Vance nodded his agreement. Paul continued. "The point is they're up walking around when a minute before they were dead. They retain some of their faculties, which, to what degree, we don't know. People are different. It's reasonable to assume this infection impacts each of them differently."

"Why are they eating people?"

All eyes fell on Angela who seemed on the edge of losing it.

"Take it easy," Paul told her. "Are you all right?"

She folded her hands atop her head and took a breath. She nodded. "I'm fine."

"Okay." Paul turned to the others. "I was saying, the same element that rejuvenates them–"

"What element?!"

"I don't know, Angela. The police chief is showing symptoms of radiation sickness. Maybe it's radiation. Maybe bacteria or a virus. Maybe it's Hilda's Big Band music! How should I know?"

"Let's calm down," Vance told them both.

Paul took a breath. "If I had to bet, I'd say it's radiation. But I don't know. Whatever started this night of bloody horror, whatever brings these bodies back to life, also makes them deteriorate. In this second stage, they suffer rapid cellular breakdown. Their burns worsen, grotesque mutations develop, they rot before our eyes. That's why they're flesh eaters."

"I missed the transition," Angela said. "How does cannibalism–"

"It's not cannibalism," Paul insisted, cutting her off. "Whatever those things are, they're not human. They feed on human blood and tissue. When their victim dies–"

"Victims," Dex put in with a derisive laugh. "Aren't we all?"

Paul and Vance frowned at the interruption. Paul cleared his throat and repeated, "When their victim dies, they stop feeding. They're not eaters of the dead and they're not interested in each other."

"Okay," Vance agreed. "They're not cannibals. Where's this going?"

"They are consuming flesh and blood for nourishment," Paul told him. "Their physical conditions improve after they've eaten."

"Human flesh reverses the decay?" Angela asked.

"It seems to."

"What? You're saying that to them we're just… protein shakes?"

"Not in a million years," Paul told her, "would I have phrased it that way."

"You don't know!" she screamed. "You're not even a scientist. You're an archeologist."

"I'm a geologist," Paul shouted back. "It's a science. And I have a degree, so it's unlikely I'm an idiot."

Angela was shaking. "Lots of college graduates are idiots!"

"Stop!" Vance barked. He sighed and turned to Paul. "Go on with your theory."

"Fine! By the third stage, and I grant this *is* a theory, they've lost orientation to person, place, or time. Speech becomes difficult; for some impossible. The rate of decay increases and their core temps spike; they're virtually melting. The flesh eating becomes ravenous as if it's their only hope for survival."

"And what," Angela calmly asked, "is our hope for survival?"

Paul would have loved to have answered. More, he would have wished for the time to answer. But, before he could, the big window behind Angela shattered.

In the dark there was chaos; the sound of the huge pane breaking, the rain of glass shrapnel flying over top of the blockade, and screaming. Lots of screaming, male and female, living and undead. Then came a particularly impressive shriek as Gar leaped from the porch, against the tables and in, through the massive jagged hole. Everything thereafter happened in a horrifying flash.

The tables fell and Gar grabbed Angela by the hair. Paul saw it, grabbed the rifle, and shot Gar in the stomach – to virtually no effect. Vance saw that and shouted, "You're so damn smart, stop wasting ammunition." The sergeant shot Gar in the forehead. The blow knocked the leather-clad monster back through the window, taking more broken glass with him, onto his back on the porch. "Shoot them in the head, for Christ's sake."

"The head. Right. Got it."

Paul and Vance, of like minds now the professor had been schooled, grabbed a folded table and threw it up to block the window again. They shoved stacks of chairs behind that as the things outside shrieked wildly.

Dex, by his wild eyes, looked to be teetering at the crumbling edge of sanity. In what seemed an effort to prove it, he suddenly began to sing, a heavy metal song that nobody (save Norene) knew or cared about. The lyrics, heard above the growls and hisses from outside, mentioned *"Demons in his head," "not feeling well,"* and *"being in a mental hell."* Maybe Dex wasn't crazy after all. Outside of his breakdown, the chaos continued.

Chief Cross, back from wherever he'd gone when he died, sat up on his makeshift bed. As at the time of his passing, no one in the room noticed or paid him any mind. He staggered to his feet and found his balance. Then he turned and, blinking through glowing eyes, grabbed Norene from behind.

Her scream interrupted Dex's song and jerked him back to reality. He turned to the chief, shouted, "Get away from her, you bitch," and leaped. Dex tackled the undead Cross to the floor. Struggling to keep the zombie-pig from biting him, Dex caught a glimpse of his freed girlfriend just standing there. "Run, Norene," Dex hollered. "Run!"

Outside on the porch, Falcon hurdled Gar's body, shoved against the table blocking the broken window, and pushed past and through the hole in the glass. The little vicious Caleb-thing was right behind her, waiting to get through, snapping his jowls and howling like a crazed Chihuahua.

"Death has climbed in through our windows," the reverend screamed in the dark, "and has entered our fortresses!"

Vance grabbed the ranting man of God and shoved him toward the campus door. But they didn't get far. Dex and Norene had beat them there and, fumbling with the blockade, jammed the exit. With no intention of waiting in line while the creatures attacked, Vance spun the reverend and pushed him toward the kitchen instead.

Angela, trying to find her bearings in the dark, found the undead police chief instead, behind her, reaching in her direction. She screamed. Paul appeared on her other side, poked past her with the barrel of Arthur's rifle, and shot Cross in the eye. The white-orange flash was blinding, the report deafening. Angela threw her hands up trying, unsuccessfully, to block both. She couldn't see a thing and, with the ringing in her ears, couldn't hear Carter Cross groan as he dropped dead – again.

Falcon had cleared the barricade, was inside, and looking for a victim. Vance, heading past with Reverend Snow, paused to bust her in the face with his pistol grip. The blow sent the Goth creature hurtling backwards through the window she'd only just accessed. She bowled into Caleb on the porch and, as one, landed atop Gar's corpse. The two wrestled, kicking and scratching; both starving, melting, and making a hell of a mess of Gar underneath.

"We're losing the hall," Vance screamed. "Let's get out of here. Abandon the building." He grabbed the reverend and, once more, shoved toward the kitchen.

Dex and his rescued Norene, panicked and exasperated, had thrown the blockade at the door down when the sergeant's order came. Both were more than happy to comply. They pulled the door open, and were heading out, when a melting claw snapped the front of Norene's shirt and the mutilated Ben Nath shoved in from outside. Norene screamed. But Ben had his irradiated sights on a bigger fish. He pushed past the startled girl, grabbed Dex was his good hand and, despite having half the teeth of the other mutants, bit him savagely in the throat. Norene pulled away, screaming, and ran out the door.

Norene hated leaving Dex behind. She liked Dex. But she was out of there. She cleared the porch in two strides, hit the ground running, and jumped over the supine corpse of John P. Not a thing had gone right for Norene all day. So it should come as no surprise that, as she passed over him, the fisherman returned to life. John opened his glowing eyes and grabbed the leaping Norene by her legs.

Inside, Paul fired a shot that missed its target and hit the wall above Ben's head. Drywall flew like rice at a wedding. In the swirl of plaster powder, the oblivious Ben-thing continued to feed on Dex.

Falcon, free from her scuffle with Caleb and on her feet again, vaulted once more through the broken window. She grabbed for Angela. Paul intervened by swatting her with the rifle. This time Falcon fell *into* the room and landed atop Cross' body. In a frenzy, she bit a chunk from the chief's shoulder. An instant later, realizing he was dead, retching and choking, she spit the bloody bite out.

In the meantime Angela had turned and, leading their escape, kicked the remaining glass shards from the big window and climbed onto the sill.

"Watch for Caleb," Paul shouted. "He was right there!" He joined Angela outside, stepping over Gar's mutilated corpse. Both looked around to see that Caleb was gone.

While the others abandoned the community house by the hall's front door and window, Vance had thrown aside the kitchen barricade and was shoving the reverend out the back. The rear of the campus between the house, the caretaker's tool shed, and the north woods was pitch black, and so quiet it was frightening. Vance hustled the reverend out and toward the west side of the building. As they neared the corner a blur came at them from the dark shadows of the shed. It was Arthur and Hilda, together, on the attack.

"When I snuff you out," the reverend cried, "I will cover the heavens and darken their stars."

"Talk is cheap, rev," Vance hollered as he slapped Hilda, shoving her past them. He kicked Arthur the other direction. "Snuff 'em already!"

"I will cover the sun with a cloud, and the moon will not give its light. All the shining lights in the heavens I will darken over you."

Arthur growled and came at them again, a rabid animal. Vance knocked the old boy atop the rising Hilda and both went down in a pile.

"I will bring darkness over your land, declares the Sovereign Lord."

The sergeant gave the reverend a look to kill, grabbed him, and ran. He pushed the minister around the corner of the house where, with a high-pitched shriek, Caleb leaped out of the dark.

# TWENTY-THREE

The monstrous child grabbed Vance by the leg, his touch setting the sergeant's thigh on fire. Caleb laughed like a kid in a candy store and struggled to bite him. Vance, terrified and in pain, kept his head – and controlled the boy's. He'd grabbed Caleb by the hair and was yanking the feral child's head back to prevent him latching on.

In the dead of night, Vance could barely see his hand before his face. He had to find light. More, he needed to rid himself of Caleb. Possessed with those thoughts the sergeant ran for the front of the building, pushing the handcuffed reverend ahead of him, with the melting, laughing Caleb on his foot, riding his leg.

Out front, tripped up by the newly awakened dead, Norene fell hard to the ground. John P, one-time fisherman, four-time water taxi, part-time deputy, and full-time henpecked hubby, used to a steady diet of cold shoulder, was now a slathering thing looking for something warm with meat on it. He gripped one of Norene's shoes in each hand and crawled between her legs with his blue tongue wagging.

Norene, struggled up on her elbows and screamed, trying to scooch away.

Shrieking, eyes blazing, drawing nearer, John lifted his head to bite. Then his forehead exploded. A wide hole appeared above his left brow. Gore showered Norene and ran in a fall from the wound. John gurgled, released his grip as his eyes went dead again, and dropped face-first to the ground between her knees.

A shocked Norene stared in awe at the dead thing, then turned gaping to see from where the shot had come. Behind her, the one Vance had called Melissa, the female deputy, stood with a smoking gun in her hands. The lady creature had shot the other one! For an instant, Norene's terror turned to exhausted relief. Then the question hit her full force – why? Why would one zombie kill another? Her answer came when Melissa holstered the weapon, locked her red eyes on Norene, and hissed her own unholy hunger. The deputy, Norene realized, had destroyed John to have her for herself. With a scream of fear, Norene jumped to her feet and ran. Melissa took chase, caught her in four long strides, and leaped on the girl taking her to the ground from behind. The shrieks and screams already in the air were joined by theirs – and the sounds of Norene's tearing clothes.

Had he been safely at home, in his lonely shack across the river, the tumultuous noise would have driven Ben Nath insane. But there, howling with glee in the house commons after having drained Dex of his life blood, the crotchety old undead thing was part of the concert.

Vance exploded from the darkness behind the community house into the pale light of the campus clearing like a character running a sack-race in a John Waters film. The reverend had fallen behind and Vance was dragging him with one hand. With the other, he had Caleb's hair. (And had to establish his grip again and again as, sickeningly, it kept coming out in bunches.) Caleb, atop Vance's foot, riding his leg, laughing hysterically, struggled with all his might to bite a chunk from the harried officer.

"I will wipe mankind, whom I have created, from the face of the earth," the reverend ranted. "Men and animals, and creatures that move along the ground, and birds of the air, for I am grieved that I have made them."

Vance growled, "Shut the fuck up!" Then he screamed. His leg was burning beneath Caleb's melting grip – but this was something else. The sergeant couldn't take the searing pain any longer. If he didn't get the little bastard off, he was a goner and knew it. He let go of the mumbling reverend and grabbed Caleb by his arms. He ripped him off of his leg and hurled him away with all of his strength. Caleb's body hit the outside wall of the community house and ruptured like an exploding paint ball.

"So who's laughing now?" Vance shouted. "Who's laughing now?"

Red and green gore splattered the siding, scorching it, running in smoking rivers to the ground. Caleb, gone the way of his daddy with his shriek and his laugh, left only a puddle of burning goo.

Half of the unearthly creatures had traded places with the living. The melting dead were inside the house and the humans had escaped outside. One of those now in the commons was Falcon. Having gotten the nasty taste of the chief out of her twisted maw, she saw the others were gone. She leaped back up onto the frame of the broken front window, staring out into the campus, ready to spring back onto the porch. Behind her, Ben stepped into the doorway looking out with gore dripping from his chin. Dex, eyes glowing, rose from the floor and joined him. All gauged the reversed situation considering, it seemed, their revenge.

Vance, with the reverend, looked up from the putrid mess that had once been the little Harper boy to the wide campus clearing. He too was trying to figure where everyone, alive or dead, was and how each stood. The monsters remained close, as ravenous as ever, and coming on. His people were scattered and needed to regroup quickly.

Then Vance saw the barn. "The theater!" he cried to everyone still alive. "Get to the theater!"

The race with the devil was on.

Norene, wrestling for her life, her clothes nearly torn away, saw a flash of bright pink at Melissa's ankle. She grabbed for it out of desperation and, somehow, pulled the deputy's compact .380 from her back-up holster. She fired a haphazard shot. It missed the creature by a country mile but got her attention nonetheless.

Paul and Angela, in the lead and headed for the theater, heard the *pop* of gunfire and slowed to look.

Norene pulled away from Melissa, got to her feet and, screaming, fired off two more rounds at the maniac cop. *Pop, pop.* Both missed but, for the moment, the melting Melissa-thing had stopped grabbing at her. The southern belle heard the sergeant shout again, "Get to the barn," and heard Paul calling her by name. She dropped the gun in the grass and took off running.

"She threw the gun down," Angela cried with a groan. Paul grabbed the director and yanked her toward the theater. Running again, Angela continued to complain. "Did you see that? She threw down a perfectly good gun. Hasn't she ever seen a horror film, for God's sake?"

Paul and Angela were almost to the barn with the terrified Norene, unarmed again, following. Vance, back to hurrying the handcuffed reverend, brought up the rear. Not far behind them, certainly not far enough, Melissa was back on her feet and leading the pursuit. She was trailed by the creatures that once had been Falcon, Dex, and Ben. Arthur and Hilda, bringing up a distant rear, joined the chase from behind the community house.

Paul yanked the theater door open and, screaming, "Come on," ushered Angela and Norene through. Then, fighting every urge for self-preservation, he stopped and stared back to the cop and the minister with pleading eyes.

"Don't wait for me," Vance shouted.

Paul didn't need to be convinced. He hurried into the renovated barn as the last two humans hurried toward it.

Melissa stopped, awkwardly pulled her service pistol from her holster and, as the other melters passed her up, fired in the direction of the barn. The shot tore through Falcon's back. The ghoulish Goth girl, halted in her tracks and looked down to examine the 'exit wound' damage between her breasts. She glared red-eyed daggers at the melting deputy, then returned to the chase. Unfazed, the Melissa-creature merely crouched and fired again. Her second shot hit the door frame of the barn's entrance, sending splinters flying, as Vance shoved Snow through. The sergeant dove on the reverend's heels, pushed the door closed, and fell against it.

"More gunshots," Angela shouted. "Did you hear? More gunshots." She glared at Norene. "From someone with brains enough to *not* toss away their gun. Maybe the cavalry's arrived!" She started for one of the two small windows near the door with Paul behind her. Norene, aware she was now on Angela's frayed nerves, headed for the window opposite.

"It's not the cavalry," the winded Vance gasped. "Stay away from the glass. Keep your heads down."

Outside, Melissa's gun barked again. The window beside Norene shattered and she unleashed a scream. Behind her, the reverend cried out and grabbed his shoulder. He fell to the floor, shouting, "This is my blood of the covenant, which is poured out for many for the forgiveness of sins."

Paul grabbed Angela and pulled her down beneath their still-intact window. On the floor, he shook his head. "Good gravy, how many guns does she have?"

"If I remember correctly," Angela said, trying to catch her breath, "You're the one who said 'Challenges are good for you'."

"I never said that." Paul turned and shouted at the sergeant. "How many guns does she have?"

"She was wearing two," Vance said. "But *how many* isn't the issue. Our problem is, if she retained her skills from when she was alive, she knows how to use them."

The wall splintered beside them as another bullet tore through from outside. "Get down!" Everyone did – and held their collective breath.

The shooting stopped.

They lay there in silence, waiting. The shooting had stopped, at least for the moment. Vance sat up. He leaned on the door, groaned in pain, and took in his motley crew. Everyone was torn up, filthy, and splattered in blood. There sat the crazy minister trying to reach his wounded shoulder in handcuffs. Whatever had happened there on the island, Vance knew, that poor guy hadn't been the cause. He dug out his handcuff key and, in pain, crawled to the reverend. "It looks like Carter got it wrong, old boy," he told him. "I don't think you're responsible for Arthur. And you certainly aren't at fault for the rest of this nonsense." He unlocked the cuffs and let Snow rub his bruised wrists. He drew out a handkerchief and applied it to the bullet wound in the holy man's shoulder. "Here, hold that."

The reverend did, saying, "Blessed is the man who perseveres under trial, because when he has stood the test, he will receive the crown of life that God has promised to those who love him."

"I hope you're right, Reverend Snow," Vance said. "I hope you're right." Barely had the sergeant voiced his wish than another hair-raising scream, outside, put the question back in doubt.

Hair-raising didn't cover it. This scream came from the pit of a dying soul, pained, stunned, and very male. It was the scream of the Jackson County Sheriff, Rufus 'Rough' Nelson. A peek through a theater window showed Rough running into the clearing from the south woods with someone, something, atop his back, riding him like Death riding the pale horse of the Apocalypse. They barreled beneath a nearby pole fixture and into the middle of the group of staggering melting dead. Only then, in the dim amber pool of light, could those trapped in the barn make out Rough's rider. It was Crystal Harper. Her fingers were locked in his hair and her mouth fastened on his neck. The screaming sheriff had, it appeared, changed his opinion. Moving fast was no longer an activity reserved for felons. Rough toppled over and Crystal, still feeding, rode him to the ground. The others melters moved in.

Vance pulled himself from the sight, closed his eyes, and took a deep breath. When he opened them again, he found himself staring at Norene on the floor beneath the shattered window. "That was the Sabula sheriff," he told her through clenched teeth. "He was here because of you and your friends? He's dead now." He had more to tell her but bit it off. Norene hung her head without offering a reply.

Vance felt like hanging his head too. Anger did nothing to help them and he knew it. He sank to the floor with the others as the realization of their situation dawned. The siege had started anew.

Soon after, his mind back on business, his sidearm reloaded, Vance was putting the weapon away when a high-pitched voice stole in from outside. It pricked the ears and raised the hackles of everyone present, but assaulted the sergeant's particularly. The sing-song message was aimed at him.

"Va – ance!"

Curious, and not a little frightened, the sergeant sneaked back up and peeked out. As before, the melters roamed in and out of the shadows groaning in pain and grumbling in hunger. The others had moved away but Crystal was still straddling the sheriff. She'd bitten a chunk from the back of Rough's neck and sat merrily chewing away. Numbed by the sight, it took Vance a moment to locate the source of the musical call. It was Melissa, the thing Melissa had become, nearer to the theater door than the others in the clearing. She'd holstered her gun and was staring at the barn waiting. Her eyes glowed and she smiled as she called again, "Va – ance! Va-ance! You owe me a da-ance."

Behind her, Crystal finished licking the blood from her lips and climbed off of the sheriff. She wandered into the shadows relishing the rejuvenating afterglow. The dead Rough, lying face-down in the mud, suddenly convulsed and slowly stood up. Eyes glowing, he stumbled to Melissa's side, sheriff and deputy reunited. Awed and sickened by the sight of his former friends and colleagues, unwilling to stand it another minute, Vance looked away. He missed seeing Gar stagger from the dark to rejoin the group. He also missed seeing the Arthur-creature wander from the light, with his Hilda in tow, to disappear around the side of the barn.

Melissa's serenade was unsettling. Vance tried to ignore it, to put it out of mind, and called for everyone to regroup. Though he was counting on little input from either the criminal or the loon, he suggested Paul and Angela return with him to formulating a plan of action. "If I remember correctly," the sergeant said. "Professor Regas was elaborating on his theory when we were interrupted. If there's anything there…" He paused to catch a needed breath, unable to hide the fact he was hurting. "I mean anything to help." He turned to Paul. "You were saying?"

"I was ruminating on the stages this curse of the demon seems to put a dead body through. I reached what I imagined as stage three when, for whatever reason, Dex started his concert. Then the window broke and everything went crazy."

Norene, reminded suddenly and not too subtly of Dex's death, began crying uncontrollably. Angela stared daggers at Paul and went to her. The loss of everyone, dead in the woods but still roaming, hit them all. The theater fell into silence. But the silence didn't last. It was soon broken by the thunderous sound of a *crash* up on the stage.

# TWENTY-FOUR

All eyes turned. But the theater stage was empty.

One by one the realization came that the crash had come from further away in the wing. A dozen alarmed glances darted between those in the small group of frightened humans, not counting the facial contortions of Reverend Snow (in his own world), but nobody moved. Then Paul gulped and said, "I'll check it." He reaffirmed his grip on Arthur's rifle and told Vance, "You better stay up front," and started for the stage. As he passed Angela, Paul wasted his time telling her, "Stay here."

"I've had all of *that* I can stand," she replied shaking her head. "If you're going, I'm going. End of discussion." Paul frowned but said nothing. Angela joined him.

One step at a time they made their way to the stage, on pins and needles, rifle before them like military colors; so different from their giddy run that morning. Their meeting now seemed a lifetime ago. Like cartoon characters, Paul and Angela peered into the stage right wing. They looked silly, they knew, but it wasn't to be helped. They looked sillier still when they froze in shock. The area should have been dark, but was not. A sliver of amber light intruded from the campus. The stage door was standing open.

"How did that get unlocked?" Paul whispered to the gods. They didn't answer. He gulped again, licked his lips, and strained his eyes. "Do you see anything?"

Angela, scanning the gloom, whispered back, "No. Nothing."

"I've got to close the door and lock it. You stay here."

"Yes. And no."

"What?" Paul demanded, furling his brow at Angela's newest display of goofiness.

"Yes," she said. "It must be locked. And, no, I won't stay here. I'm coming with you."

Paul frowned again, but only on the outside; inside he was delighted. He nodded and they moved, across the wing, following the amber light to the door. Paul yanked it closed and Angela turned the lock. Enveloped again in darkness both heaved sighs of relief.

That was when Hilda, camp cook, Big Band groupie, and undead monster, like Karloff's corpse in the climax to *The Body Snatcher*, leaned from the black corner to their left, slapped the rifle away, and grabbed Paul by the arm. The geologist screamed louder than the director, but with reason. The old biddy had a killer grip. Paul yanked his arm back, surprising even himself with his violence but, really, hadn't he had enough? "Back away, Angela," he cried, practicing what he preached.

Angela obeyed. And backed into Arthur coming from the opposite corner. His skin bubbled like a well-baked pizza, a gurgle escaped his sagging lips. She screamed and retreated, with Paul, away from the door and into the middle of the wing. The elderly pair of melters came together, blocking the door, staring with flaming red eyes. Backlit by the matching red 'EXIT' light, above and behind them, they looked like American Gothic after the old homestead burned down. Arthur held his jingling custodial key ring in his melting hand. So much for locked doors.

For a moment, they stared in a bizarre showdown. Then the dam broke. With a feral growl, Hilda went after Paul and Arthur took after Angela.

Across the barn, at the entrance to the theater, Vance heard the backstage commotion and rose to the occasion. He managed two steps before regretting it. Another of Melissa's bullets raced through the already broken window, missed him by whiskers, and ricocheted off the fireplace grate. The sergeant hit the deck again and, slowly and painfully, crawled back to the wall. For the moment, his friends on the stage would have to fight their own battle.

And they did.

Hilda stayed after Paul, intent on his flesh and blood, all the way across the stage. The professor backed into, and around, a collection of prop furniture. He kept his distance from the old girl as best he could, initiating without meaning to, a dark sort of schoolyard tag. The difference being, in this instance, 'You're it!' meant the end – and an awakening to something unimaginable.

On her side of the stage, Angela had nowhere to run. She couldn't take to the floor. That would lead Arthur to Vance, Norene, and the raving reverend. She couldn't cross over to Paul, who had trouble enough of his own and didn't need more. The stage door was out. It led only to more of those things. There was no way out; only deeper in. That's where she went. Stalked by the smoking glob-dripping groundskeeper, Angela started up the ladder to the crow's nest.

To her horror and anger, Arthur followed. "Hey," she screamed down at him in disgust. "You don't mess with someone when they're on a ladder!"

Arthur paused, staring up. His eyes glowed. His cheeks were melted jowls. His nose slipped, slid down his face, and dropped. It landed with a splat. The wooden rungs beneath the caretaker's hands were scorched and beginning to smoke. He grabbed a rung near Angela's ankle and reached for her. She shrieked and pulled away. Arthur lost his grip and fell to the floor.

Paul and Hilda continued round the Mulberry bush; the professor backing off, blocking her claws, and uselessly pleading for her to stop. The cook came relentlessly on. It was a shame. Paul couldn't fight her and no longer had the rifle with which to shoot her. Some hero he turned out to be. At least he had the satisfaction of knowing he'd been right all along; vacations never worked out for him.

For her part, Hilda had one thought in her burning mind. *"Oh, yes, there will be blood!"*

Oozing, smoldering like a dying campfire, melting horribly, Arthur struggled up and jumped for the ladder again. Angela had gained the crow's nest and, staring down, was trying to catch her breath. The groundskeeper started up. His core temperature, as his body broke down, increased rapidly. And, unbelievably, the rungs beneath his gummy hands caught fire as he climbed.

Paul threw a footstool to slow Hilda. It didn't. He hit her in the head with a potted plant. What kind, he didn't know; something from the *Little Shop of Horrors*, no doubt. He wasn't a botanist and it wasn't real. That slowed her for an instant, more from surprise than anything, but she quickly returned to the chase. The professor tripped over an end table, hustled back to his feet, turned, and ran face-first into a huge paper mâché elephant's ass. (From a production of *Around the World in 80 Days*.) Hilda was around the table in eight seconds. Paul had nowhere to go.

Arthur, struggling, smoking like a forgotten cigar, was nearly to the top of the ladder.

In the crow's nest, Angela (like Paul) had nowhere to go. She pawed through the wall flats, and dug through the hanging and scattered props, looking for something with which to defend herself. She had it all, knives, swords, and blunt instruments aplenty. But nothing was real! Her chosen profession, her home, her life; the theater – and nothing about it was solid, real, or of the slightest value. She spotted the costume trunk. It contained everything Paul had needed to recreate Chaney's masque of the Red Death. But it held nothing to stop Arthur or the dinner he was about to hold in her honor.

But what was she thinking? What was she doing? Of course!

Angela reached into the box, threw aside the red cape, a robe, and the musketeer's hat. "Yes!" she exclaimed, and pulled out the long walking stick. Paul's heavy cane. She rapped it on the side of the trunk. She'd been hasty, Angela knew. She'd been hysterical. She wasn't anymore. She wasn't going to her grave without a fight. Come to think of it, there wasn't a damn thing wrong with the theater!

With Paul's rod of Asclepius in hand, Angela swore her own Hippocratic Oath, promising the gods of Greece she'd absolutely do as much harm as humanly possible. Thus armed, with nothing remotely like healing on her mind, Angela hurried back to the ladder.

Arthur, what remained of him, reached for the top rung. Angela saw him and gasped. Then she gritted her teeth and, like Leatherface swinging his mallet, lowered the boom. She didn't know what to expect. The snap of the walking stick breaking? The crack of the old man's skull? She got neither. Instead, the rod sank into Arthur's crown like a hot knife into butter. Stunned and appalled, Angela yanked the stick back. Gore flew.

Arthur howled. Despite his tight grip on the ladder, he teetered back, his melting wrists stretching like taffy. His body weight pulled his right arm away, just his arm. His disembodied hand stayed, still clutching the rung. The hand and rung caught fire. Arthur fell again, the full distance to the floor. He rose up ponderously, wobbling, and tried for the ladder once more. He jumped, missed, and fell. He stood again, issuing a low moan, jumped, and fell again. On a third try, his feet melted. For an instant, the old man stood balanced on the stalks of his legs. Then his body collapsed in on itself. He dropped to the floor in a pile of putrid sludge.

Across the stage Hilda, maw wide open, moved forward to bite Paul.

But, before she reached him, her forehead erupted. The lamps behind her red eyes went out and she fell forward, revealing Sergeant Vance behind her with his smoking gun in his hands. Paul, covered in her hot goo, gray matter, and shards of her softened skull, freaked out.

Figuring everyone's entitled to one good scare or, for that matter, a well-earned breakdown, Vance left the professor to it and raced across the stage to the other wing.

He arrived at the base of the crow's nest ladder to find what was left of Arthur Aaron, namely his dentures, laying in the middle of a bubbling puddle of bloody fire. The ladder dripped with red and green ooze. Several rungs were burned through. Angela hung over the rail above, freaking out too. It had been a hell of a show, unlike anything seen in that little theater before.

Some time later, when the freaking out had run its course and sanity been reclaimed, Paul extinguished the ladder and helped Angela down on what remained of the rungs. They met Vance at center stage. Like many that had trod the boards before them, in comedy and in tragedy, they were accompanied by a Greek chorus as, from the other side of the theater, the reverend shouted, "Our God is a God who saves; from the Sovereign Lord comes escape from death."

"Here, here," Vance shouted back. "Hang on to that thought, reverend." He paused to consider the smoking mound of glop that once had been Arthur. He examined the back wall on the other side where Hilda's body lay in its own gore. When he got his chin working, Vance told his companions, "I try to watch my language when I'm in uniform but, really, what the fuck? Can you believe this?"

"What I can believe," Paul said. "Is that I was wrong. These things don't exist in three stages. They exist in four. They burn out!"

"What?" Vance asked. "You mean like... What do they call it? Spontaneous human combustion?"

"No. They're not human. We've been over that." Paul stepped to the edge of the stage and sat. "Look, we just saw it again. Whatever they are, this ionizing radiation... I believe that's what it is. It burns them up. In the end they're like taffy."

"But they're still dangerous," Vance insisted.

"Incredibly dangerous. They're ravenous. They're highly radioactive. They're incendiary; they're so hot they start fires by touch. And they're unstable. Arthur, literally, melted."

Angela smiled ear to ear. Vance stared, Paul asked if they were missing a joke. She shook her head and waved him away. "No," Paul insisted. "What is it?"

"An idea came to me. But right away I thought, no… They're all gonna laugh at you! They're all gonna laugh!"

"Well, what is it?" She tried to wave it off again. "Come on, for cripes sake. No one feels like laughing, so give. All ideas are welcome."

"Didn't you hear what you just said? They're unstable. These things, they melt and burn up. Do you see what that means? All we have to do is outlast them."

"Sounds easier said than done," Vance growled. "How long would that take?"

"I don't know. Paul's the scientist."

The professor frowned. "There certainly are no experts regarding these creatures. They come back at different speeds. Some speak, some don't. They burn at different rates."

"Okay," Angela said. "But, if we can avoid them, avoid infection, will they melt on their own?"

Vance looked horrified. "My God, that could take forever!"

"That's why I smiled," Angela said, smiling wider now. "What if we could speed it up? There was this movie… *The Giant Spider Invasion*. This gigantic spider, well, really it was a Volkswagen chassis covered in fur, but anyhow, Steve Brodie and Barbara Hale bombarded the creature's space portal with a neutron bomb to overload it and choke it off."

Paul rolled his eyes. "What the hell are you talking about?"

"No, wait." She snapped her fingers, ignoring the cynic, drawing on her memory. "Better yet. Ray Harryhausen. *The Beast From 20,000 Fathoms*. Yes, much closer, a radioactive dinosaur!"

"Geek girl," Paul cried. "This isn't a movie."

"Oh, you give me a pain."

"I'm glad to hear it. Since when did you go in for crusading in the cause of science? This isn't *Jurassic Park*. So why are you rambling about dinosaurs?"

"Forget the dinosaurs," Angela screamed. She turned away, fighting tears and, perhaps, her own breakdown. "I'm talking about radiation."

"Come here." Paul laid his hand on her shoulder and, when she wouldn't turn, turned her. "Come here, sob sister. All right, go ahead, tell it your way."

"You said there was radiation. If these things are radioactive."

"I said Chief Cross seemed to be suffering–"

"From radiation poisoning," Angela said, interrupting.

"It's a guess."

"Yes. But a good one, I think."

"You do? Based on what?"

"Based on what you said," she told Paul, forcing a smile. He considered a second, realized she'd complimented him, and beamed. She laid a hand on his. Vance, in pain, watching impatiently, cleared his throat loudly at their sappy display of love in bloom. "Do you two mind?"

"Sorry," Angela said. "What I'm saying is, if their bite is radioactive..."

Vance shook his head. "The chief wasn't bitten."

"No, that's true. He wasn't," Paul said. He looked to Angela, she waved back giving him the stage. "But he had an open wound. If it's radiation, it's Beta at least, possibly Gamma because it's airborne and penetrating." He glared at Angela. "*Hah.* Science!"

She raised a palm to his face. "I gave you all the credit you're getting."

"We need to get the hell off this island," Paul said.

"Isn't that where we started?" Angela asked. "What are the odds of that? My point, all along, has been there's another option. We could find the radioactive source and bring it here."

"Why?" Vance asked. "For what?"

"They consume flesh to fight the effects of the radiation," Angela said. "An increase in the radiation should speed up their disintegration. Shouldn't it?"

Paul nodded. "I hate to admit it, but she might be right."

"Why not just lead them to the source?" Vance asked. "Wouldn't that be quicker? Safer?"

"No. No, it wouldn't. Angela is right. The source, the meteorite, if it really is a meteorite, is surely in the open. Even if we could find a way to lead these things to it, there would be no way to concentrate the radiation. They won't grab hands and dance around it until the melt. But if we can find the source and bring it here..." He pointed to the floor. "Right here. And lock them in. There would be no escape."

Vance looked doubtful.

Angela chimed in. "The radiation could do its voodoo, man."

Vance raised an eyebrow. "How do we find the source?"

"Geology," Paul said. "There's no radioactive ore in the Mississippi Valley. Just iron, lead, and unending limestone. We're looking for Caleb Harper's space rocks. Isn't that what Hilda called them?"

"I'm certainly no scientist," Vance said. "But there may be something to this. I don't know if you're aware but there is an odd electromagnetic field on this island. I saw it on the river coming down here. Compasses, watches, radios, phones; nothing works. And the Harpers suffered first."

"The meteorites you saw," Paul told Angela. He turned to Vance. "Point me to Harper's Cove."

"No," the cop said with finality. "I'm going."

"Wait a minute!" Angela stared as if they were both crazy. "I know it's my idea. But I just realized how ridiculous it is. It's radiation. The characters in the movies had lead-lined containers, air tanks, rubber coveralls. We don't have any protective gear. Whoever goes is going to die. *If* you make it there, *if* you make it back, *if* it even works, you're going to be irradiated terribly. You're going to die. Why don't we just wait here for awhile; see what happens."

There came a growl from outside and an eruption at the theater's main entrance. Something slammed into the door. A chunk of wood flew as a melter's hand shot through the busted slat, missing Norene's face by inches. "Boy!" she screamed. "Did you see that?"

The disfigured hand, caught sticking through the broken door, snatched blindly.

The trio left the stage and raced to the entrance. Vance pulled Norene from the door, and the grasping claw, and drew his handgun. From the size, even as it melted, it was obvious the hand belonged to the creature that had been Rough Nelson. The sergeant wasted no time firing through it. Rough howled. He pulled back violently, withdrawing his arm, and leaving behind a splatter of blood, a scorched hole, and the hand. It plopped to the floor like a wet fish.

The howl outside became something else, a guttural grunt that fought to be words. "Give… me… back… my hand. Give… me back… my hand!" But the Rough-thing's demand was out of the question. Not only wouldn't they, they couldn't. The amputated appendage had already deteriorated to a smoking stew on the floor.

"You were right before, Angela. We've got to try it; bring the radiation source here. It's got to be done," Paul said staring at the marred door. "The alternative is we all die."

"It was a stupid idea," she replied. "No one can survive out there." Then a light shown in her eyes. "But if anyone goes," Angela said. "It should be me. I run marathons. I can go without stopping farther than either of you. I can get there and back faster."

"I'm going." Paul raised his fingers to count. "One: This idiotic idea, with virtually no chance of success, came to you because of what I said. The responsibility is mine. Two: I'm the geologist. I'll know what rock to look for. Three: You're the nurse and Vance is the real defense around here. I'm the most expendable."

"You can both forget it," Vance said. "I'm going." He raised his fingers to count. "One: I'm what's left of the law and it's my responsibility. Two: I can get to the cove, in the dark, in half the time either of you could. I'd know the way blindfolded. Three: I know what Harper's place looks like and don't need a degree in geology to figure out which new thing is a meteorite. And, Four…" He pulled up his bloody shirt displaying a small but vicious infected bite on his side.

Paul, Angela, and Norene, gasped as one in horror and disbelief.

"It's already too late for me. That little bastard Caleb bit me. I've got to do what I can… while I can. All right?"

"Vance, I had…" Paul paused and bit his lower lip. "Yes."

The sergeant turned to Angela. "All right?"

Feeling herself welling up, she managed a nod.

"All right," Vance said with a sigh.

"The Spirit, the water and the blood," the reverend called from across the theater, "and the three are in agreement."

Vance, Paul, Angela, and from a distance Norene, shared a weary and pained laugh.

# TWENTY-FIVE

"Cover that front door up, will you?" Vance said, pointing to the scorched hole the Rough creature had left. "Make sure it's secure."

Moving in a crouch, Paul and Angela set about it while Vance returned to the stage. He collected a tarp from the back and threw it over Hilda's remains, then disappeared into the wing. A chorus of slams and bangs followed as he located a tool box and dumped its contents. He reappeared displaying the empty box. "It's what everyone is carrying their meteorites in nowadays."

Vance set the box down and, returning to the theater floor, pulled another item from his back pocket. "Found something else up there," he said, displaying the prize. It was a hip flask.

"Another one?" Paul asked in amazement.

"Good ol' Arthur," Angela said. "Every day was Easter."

"It gave him a one up on this space virus," Paul said with a chuckle. "No matter what it did to him, it couldn't hurt his liver."

Vance took a slug, winced at the joy, then offered it over. "Do you think that you could join me in a drink?"

"Mr. Vance," Paul said, "I honestly believe that I could join you in a drink."

Angela, looking grim, shook her head.

"It's only gin, you know," Vance told her. "I like gin."

"I don't," Paul said, reaching for the flask. "But I'll join you all the same."

Angela grabbed his hand. She shook her head again. All three traded looks, then Vance smiled. "She's probably right. The less we share our radioactivity, most likely, the better. All right, I'll toast the both of you instead." He lifted the flask. "Though you might not appreciate it, I give you–"

"Illusion," Angela said.

"Illusion?"

She nodded. "Under the circumstances, believe me, that's precisely the right toast."

Vance took another jolt, capped the flask, and tossed it down. He paused for a breather, seemed to get an idea, and moved to Norene, who was tamping the reverend's gunshot wound. "How is he?"

She released the bloody handkerchief and the minister took over holding it in place on his own. "Aw-right, I guess. Good as can be, things bein' the way they are."

Vance nodded, sighed deeply, and asked her, "Are you sorry for what you did?"

Taken aback, Norene stared, wide-eyed and wary. "The robb-ry, ya mean?"

"Yes, the armed robbery you helped to commit. Are you sorry?"

"Yes, sir. Yes, sir." She tried to hold it off, but couldn't. Norene began to cry again. "Yes, sir. More sorry 'n you know. I sure am."

"I find you guilty as charged, but I'm suspending your sentence. Don't do it again."

Norene gawped. "I won't," she said in a whisper. "I surely won't. I just want to go home."

"Do that. When you get out of here, go home." Vance nodded, done with her. He leaned over the reverend, and whispered, "Say a prayer for me, you crazy bastard." The reverend began to mumble and Vance shrugged. Who knew? Maybe it was a prayer. The sergeant turned to Paul and Angela and said, "Let's do this."

They followed him to the stage. He retrieved the tool box and headed for the back door.

"Lock it when I leave," he told them. "Do what you can to hold them off. And be patient. I'll be back in two shakes of a lambs tail."

"Really?" Angela asked.

"They just talk that way in the sticks," Paul said.

Vance smiled. "That's right. You two aren't from around here, are you?"

Angela opened the door for him. With his tool box, Vance slipped out and she quickly pulled it closed. The lock clicked with a frightening finality.

Outside, Vance leaned back against the stage door and took a breath to steady himself. He wouldn't have let on to any of those he'd left behind, but his side was on fire. The pain was excruciating. It was all he could do not to vomit or pass out. His guts swam, his head spun and, truth be told, he felt worse than like hell.

But the time had come. The creatures, the melting dead, were just around the bend, milling and grumbling. He would stick to the shadows on his side and slip quietly into the woods behind the theater. He could pick up the trail to the Harper's place further down out of sight. For whatever good it would do, he would find the source of this ridiculous infection, the meteorite, and return with it or die trying. He paused, accepting the reality that he *would* die trying. To hell with it. He took off while he still could.

Before he'd left, Vance had requested the reverend bend the Lord's ear for him. Though he had no clue whether or not the crazy man of God would come through, he had hopes.

"Your word is a lamp to my feet and a light for my path."

While the sergeant raced, hurdled, dodged, and hustled through the dark south woods of the Rock Island, the mad minister poured it on. Vance couldn't hear him praying, or spouting scripture, but the old boy was about it all the same.

"The light of the righteous shines brightly, but the lamp of the wicked is snuffed out."

Vance paused, breathing hard, having heard – something. He gripped his aching side and leaned heavily on a tree near the path. He could hear the melters behind him, at the theater, groaning and grumbling, sounding at that distance like nothing so much as an ill wind. But that background noise had been there since he'd stepped from the barn. No. Now he heard something else. Before him? Perhaps. Or very near by.

It suddenly dawned he wasn't certain all of the melters were still at the campus. Perhaps he'd been seen leaving? Maybe he'd been followed? Maybe they were moving to cut him off? Perhaps it wasn't the old gang of creatures at all? Hadn't new ones, former friends and associates, irradiated monsters now, been popping up unexpectedly all night? Who knew who–

A rustle in the brush off the path to his right interrupted his thoughts, shook him.

Who knew who, or what, roamed the black timber?

A low growl issued from the darkness. An animal's growl, menacing, terrifying; made more so by the fact Vance had neither seen nor heard any birds or animals since coming to the island, not one. He didn't need this. He didn't have time for this – in many ways. He scanned the woods and path ahead as best he could in the dark. He saw nothing but heard, whatever it was, still growling. He had no choice. He had to move on. Damn it! He'd deal with his new nemesis when it showed itself. Chilled, with fear probably, with fever definitely, he hugged the tool box, got his bearings, and started off again.

Vance didn't know but, in the theater, far behind him now, the reverend kept his mumbled promise. "A little while, and the wicked will be no more. Though you look for them, they will not be found."

What Vance did know was… he'd arrived at the clearing where once the Harper's shack stood. Nothing remained but a burned out ruin. He set down the tool box and, wasting no time, started searching for the meteorite. He circled the outhouse, finding nothing. He kicked through the high grass and threw back tarps exposing the treasures of the late Harper clan, but nothing else. He lifted a sheet of plywood – and was startled by movement beneath.

It was Jay Harper, or all that remained of him. He had no lower body at all. His coveralls had burned away and a puddle of smoking glop covered the dead grass where his legs had been. He appeared to be in his death throes. But the head and shoulders were still undead and, unbelievably, trying to bite him. The scene was right out of a *Monty Python* film. Vance thought he might laugh; then started to cry. Sickened by the sight, stunned by his own reaction, the sergeant pulled his gun and fired into Jay's head – like shooting a red-eyed jack-o'-lantern on your neighbor's porch railing. The head dropped to the ground. Then it melted into goo. Vance fell to his knee, gasping and sobbing.

("Then the Lord rained down burning sulfur on Sodom and Gomorrah – from the Lord out of the heavens.")

The pain, the terror, were almost too much and Vance fought to catch his breath. But his battles weren't over. He heard it now, again, the thing that had come upon him in the woods. It had followed him and, apparently, had ideas of its own. The familiar low growl erupted from the trail head. The creature, long unseen, burst from the woods on four feet, low to the ground, barking. It came at him with gleaming red eyes and snapping, obscene yellow teeth.

Vance pulled his trigger. *Click.* He threw the empty gun down as the beast leaped. He grabbed the creature, the thing that once had been Spot, a German Shepherd, a family pet, a new and loving mother. Thank goodness, thank Reverend Snow's God, the vicious monster, beneath the scorched and melted flesh of its thick throat, was still wearing a collar. (No registration tags, of course, it had belonged to the Harpers.) Gripping the leather choker, struggling to hold its snapping head at bay, forcing himself to his feet, and spinning for momentum, Vance hurled the animal up and away. The monster dog howled, cartwheeling toward the cabin ruin. It landed in a burst of flames.

Night blindness followed. But Vance's brain was still functioning. The dog hadn't blown up on its own. Something within the cabin debris had caused that eruption! The sergeant gathered his strength and climbed atop the stifling cabin wreck. He lifted a sheet of dented tin, burning his hands. He threw the cover back and shielded his face against the glow. There lay the radiating meteorite.

("When he opened the Abyss," Reverend Snow prayed, "smoke rose from it like the smoke from a gigantic furnace. The sun and sky were darkened by the smoke from the Abyss.")

Stunned, sick, and burned, Vance looked from the debris pit to the small tool box on the ground and realized there was no way on earth the radiating rock was going to fit. "Balls!" he screamed. He rolled off the wrecked porch, fell to the cool ground, and stared into the black sky. Had He, the reverend's God, the sergeant wondered, created him, ladled him from the primordial soup, then dug him out of the toy box, merely for this little evening of fun? Or was there a point to all this shit? A star shined though the clouds and Vance couldn't help but realize that everything could have been worse.

"Could still be raining," he shouted, laughing and crying at once.

On adrenaline alone, he rummaged about near the bubbling Jay Harper puddle, and found a tarp he was able to pull free. Vance returned to the cabin and, fighting the pain and heat, threw the canvas over the meteorite. He bundled the heavy rock up, tossed it over his shoulder like a demented Santa Claus, and headed back into the woods.

The melting dead were in an all out assault on the theater when Vance emerged from the woods. None of them looked good, but a couple were appallingly decayed and near panic for sustenance. The Ben-thing pounded on the door with both hands; neither of which now had the correct number of fingers. Several on his good hand had melted off. He hollered at the top of his lungs without forming words and, while it no longer concerned him, no doubt was disturbing folks in both Iowa and Illinois with his outrageous noise. Rough Nelson, who'd risen from the dead much faster than the others, was falling apart faster too. He'd broken the glass from the other small window near the theater door, but was too fat and too far gone to get up and in. Paul kept him out with a metal chair while one of the girls, Vance couldn't tell which, threw up a table to block the hole. The rest of the melters were there, with bloody intent, but less notable hysteria. Falcon and Gar paced together. The Dex-thing and Crystal were on their own, on opposite sides of the clearing, looking forlorn. Melissa stood exactly where she'd been before, still holding her gun (though now with a droop), watching the door like a vulture eyes a dying man.

Vance felt himself failing. It was now or never. He could only hope Angela's silly 'horror movie' idea had a chance of working. He took a breath, though breathing was becoming a real chore, shouldered the jury-rigged sack again, and – staggering from the weight and heat of the meteorite – stumbled into the clearing outside of the theater entrance.

The melting dead turned on Vance.

The creatures hesitated, strangely silent as if *they* were startled, recovered quickly, and advanced on the bedraggled policeman. Vance dropped to a knee, pulled the satchel from his shoulder, and set it on the ground before him. The meteorite glowed hot through the canvas. The creatures, those that could, hissed and growled their anger and pain. All halted their progress; several backed away.

It was a stand-off. The monsters wanted the sergeant's rejuvenating flesh and warm blood, but they wanted nothing to do with the meteorite. The rock prevented their getting to him. But they prevented Vance from getting to the theater. Not that he didn't try. Again and again, the officer gathered his strength, and the space rock, to make his way around the corps of walking corpses and reach the old barn. Each time, he was cut off and pushed back to the edge of the timber by the ravenous melters. The monsters, meanwhile, repeatedly moved in to grab at Vance, forcing him to brandish his radioactive bundle to frighten them back.

Vance felt himself running out of time.

Not all of the creatures could afford to wait either. Ben staggered through the group, toward Vance, horrendously decomposed and shrieking in pain and terror. He began to run in what appeared a final attempt to save himself. He leaped for the sergeant and, as he went airborne, burst into flames. He fell well-short of Vance and landed, disintegrating, with a fiery splash. All that remained, burning denim in a disgusting puddle, smoked the grass.

There was nothing funny about it. Still Vance couldn't help but laugh. Angela, and her silly 'monster movie' plot point, had been right. If they could wait long enough, the freaks would burn themselves out. He looked at the mess that had been Ben Nath and relished their group being one monster down. If he could get them all to take their medicine, he thought, turning again to the canvas-wrapped rock, the rest could join him. Barely had the smile appeared on Vance's tortured face than it vanished. From the darkness, a rejuvenated John P, hunger and curiosity on his twisted mug, the bullet wound in his head still leaking, stepped out and rejoined the crowd of melters. There was no end to them. Vance shook his head in disgust wondering who exactly he had to screw to escape this nightmare.

It went that way too long. The melting dead moved in on Vance. He drove them back. With each passing moment, the creatures deteriorated further and grew hungrier, and the sergeant grew sicker and edged nearer to death. It couldn't go on, Vance knew. His hope faded.

The sergeant had no way of knowing for sure that Paul, Angela, or Norene were watching from inside the theater. Watching helplessly, but intently.

"They won't let him near the building," Paul said.

"We've got to help," Angela cried. "He's going to–"

"He's going to die no matter what," Paul told her. "It's a cold, hard fact. There's nothing anyone can do about that. Another fact, and our real problem, is that at this rate, he's going to die before he can destroy those things."

"Or save us," the crying Norene couldn't help but add.

Though nobody could have imagined it, or would have believed it, by then… The Reverend Snow, forgotten and alone on the barn floor by the theater fireplace, had an idea. An idea he had no choice but to act upon, as it had come to him from the Lord. That made it his solemn duty. The reverend let his bloodied handkerchief fall to the floor, whispering, "They overcame him by the blood of the Lamb and by the word of their testimony."

Everyone else in the barn had grown used to Snow or, more accurately, completely exhausted by him and had long since tuned him out like a dripping faucet. No one paid his newest mutterings the slightest attention. Nor did they bother to notice as he rose stealthily to his feet. "They did not love their lives so much as to shrink from death."

Still bleeding from his shot shoulder, guided by heaven, or hell, or perhaps merely by the mania that had seized him, unseen, the reverend quietly extracted two sturdy logs from the nearby wood pile. Two logs as commanded. Moving quietly along the wall, he reached the door. So far, so good.

The others, the sinners on whose behalf he was called to act, were busy at their window watching all that unfolded outside. None paid him any mind. And, as he unlocked the door, the reverend knew that none would intervene. "The night is nearly over; the day is almost here," he said in a whisper, still ignored. "So let us put aside the deeds of darkness and put on the armor of light." He opened the door and, carrying his logs, slipped outside.

The melting dead, like moths around the fateful flame, were mesmerized by Vance and his hateful canvas package. Not one of them noticed the reverend as he stepped from the theater. He gained the other side of the clearing, behind the monsters, directly opposite of the sickly policeman, without being molested or seen. Snow stopped there; God told him to. He drew a deep breath and, with no sign of a mutter, loudly proclaimed, "The Lord is my shepherd..."

The creatures turned en masse.

"I shall not want."

"Reverend!" Angela found the theater door ajar and now stood in the doorway screaming.

The starving melters turned from the minister to her. Paul appeared behind the director, grabbed Angela, pulled her back, and slammed the door. Groans escaped several of the creatures. They began to turn in place, their attention split between the barn on their left, the reverend before them, and Vance and his bundle at the edge of the clearing behind.

The girl had nearly mucked things up, trying to steal the glory from God. But the Lord would not be mocked. Reverend Snow knew his duty. "He makes me to lie down in green pastures," he called out. "He leads me beside the still waters." The melters turned back to the minister. They turned to Vance. They traded looks amongst themselves, unsure what to make of the situation. "He restores my soul. He leads me in the paths of righteousness for his name's sake."

Several of the creatures started toward the minister. Several others moved back toward Vance. The police sergeant, in agony, held up the satchel. The heat, the radiation, was stunning – to the lawman and the monsters. Convinced by his formidable weapon, they backed off again and turned once more on the reverend.

Just as The Almighty wanted it, Snow knew. The minister raised his voice again, shouting, "Yes, though I walk through the valley of the shadow of death,

I will fear no evil, for you are with me; your rod and your staff they comfort me." He lifted the logs, one in each hand, as the melting dead began shambling toward him.

Seeing what was taking place, recognizing the sacrifice the, either not as crazy or more crazy than they'd realized, minister was making, Vance again hoisted the canvas sack over his shoulder. The shouting minister, across the clearing, had the monsters' full attention and, using the diversion, the sergeant moved toward the theater door.

"You prepare a table before me in the presence of my enemies. You anoint my head with oil. My cup runs over." The reverend crossed one log over the other before him forming a large cross. The melters saw the move and hesitated.

Vance, half-way to the theater, hesitated too, wondering if they'd turn back.

Snow held their attention. "Surely goodness and mercy will follow me all the days of my life."

The creature that long ago had been Rough Nelson, but now was a bubbling bloody horror, moved in and grabbed hold of the makeshift cross with his remaining hand. The reverend fought back struggling, not with the monster, but to keep the logs together in the shape of the cross. Not that the symbol of Christ's suffering had any shielding effects or that Snow believed it did. It didn't repulse the creatures. They weren't the vampires of legend after all. They were genetic messes, walking piles of radioactive sludge, with a deadly hunger and the teeth to feed it. But what had the reverend told the children of his church for all those years? "Glow! And give the glory to God." This was his commanded Passion and he would obey. He would lead the melting dead through Golgotha.

Peeking at the window, in awe of his bravery, alarmed by the depth of his lunacy, still the overriding thought in Angela's mind was, "What an excellent day for an exorcism." She was a horror fanatic until the end.

Against the searing pain, the reverend redoubled his efforts to hold the cross together, telling Rough Nelson, "And I will live in the house of the Lord for ever."

Under the grip of the melting sheriff, the makeshift cross finally burst into flames in the reverend's hands. The startled Rough-creature backed off shielding his new, dramatically sensitive, red eyes. The others did likewise, repelled, not by the religious prop but by the light of its immolation and their own fear. Reverend Snow screamed in pain but held onto the burning symbol through sheer force of will.

Following a moment's hesitation, and recognition the flame had done him no harm, the ravenous Rough moved back in. The other monsters swarmed in behind him. The reverend held his burning cross as the melting dead took hold of him and dragged him screaming to the ground. He held his burning cross as the irradiated creatures, like a pack of rats, tore him to shreds.

## TWENTY-SIX

For all of its horror and sadness, the minister's immolation achieved his goal. Vance was just outside the theater door when Paul threw it open. The burned cop raised a blistered hand and told the professor, "Get back, Paul. As far back as you can. All of you."

Paul ushered Angela and Norene to the center of the theater, hesitated there, then moved them back to the stage, clearing the entrance. Vance hurried the satchel into the theater, closed the door behind him, and fell against it. Paul and Angela started toward him.

"No! Stay back!" Vance caught his breath with difficulty and lifted the satchel again. "Stay back." He moved, staggering, reached the center of the open floor and dropped the canvas bag. Then, drawing on reserves of strength he did not know he possessed, Vance stumbled back to the door. "I'm going to open it again," he called out. "I'm going to lure those things in here. When they start in the front, Paul, get yourselves the hell out the back."

Paul stepped forward again.

"No!" Vance shouted, desperately fighting the pain, waving him back again. "Stay there. Once they're inside, I'll need you to come around front from the outside and bar the door behind them. Lock them in here."

"What about you?" Angela cried.

Norene added her plea, "Y' just cain't stay here."

"It's over, ladies," the sergeant told them. "Another few minutes, I'm going to be one of those things. Please, if you have any heart at all, don't waste another second. Go."

Though none wanted to, all three hustled up the steps and into the wing. Paul called for the women to get to the back door then returned far enough to see Vance from the stage.

Leaning heavily, Vance cracked the theater door and peered out. The reverend's fiery cross had gone out. The melting dead, dripping blood and to varying extents temporarily rejuvenated, milled around the minister's corpse. Vance watched, fighting the pain, holding on to life. "Come on, reverend," he whispered, pleading. "Come on. Come on."

"What are you waiting for?" Paul shouted across the barn.

"All... of... 'em," Vance said, in a strained whisper. "Got... to be... all of... 'em."

He waited, more afraid now than he'd been all night. Terrified not that he would die (that was a foregone conclusion), but that he'd die too soon. "Come on," he whispered.

Finally, as if in answer to Vance's plea, the reverend's eyes came open with the tell-tale glow of his radioactive damnation. A bitten and bloodied wreck, the minister sat up, clumsily stood, and joined the others. All of the surviving creatures, including Snow, were finally together. The ailing sergeant threw the theater door open with a *bang*. The dripping monsters turned in his direction. Vance took a breath, found what remained of his voice, and shouted, "Supper time, you pricks!"

The melters, as one, moved. Vance, his guts on fire, waited patiently in the door as they advanced on the theater. When Satan's shambling brotherhood were nearly upon him, he backed inside, leading the creatures in with him. He continued back, staggering as much as his grotesque followers, to the center of the floor and to the tarp-wrapped meteorite.

Angela and Norene waited blindly in the dark theater wing. They could hear the slathering, hissing things as they piled after Vance. But they'd promised the sergeant not to take a hand or even look. Their only job now was to be ready to run.

Paul, outside the stage door, watched with baited breath as the last of the melting dead disappeared through the theater's front door. Once all of the stumbling wrecks were in, he waved to Angela and Norene, ordering them in a heightened whisper, "Get out of here. Now. Run."

"Paul, what are you–"

"Go," he said, cutting Angela off. She may have been the greatest actress, the best director, in the world. It made no difference. There was no time for drama. "Go!"

Angela and Norene ran. Of course, within twenty strides Norene veered off, heading in a different direction. Angela pulled up. "No," she cried in a whisper, desperately wishing she could shout. "Stay together!" She shook her head, turned back to Paul, and muttered in disgust, "You'd think that girl had never seen a horror film."

Paul waved for the trees. "Run, for God's sake."

Angela disappeared into the dark.

Paul had Arthur's key ring. He'd wiped the gooey remains of the groundskeeper off on a costume backstage and used them now to lock the back door. Then he took a breath (as much for courage as for air) and raced around the barn. He reached the front door, reminded himself there was nothing to be gained by looking in, then ignored his own advice and looked. The gory melting dead had surrounded Vance and were mercilessly moving in. That was all Paul could take.

Recognizing Vance's helpless situation, fighting every totally human, completely illogical message firing in his brain, Paul shuddered and pushed the door closed. He flipped through the unmarked keys, searching for the right one, longing for the good old days of the skeleton key, but soon gave it up. He grabbed up several broken branches lying nearby, eyeballed them for size, and discarded one. The other he jammed into the dirt at the base of the door, on angle, and shoved the upper end under the handle. The door wasn't going anywhere. Neither were the melting dead.

Sadly, Paul knew, neither was Vance.

Inside, the melters set upon the sergeant. He was crouched before the package he'd struggled so desperately to bring to them and, as they grabbed for him, yanked off the top wrap of canvas. The meteorite, cooled considerably from the time of its arrival, the previous morning, was still plenty hot and glowed with alien radiations. Vance exhaled, awash in the sudden wave of heat. His head and shoulders sagged in surrender and he fell to his knees in exhaustion.

The creatures, already on him, shrieked and shouted, hissed, cried, and scrambled to get away. Or tried to. Gar, the nearest, who already had Vance by what remained of his shirt sleeve, got in just two backwards steps before bursting into flame. The others tried to bolt but all were too late. They dropped over, burning, then exploding in every direction. Crystal and Falcon ran for the stage and set the curtains on fire in passing. The proscenium went up as both disintegrated into puddles of goo.

Melissa and Rough were in agony. She wrestled her service pistol out a final time, gurgled at the sheriff, shot herself in the head, and disintegrated. Rough stared at the glop that had been his deputy and at her weapon lying in the center of the smoking pool. He looked to his own empty holster, then howled to the rafters as he melted away. Dex struggled to move the up-ended table from in front of the window but burned up before he was able. John P merely stood in place, his fevered, shot brain, turning over the foggy notion his wife was going to be mad. Then he was gone. Vance died too, as he knew he would. And, as he had feared, rose from the dead soon after. Eyes glowing, the sergeant-thing took in the devastation, the space rock before him, the consuming fire. Then like the others, he decomposed, providing a funeral dirge with his own shrieks and howls.

Only minutes after Paul had gotten the door secure, he saw from the campus clearing that the barn was on fire. The building rolled in red, orange, and yellow flames – decomposing – like the creatures he knew to be trapped inside. The theater's interior had become an unimaginable crucible of horror. Smoke raced into the night sky blotting out the few stars trying to steal a peak through the evanescent rain clouds. Paul turned away from the carnage, feeling a sudden overwhelming sense of isolation as if he were the last man on earth. Then gathering himself, he quickly, almost desperately, started to search. He scoured the campus, shouting, "Angela! Norene!" from the raging theater, to the shadowy campfire ring, to the dark bathrooms.

Somewhere, deep in the island's surrounding woods, Norene ran tripping, falling, rising, and running again. She was too scared to close her eyes for more than a few seconds and too scared to keep them open for any longer. She knew, just knew, the horror wasn't over yet. They were all going to die out there. Crying, she ran aimlessly on, to escape what she was certain was an inescapable fate. One thought raced a crooked circle in her mind. *'You're next. You're next. You're next.'*

Unable to find either of the girls and ready, finally, to admit he'd really only been searching for one all along, Paul muttered, "To hell with Norene." He turned to the devastated and abandoned community house, shouting, "Angela! Angela!" The dark commons hall, with its broken glass, slippery patches of gore, scattered plaster, and strewn tables and chairs, was as empty as an echo. The nature museum stood equally vacant and lifeless. There was no sign of the wayward theater director.

Back outside, Paul saw the theater was now fully involved and burning brilliantly, almost beautifully, in stark contrast to the last of the dying howls that escaped the inferno. Those fading screams echoed across the empty campus and into the woods. The woods? Paul wondered.

Done with the terror show the Park District had provided, no longer interested in horrors rising from the tomb, with only one thought in his head, Paul ran into the timber on that isle of the dead, shouting, "Angela!"

Hidden on the lowest of the many shelves in the darkest corner of Arthur's tool shed, Angela perked up. She listened intently and could have sworn someone in the distance was calling her name. Fear struck her heart and she couldn't help but whisper aloud, "Oh God! It knows I'm here."

But that was her mind playing tricks on her again; her goofy mind trying to cope. The creatures were gone. Vance had taken them all. He'd waited, risked his life to wait, to make sure he got them all. Then another thought occurred. Could it be possible? Could it be Paul? Could she hope Paul had survived? There again… Someone called her name. Angela slid from her hideout, crossed the shed as quietly as she was able, opened the door a crack, and slipped outside.

The theater blazed in the distance. The shrieks of the dying melters had ended. Outside of the crackling fire, the night was silent. Angela saw no one around. "Paul!" she screamed. "Paul!"

There! She heard her name again, nearby she was certain, but in a strangely distant and strangled voice, "An-gel-a. An-gel-a." It came from the community house, behind. Delighted, unable to believe her good luck, she turned to greet Paul – and saw the police chief instead.

Carter Cross resurrected, the last monster standing, the king of the melting dead, with a gunshot wound to his head still oozing, bubbled and dripped in the dark sill of the kitchen door. He licked his twisted lips, beneath his remaining red cyclopean eye, and gurgled her name again, "An-gel-a."

With the growl of a hungry animal, he started for her.

Angela screamed and ran into the woods, looking back in terror for a glimpse of the melting Cross-thing in pursuit. She thought of her horrible dream and, as suddenly, realized, *This is no dream. This is really happening!* She was living the nightmare from which she'd awakened in a start each of the last four mornings. But this was real. She was running for her life.

Angela looked as if she'd been yanked through a knothole. Her eyes swam in pink puffs of flesh, tears streaked her cheeks, a smudge marred her jaw. Her hair was disheveled, her clothes filthy, torn, blood spattered, and even burned in spots. She was running like she'd never run before. Uphill through the woods, out of breath, running on her last ounce of strength. She hadn't a step left in her, still she ran on, gasping, shooting terrified glances into the darkness behind.

She failed to hear any of the *normal* sounds of night. No nocturnal animals scampering in the brush, no creatures slithering in the grass, nothing flitting past on night wings. Not even crickets. Nothing but her gasps, her footfalls – and the unearthly sounds of the thing chasing her. The leaves crunched and branches snapped to his uneven step as the melting dead police chief pounded the brush behind. His occluded breath, growing louder, drawing nearer, threatened Angela like an opening theme from a horror flick; music to scream by, music to die by. His panting gave way to a guttural howl. The Cross-thing was on her heels and closing.

All seemed lost… when the dawn arrived.

Angela experienced a rush of hope as brilliant rays of orange, white, and gold burst through the trees. But that hope was fleeting. The cavalry had not arrived in time. It wasn't the light of salvation. It was the dawn of the dead. It cast long shadows through the woods while ominously lighting the clearing ahead like a spotlight on a stage. Lights up, she knew, on the final act in the theater of blood. Angela had no choice. She left the path, crossed the clearing in eight panicked strides then, gasping, pulled up with no more room to run.

"No!"

She caught her balance at the brink of the rock, the sheer drop-off of her nightmare, the cliff of the Rock Island. She swallowed hard and gaped over the edge taking in the hundred foot fall to the little cove and the surging Mississippi River below. Her mind reeled. Her stomach rolled. She took an involuntary step back. As in her dream, she was trapped.

She turned, stared across the clearing to the woods on the downhill side, and realized she'd never seen the end of the dream. Each time, she had awakened screaming. Her attacker had never reached her. Now that she knew who and what her assailant was, she couldn't help but wonder how it would end. Couldn't help but think, how could it end? She dropped her arms to her sides, flexed her fists, and governed her breathing. Was she afraid? YES! But let it come. She'd fought this horror all night. She'd meet the climax, for herself, for Paul, like she met every challenge in life – head on.

The morning breeze chilled her, blew through her hair and torn clothes, brushed her beads of sweat, turning her skin to goose-flesh, and sending a shudder through her small athletic frame. Behind her, Angela heard the water surging below. At the timber line, before her, she heard the snap of twigs and crunch of leaves heralding the arrival of her pursuer. And, from the shadows of the park trail, she heard an odd and hollow sound: '*thunk.*'

Paul's rappelling helmet flew out of the trees like a kicked football. Angela remembered Paul having dropped it on the trail the previous day. She'd had to jump over it not to fall, and had to duck to avoid being hit now, as it arced over her head. The melting monster had apparently kicked it coming up the path. The soaring helmet glinted in the morning light and plunged to the river. Angela watched it land with a splash a hundred feet below. Despite her terror, the overwhelming thought in her mind was… *That didn't happen in my dream.*

The thing that used to be Chief Cross broke through the trees and into the clearing.

# TWENTY-SEVEN

Smoking like a poorly extinguished campfire, a portion of his head missing from his gunshot wound, oozing green rot, dripping bloody gore, and covered in burnt and bubbling flesh, the Cross-thing came to a stop at the edge of the clearing. He spotted Angela with his deteriorating yet still dimly glowing eye, gasped, then rose to his full height and let fly with an otherworldly shriek.

Terror registered on Angela's face, the blood froze in her veins and, as pathetic as the cliché might be, the horrifying events of the past twenty-four hours flashed through her mind like a picture on a theater screen. It was her dream, come to life in every detail; the island, the hill, the sheer cliff to the pounding river, and this screaming creature of destruction. Her prophecy, though she hadn't recognized it as such, had come true. Her last day, as she'd innocently predicted, had been one big trip through hell.

The images of the previous day vanished as the last melting dead monster started toward her.

Still searching the island for the missing, and missed, little theater director, Paul had heard the unearthly cries of another creature – and knew the horror had yet to end.

Then he'd heard Angela's screams.

Now he raced through the timber, up the hill, nearing the rock peak, but sadly certain his heart would rupture before he got there. Gasping for breath, aching from tip to toe, he left the trees for the hilltop clearing. Then he stopped, slapped in the face by the scene before him. Angela teetered at the cliff's edge, trapped with nowhere to go, while the burning remains of what had been Chief Cross howled and murderously bore down on her.

Paul quickly scoured the area for anything he might use as a weapon. There was, of course, nothing. He'd picked up the loose debris, every stick and stone, when they'd been there the previous morning. Angela had had a blast, in fact, making fun of his cleaning up the island by hand. She'd laughed her shapely ass off, just because he'd wanted to make the rappel safe for both of them. God, she was aggravating. Now there was nothing left with which to save her.

Then he saw it – and a crazy idea exploded in the professor's mind.

It was right where he'd dropped it, what seemed a lifetime ago, when Hilda's scream had torn through the trees. His rappelling harness, still attached to the climbing rope by the descender, still anchored to the trees on his side of the clearing, lay there on the ground.

The creature's shriek jolted him from his examination of their surroundings. The melting thing was almost on top of Angela. She screamed what, if he didn't do something, could be her final scream. What the hell, Paul thought. He wasn't Don Quixote. He didn't have the courage to run into hell for a heavenly cause. But he wasn't a coward. And, really, was life worth a damn if you wouldn't take any risks? He scooped up the harness by the arm loops, slid them over his shoulders, grabbed the belay rope well-clear of the descender, and ran. He bounded across the clearing straight at the melter, at Angela, and at the precipice. Paul gave a primal scream, raced under the Cross-thing's arm, snatched Angela from his clutches on the run, and pushed both Angela and himself over the edge of the cliff.

The former chief of police had no room to alter his course and no time to slow his momentum. Grasping, the melting terror toppled over the edge, falling after them.

Angela joined Paul in a joint scream as the rope paid through the belay. And, an instant later, the professor's well-tied Prusik Knot hit the descender's breaking teeth. The rope jammed – as it was meant to do. Their fall ended with bone-jarring suddenness. Paul clutched Angela as a black widow would her mate while the haphazardly donned rappelling harness did its best to tear his arms from their sockets.

The melting creature fell past them hurtling toward the river below. His legs hit the Mississippi first and exploded like a bag of manure in the parking lot of the Bait and Switch. His howl ended abruptly as he vanished beneath the surface.

Angela dangled in Paul's arms. Paul dangled from the harness. Both swayed back and forth on the climbing rope before the cliff face like a pendulum over a Poe victim. Together, from on high, aghast, they watched the spot on the river where the monster had disappeared.

What was left of the melter burst back to the surface. It struggled, splashing and shrieking, as the water bubbled and steam hissed into the air. Like a foaming volcano in a science fair project the river churned and convulsed around the Cross-creature. His scream was filled with water, and worse, as he effervesced and dissolved. His horrendous immolation left only a tiny island of foaming green and red goo, a slick of gore, that immediately began to drift down river.

"Look what you did to him," Angela squeaked, staring below. "Look what you did to him!"

Paul frowned and, with the screaming thankfully over, turned his mind toward keeping them alive. He took a breath and lifted Angela. (Thank God she was small.) She saw his intent and helped by slipping her arms through the leg loops of the harness and putting her weight on the belt instead of on Paul. He looped his anchor lanyard, already hanging from the belt, around her and fastened the carabiner. The result, while less than cozy, eliminated any immediate danger of either falling. They continued to sway, suspended before the face of the cliff, but slower now; children clutching each other on a playground swing. Sadly, it occurred to Angela, there was no one left alive on the island to check the children.

"See," Paul said, now that he'd caught his breath. "I was right. I told you I'd get you to rappel."

"No, you were wrong," Angela replied. "I told you the only way I'd go abseiling would be for you to push me off the cliff."

They laughed, breathed deeply, then laughed louder as the flood gates opened. They laughed until a new sound interrupted; a foreign sound, high-pitched and whining. A second whine, almost identical, joined in. Both turned to look up and around, fearfully searching the dawn sky for another barrage of space rocks. But there was nothing to see, nothing but a wide field of blue dotted with white clouds. Still the odd whines from above persisted.

"Oh, look!" Angela exclaimed, gripping the rope and staring up, past their harness, to the cliff edge just out of their reach. Paul followed her gaze to see two adorable German Shepherd puppies, Caleb Harper's puppies, hungrily whining, scratching the turf, and looking down the swaying rope at them from the cliff above.

"Where did they come from?"

"I don't know," Angela said, laughing, then crying at the same time.

"What's so funny? What's the matter?"

"It's just…" Angela's tears flowed now, like the river far below, and she was laughing. "This is just such… a Lon Chaney Jr. moment."

Paul stared back, flummoxed. "You mean the one with the red cape and the feather?"

"No," she barked in disgust. Tears were obviously wasted around this idiot. She wiped them away as best she was able, hanging there like meat. "That's Lon Chaney. I meant Chaney Junior… The Wolf Man. He was Lenny from Of Mice and– You don't…" Angela shook her head. "Oh, never mind."

"Your mother did this to you, huh?"

Angela nodded. "You'll like my mother."

Paul opened his mouth, but didn't get the chance to respond.

"Hey, y'all!"

Both Paul and Angela heard it and, startled anew, followed the voice up. It wasn't a puppy's whine. It was a human shout, female, and southern like dripping molasses."

"Here," Paul shouted. "Down here."

"I heard y'all laughin'." Norene's dirt-smudged face appeared, above the puppies, peering over the edge. "Are you guys aw-right?" Paul and Angela were too surprised to answer. Norene scooped one of the puppies into her arms, grimaced at the height from her perspective, and asked again, "Y'all aw-right?"

"Great," Paul said. "We're great."

It had been one hell of a night as far as Norene was concerned. So many dead, including her Dex. She'd only known him for six weeks but he was real nice and she liked him a lot. Now he was gone, really gone. She'd thought about it all through the early morning, when she'd been hiding, and crying, and praying for the sun to come up. With Dex gone there wasn't nothing there for her. And she was lucky to be alive and all. And hadn't she told that police officer, Vance, she would? Maybe she'd just go home, see if she couldn't get the court to give her son back. Momma would let her move back in, she knew that. She could start over. It would be a relief to start over.

Though they didn't know Norene's thoughts, Paul and Angela, dangling below, shared her relief, her exhaustion, and her gratitude at being alive. They would need to be seen to, decontaminated, treated, but they were alive. They turned from the Georgia peach and her adopted puppies on the cliff above. The fear seemed to drain from them. They laid their heads together, felt each other's closeness. They looked at each other, inches apart; a look that lingered becoming something more.

"If this were a movie," Angela finally whispered, "we'd probably kiss now."

They stared deeply into each other's eyes and, for a moment, it appeared they might. The moment lingered. The time for it came – and went – and they were still staring.

"Give it some thought," Angela said.

Paul nodded. "I will."

Down river of the Rock Island, this side of the closed lock and dam, the dredger operator fired up his machine. The silt beneath the metal behemoth was drawn from the Mississippi bed by the vacuum and dragged toward its maw-like intake. Seconds later, an explosion of mud and silt arced from the exhaust tower, cascaded down, and plopped in a wet pile on the west bank like a cow pie on a prairie. The new day's work (Sunday morning, premium pay!) had begun.

The surface waters of the Old Man River were caught up in the man-made current and disappeared below in a multitude of miniature whirlpools. With it, without anyone paying the slightest notice, went a rotted green, burnt black, and bloody red swirl of steaming flotsam that had only been drifting by. The operator missed seeing it, consumed as he was wrestling the lid from his Thermos of badly needed coffee. Missed seeing too the same gore, cooled and clumped and mixed with silt and mud, as it was jettisoned to land in a slimy mound on the river's distant bank. And, as the operator finally managed his first sip of morning brew, missed the silver glint of a police chief's badge as it left the exhaust shoot, arced through the sunlight, and landed with a dull *tink* atop the sludge.

North of the dredger, north of the Rock Island, the Mississippi River between Savanna, Illinois and Sabula, Iowa slowly came to life. The fish began to jump and the birds to fly. Soon the fishermen and barge men would join them. Eventually Ferenc Blasko and Billy Pratt would start to sweep up broken glass and, among the rubber-neckers watching them, someone would gaze south and notice smoke rising from the Rock Island. But that would be in just a little while. Now as things began to stir, from boats, and cars, and across the river, came the sound of a radio jingle playing on the breeze and a chorus singing, "W-O-M-R. Old man river radio!"

"Yes, it is, moms and dads, boys and girls… This is your charming and delightful, ol' Aunt Sal. And right over there, pushing an entire Suzie Q into his frightening gaping face hole like he's some kind of anaconda, is my sidekick, little runny-nosed Eddie. Hi, Eddie!"

"Hey, Aunt Sal," Eddie said through cake and creamy filling.

"Well," Sal said in her tobacco rasp. "It seems we *were* bombarded with a meteorite shower yesterday. And, as predicted, absolutely nothing came of it."

"No devastation, Aunt Sal?"

"Zero, zip, zilch, Little Eddie."

There followed the wheezy sigh of Eddie's disheartened kazoo.

"Yeah, sad," Aunt Sal agreed. "The folks who track these sort of things say nobody saw any meteorites hit the ground. And only a handful of people reported seeing anything at all."

"Wow, what a crappy meteor shower."

"*Uh-oh.* Throw a shiny quarter in the potty mouth jar there, Eddie."

"Really? Just for saying 'crappy'? Come on, Aunt Sal."

"Yes, siree, Bob. Go ahead and hit her twice for repeating it, you little freak!"

The sad kazoo wheezed.

"While Eddie surrenders his cold cash to pay for his filthy cake hole, this is your ol' Aunt Sal wishing you a beau-ti-ful morning on the river, and hoping your next clash with the cosmos ends up being a bit more interesting. But, let not your hearts be troubled, folks, the experts assure us that space rocks hit our atmosphere constantly."

Two quarters *tinked* in a glass jar and, distantly, Little Eddie asked, "Really?"

"Oh, yes," Aunt Sal croaked, "You can bet your bottom dollar. It will happen again."

THE END
?

# About the Author

Doug Lamoreux is a father of three, a grandfather, a writer, and actor. A former professional firefighter, he is the author of seven novels, a novella, and a contributor to anthologies and non-fiction works including the Rondo Award-nominated Horror 101, and its companion, the Rondo Award-winning Hidden Horror. He has been nominated for a Rondo, a Lord Ruthven Award, a Pushcart Prize, and is the first-ever recipient of The Horror Society's Igor Award for fiction. Lamoreux starred in the 2006 Peter O'Keefe film, Infidel, and appeared in the Mark Anthony Vadik horror films The Thirsting (aka Lilith) and Hag.

*Other Books by the Author*

The Devil's Bed
Dracula's Demeter
When the Tik-Tik Sings
Seven for the Slab: A Horror Portmanteau
Corpses Say the Darndest Things (A Nod Blake Mystery)
Red Herrings Can't Swim (A Nod Blake Mystery)

**Co-authored**
Apparition Lake (with Daniel D. Lamoreux)
Obsidian Tears (with Daniel D. Lamoreux)

Lightning Source UK Ltd.
Milton Keynes UK
UKHW011845071220
374768UK00010B/748/J